# dear yesterday

# dear yesterday

*a novel*

LINDSEY RAY REDD

SAUDADE PRESS

Published by Lindsey Ray Redd

www.lindseyrayredd.com

Cover design by Lindsey Ray Redd
Cover image by Milan2099/CanvaPro

Saudade Press, LLC

*For my grandma, Marlene.*

# one

Luella despised Tuesdays. Hate was too cliché a word, and for all the things that seemed to happen to Luella on Tuesdays, it just wouldn't suffice. Tuesdays were her nemesis. Her mother left her on a Tuesday, her grandpa died on a Tuesday, and on this particular Tuesday she became unemployed.

Her boss, Ricky, didn't even have the decency to call her and fire her. He did it through an email.

*Very professional.*

The column she penned last week went viral, and theirs was the first online tabloid to release the name of a prominent figure in Atlanta who was entangled in an affair. She should have been promoted, but instead, her reward was unemployment.

Ricky must have been trying to satisfy someone's complaints, and she was replaceable. They all were. She had only been writing for *Scandalanta* for a little over a year. It wasn't her first choice in employment, but she took the job hoping it would be a stepping-stone to bigger publications. Fat chance of that now. He should have done it yesterday before she left the office.

But Ricky wasn't one for confrontation, so she received the email at eight o'clock last night.

This morning, she read it over and over again while drinking her coffee—trying to decide what to do about it.

Her fingers pecked along the keyboard as she wrote Ricky a scathing reply, read it several times for satisfaction, and then deleted the message entirely. No. Instead of responding, she would go to the office and pretend she hadn't seen it at all. Let him sweat a little.

Her cell phone buzzed across the marble countertop beside her. She looked over, but didn't recognize the number, so she let it ring. She read the last words of Ricky's email one more time, then slammed her laptop shut and shoved it inside her bag.

~

It was quiet in the office as she walked toward her cubicle. The room was cold, and it wasn't from the frigid December air.

She could feel the weight of her coworkers' eyes on her as she took off her black pea coat and sat down in her chair. When she finally looked up at them, their eyes flitted away as quickly as a flock of birds. She raised an eyebrow and gave them each a glassy stare. No one dared to say what she already knew.

She opened her laptop with her head held high. Ricky stepped out of his office, but Luella refused to look anywhere other than the screen. She sat up straighter in her chair as she began typing like it was any other day. Ricky stalked over to her cubicle. "Luella, could I see you in my office, please?" He tapped his foot rhythmically against the floor.

She pressed her lips tight, stopped typing, and got up without looking at him or anyone else. She walked into his office and waited, arms crossed over her chest, as he closed the door behind them.

"I know you got my email," he said, walking toward his desk. He sat down and leaned back in his office chair, his middle-aged belly jutting out above his brown belt.

"What email?" She didn't even try to hide the sarcasm in her voice.

He sighed. "Please don't make this any more difficult than it already is."

Luella scoffed. "Difficult. You fired me through an email, Ricky. There has to be a policy somewhere making that illegal. What kind of—"

"So, you did get my email?" He shook his head. "Probably not the most ethical thing to do. But it's certainly legal."

"I'm the best writer you've got," she said, hoping he wouldn't catch the desperation in her voice. Ricky looked past her toward the other writers working in their cubicles as if they could hear her through the glass window. She followed his gaze, then shrugged. "You and I both know it's the truth. You wouldn't have gotten the Clements story without me."

"That may be true, but we'll manage." He picked up an envelope from a pile on his desk and held it out for her. "Here's your pay stub."

She wanted to rip it up right there in front of him, but she refrained. After all, it was only a stub. Doing so wouldn't have the effect she wanted.

If she didn't need the money, she'd have quit months ago. But she did need it. This gig didn't pay much to begin with, and her roommate, Harper, was already breathing down her neck about how behind she was on paying her portion of the rent. Luella snatched the envelope out of his hand as her gaze landed on the peace lily sitting on the windowsill. She had given it to Ricky after his knee surgery several months ago. She walked over to it and picked it up, then turned to leave.

"You can't take my plant." He laughed as if she was pranking him.

Luella turned around; her face stone cold. "It may be unethical, but it's certainly not illegal." She smiled at him, then walked out of his office.

She set the plant down at her cubicle long enough to throw her laptop into her bag and put on her coat. Everyone was staring at her, but she refused to give them the satisfaction of looking upset. She threw her bag over her shoulder, shoved the pay stub inside, and picked up the plant. She acknowledged no one on her way out. She had no doubt they'd be vying for her position the second the door slammed shut behind her.

Outside, she threw the plant into a trash can with a thud. She glanced over at Ricky's office window and hoped he had watched as she did it. Maybe then he'd understand how it felt to be discarded.

She sank down onto a metal bench beside the curb, contemplating what to do next. It was just two days before Christmas. That realization made her wish she had taken up smoking like her mother. She could understand the appeal of it in moments like this when a person could use something to take the edge off. Something that was not a stiff drink.

The screech of a halting bus pulled her out of her thoughts. She looked up and noticed a woman staring at her from a few feet away, at the intersection in front of the *Scandalanta* office. Luella looked away, sure they had just made eye contact momentarily, but when she looked back, the woman's eyes were still on her. The woman was short and blonde. She looked high class in her white pantsuit and stilettos—her petite frame the opposite of Luella's pear-shaped. Her perfectly manicured hand clutched a Starbucks cup and a fancy handbag dangled from her arm. Luella watched as the woman took the lid off. She looked away when the woman looked up at her again, but Luella could see her stomping toward her from her peripheral vision. Her heels clicked on the concrete as she did.

"Are you Luella McCrae?"

"Who's asking?"

"Don't play coy with me. I know who you are," said the woman.

Luella could barely get any words out before the woman slung coffee all over her. The coffee rolled off her peacoat and dripped between the slats of the metal bench. Luella sat there, mouth agape. "You have got to be kidding me," she muttered under her breath. Luella wiped at the wetness on her coat. Thankfully, the liquid was no longer hot.

"Thanks for ruining my marriage," the woman spat.

"Yeah, no problem—thanks for ruining my coat." As soon as she said it, the woman's words clicked. Luella realized who she was. This must be Mrs. Clements.

*Freaking Tuesdays.*

Luella sighed and shook her coat, as though that might rid it of the wetness and perhaps, the woman's rage.

"I did you a favor," said Luella.

The woman bit her bottom lip, but Luella could still see the way it quivered. Luella knew how she felt. She too was an impulsive person, doing whatever felt good in the moment in the hopes of it making her feel better long term. It never did. Most of the time, it made things worse.

The woman let out a heavy sigh. The corners of her mouth turned down. "I shouldn't have dumped my coffee on you . . . but you have to understand, my marriage is over. It's two days away from Christmas. My kids won't understand why their father won't be there for Christmas morning. My entire world changed when you hit publish on that story."

Luella considered it for a moment. "Yes, but wouldn't you rather have known? Seriously. The man cheated on you in public. He wasn't hiding from the cameras or the sources who saw him out with her. It would have gotten back to you eventually."

The corners of the woman's mouth went up in a smirk. "Is that how you make yourself feel better about what you do?"

It hit a nerve. Luella was done with this day—already over whatever else the universe was going to throw at her next. She let out a laugh. She didn't have to defend what she did to anyone, least of all this woman. "It pays the bills," Luella said with a smile.

The woman's eyes went wide. "What an excuse," she said, holding her head high. "I'm sure you've heard the saying misery loves company. I think someone like you must get some weird kind of solace from knowing that others are unhappy, too."

"Lady, you know nothing about me," said Luella.

"That's true," she said. "But I know you make a living off other people's scandals like you have no skeletons in your own closet. That must be a miserable way to live."

Luella smirked. Even if there was some truth in her words, she would never give the woman the satisfaction of knowing she had shaken her up. "You know you're really mad at your husband and you're just taking it out on me because I'm the easy target. You're still gonna have to go home and deal with your side-stepping husband."

The woman stared at her for a moment. Luella just smiled back. She could tell by the woman's pinched expression that it irritated her. Finally, the woman stomped off up the stairs and into the *Scandalanta* office. Probably to have the story pulled from the website. But that was the problem with the internet. Once it was there, it was there forever—even if you took it down. People would take a screenshot, tweet it, and spread it quicker than a wildfire.

If she thought about it for too long, she did feel bad about the stories she wrote. She knew what they could do to a person. To their career. To their family. But she desensitized herself to it to get the job done. She also told herself that most of the subjects had it coming. Someone was likely to report it anyway, and she needed to pay rent. But look where that had gotten her.

Honestly, the woman had done Luella a favor. The truth was, she had gotten too comfortable at *Scandalanta*. Being a gossip columnist was never her endgame. She had her eyes on bigger opportunities. It had been her dream to get her foot in the door at *The Georgian*—a highly revered magazine, second to *The New Yorker*, and one day write stories for them. Real stories. Stories about more than whose spouse was cheating on them or who had slipped up and made a politically incorrect statement or who had recently gotten plastic surgery. She loathed everything about the job, besides the fact that she got to write. That was the reason she stayed. She told herself it was merely a stepping-stone to what she really wanted.

For months, she had been refining her portfolio and getting it into as near perfect shape as possible. Her best friend had gotten her a face-to-face meeting with one of the big bosses at *The Georgian.*

That meeting was happening tomorrow.

Now that she had lost her job and only source of income, the meeting was more important than ever.

# two

Her cell phone was dead when she woke up. The clock radio said it was nine forty-five, which meant Luella was fifteen minutes late for her meeting with Cathy from *The Georgian.*

Last night she had pep-talked herself, saying that today was going to be the day that she finally got her foot in the door. She had been through revision after revision, crafting a story about Mac Moretti—a local diner owner who worked his way up in Yelp Reviews. Cathy said she could just email it to her, but Luella wanted to give it to her in person so she could meet her and experience the perk of seeing Cathy's face as she read her story.

After waking up and realizing her alarm had never gone off, she shot out of the bed, snatching her phone up as she did. Her fingers worked frantically trying to bring the phone to life, but the black screen stared back at her.

She ran into the living room where Harper kept an extra charger by the couch and plugged the phone in to charge while she got ready. Her charger had been glitching for weeks. She meant to buy a new one, but hadn't yet. Sometimes she hated that about herself—she pushed off decisions until the last minute. It always cost her in the end.

Clothes were thrown all over the floor in her room, and there were approximately six bottles of water on the nightstand—all of which contained only one or two more sips. Harper couldn't stand that about her. She had a meltdown about it once, but right now, she was out of town for Christmas and Luella was late, so the cleaning would have to wait.

She grabbed her black slacks out of the closet and searched for the most professional-looking top she owned. The one that said, *I belong in your company.* Her eyes scanned the room and found it thrown in the corner. She picked it up and looked it over, trying to decide how many wrinkles one could get away with before looking like a hot mess. She lifted it to her nose. It smelled fine, so she pulled it over her head. The doorbell rang as she stepped into the black slacks.

"One second," she yelled, pulling her long brown hair into a bun on top of her head. It looked more like a bird's nest, but it would have to do. She tugged a few pieces loose around her face so it would make her rounded cheeks appear thinner. She slipped on her favorite pair of flats and picked up the concealer off the dresser and dabbed a little under her eyes. The doorbell rang again as she rubbed the concealer in and then quickly put on some mascara.

She already knew who it was, and he was just going to have to wait. It wouldn't kill him.

After putting on some lip gloss, she looked in the mirror at her full reflection. It was the best she could do. She went into the living room and yanked the charger out of the wall with the phone still attached and shoved it in her bag. The Coffee Shack was exactly a three-minute walk from her building. That was the beauty of the city and exactly the reason she moved to Atlanta. That among several other reasons, which she didn't have the time or the energy to think about.

The doorbell rang again as she reached for the door. She pulled it open, and there stood Benjamin with a bouquet of red roses held deliberately in front of his face. Luella rolled her eyes. He lowered the bouquet and smiled.

"Good morning, gorgeous," he said with a smirk. "I'm sorry about last night."

He held out the vase—a peace offering for his behavior. He had sent a string of constant texts all night long, to which she responded with several snarky comments before ghosting him completely. But Benjamin was nothing if not persistent. She took the vase and set it on the entryway table without even a second glance at the dark red petals. She knew plenty of men like Benjamin Wyatt, and she couldn't stand a single one of them or the way they thought they could buy a female's emotions.

"Um . . . thanks," she said. "But I don't have time for this. I'm running late for a meeting."

"I'm not here to argue," he said, holding up his hands as though it were a hostage situation. He stepped toward her. "I didn't sleep at all because I couldn't stop thinking about our argument."

She scoffed and grabbed her jacket off the rack, pulled it on, and tried not to look up at Benjamin's face. The dramatics were too much for her this morning. It hadn't really crossed her mind at all. He wasn't even a blip on her radar. She wouldn't even call it an argument so much as her blatantly turning down his advances. He just wouldn't take the hint that she was not interested. That she *couldn't* be. Besides, she had more important things on her mind.

Benjamin followed her as she flew down the three flights of stairs to the sidewalk. She wasn't paying attention to anything he was saying, and it wasn't until she reached the crosswalk that she finally focused on him just in time to see him leaning in for a kiss. *The audacity of this man.* She turned her face so that his lips landed on her cheek instead. His face fell. "I guess I deserve that . . . so, how about tonight?" he asked with a wink.

The crosswalk sign lit up, excusing her to go. "No shot unless you're dropping off dinner and leaving," she said, hustling across with several other people. When she looked back, he was still standing there, watching her walk away.

~

The Coffee Shack was busy for Christmas Eve. People stood in line waiting with bags in their hands from last-minute gift shopping. Some chatted cheerily as they waited for the extra dose of energy needed to get them through their day. The nutty, caramel smell of coffee wafted through the air and into Luella's nose. It was one of her favorite smells.

The clock on the wall above the register read ten o'clock. Thirty minutes late. She hoped the article would keep her in Cathy's good graces. She looked around and finally spotted Cathy, just as she was getting up from her table. Luella rushed over.

"Cathy, I'm so sorry I'm late," she said.

"I've been waiting forty-five minutes."

Luella wondered if she had written down the wrong time or if Cathy just arrived early, but that didn't really matter now. "I know," she said, sitting down in the chair across from Cathy. "I'm sorry. My charger must have broken because my phone was dead this morning, and I know that sounds like an excuse, but it's the honest to God truth."

Luella hoped Cathy would stay and read her story. She understood if she didn't. Luella had a knack for screwing things up for herself. Her best friend, Meggie, had gotten her this meeting. One shot to impress Cathy and maybe get her story about Mac published in *The Georgian*. She wanted it more than she had wanted anything in a long time. No, she didn't just want it; she *needed* it. One opportunity could lead to another and then maybe she could get on staff as a regular contributor. Then, she'd be someone to be proud of.

Cathy sat back down in her chair. She studied Luella for a minute without saying a word. Her eyes scanned up and down like she could measure Luella's talent by her outward appearance. Luella's cheeks grew hotter by the second. Finally, Cathy sighed. "Alright," she said. "But only because you're Meggie's best friend, and she vouched for you. Normally, I'd have already been out that door . . . but it's also Christmas Eve. So, let's see your story."

Luella couldn't help but smile. She pulled the paper out of her bag and handed it over to Cathy, who took it and settled back into her chair to read. Luella's phone started ringing again.

Cathy looked up at her.

"Sorry," Luella said, pulling the phone out of her bag. It was the same number from the day before. She declined the call, silenced her phone, and smiled at Cathy as she slipped the phone back into her bag. Cathy began reading again. Luella's eyes were glued to Cathy's face, but it gave nothing away. She didn't even move an inch while she read. Luella imagined she was probably very good at gambling because her poker face was impressive. That or Luella's story just sucked bad enough that Cathy was trying not to cringe. Either way, Luella couldn't take the pressure anymore. She scanned the coffee shop for a distraction.

A dark-haired woman in the corner sipped slowly from a coffee cup in one hand while reading a paperback in the other. Luella narrowed her eyes to help see the title, but she couldn't quite make it out. A few feet away, a mother sat sharing a pink sprinkled donut with her daughter, who looked no older than three. Luella felt a pang in her chest as she watched the way the daughter laughed as she pressed the donut to her mother's mouth, trying to feed her. They finished eating and threw away their trash before heading out the door. The mother reached for the little girl's hand, and she took it so willingly. The love between them was palpable.

Luella wondered what it felt like to love someone like that. Not only as a mother who loves her child, but as a child who knows with absolute conviction that her mother loves her back. The door slammed shut behind them. Luella noticed several people with coffee cups beside them and laptops in front of them as they typed furiously. She decided she'd rather just belong to that group of people. That was the safer way to live.

Cathy laid the story down on the table and looked over at Luella. "You're a talented writer," she said. "It's a good story."

This was it. She could feel it. Luella tried not to get too excited. "You think so?" she asked, scooting closer to the table. "I have an idea for another story where—"

"Luella," Cathy interrupted, holding a hand up. "The story is good, but good isn't enough. It needs to be great. It needs to be better than great. While you're a wonderful writer, there's something missing in this piece. I don't feel the fire in your words, and that's an absolute must for your piece to stand out. We get hundreds of submissions a week."

Luella's heart sank. She picked up the paper and looked over at Cathy. She slid the paper back into her bag. "Thanks for reading it. I know you were doing Meggie a favor."

"She's my favorite niece," Cathy said with a smile. "And I don't say that because she's my only niece, either."

Luella smiled and let out a courtesy laugh so Cathy would feel like it was okay that she didn't like Luella's story. She didn't want Cathy thinking Meggie would be mad at her. It's just business. And it wasn't the first time Luella had faced rejection.

"So, tell me about this farm where you grew up," said Cathy, still smiling. "Meggie has told me more stories than I can count about the times she spent with you there. It sounds like a magical childhood."

Magical wasn't exactly what Luella would use to describe it. She didn't want to dull the Christmas Eve spirit with her tales of abandonment and unusual upbringing. Unsure of what to say, Luella just nodded her head and said, "It was something else, that's for sure."

"You have a big family, right? Lots of brothers and sisters? I always got them confused when Meggie would tell stories because there were so many names to keep up with. Or were they cousins? Because you lived with your grandparents, right?"

"I did," said Luella. "I lived with my grandparents from the time I was seven, but they weren't my siblings or cousins. My grandparents were foster parents."

Suddenly, the room felt stuffy. This was the last thing she wanted to talk about. Cathy must have sensed that because she simply nodded. An awkward moment of silence passed between them, and then Cathy leaned forward slightly in her chair. "Have you ever thought of writing about that?"

Luella had never even considered it. She left Chipley Creek to forget, not to rehash it years later. "No, I haven't."

"There might be something there. It's an interesting dynamic and a story only you can tell because you lived it. It might be worth exploring just to see what comes of it."

Luella nodded. "I'll keep that in mind," she said, knowing she had zero intentions of following through with that idea.

"We have our 75th-anniversary edition coming up in a few months. It's going to be a double volume, and perhaps a good edition to feature that story in if you think you would consider writing it. If you do, get it to me by the end of March." Cathy looked at her watch, and Luella knew their meeting was over. Her chance to impress Cathy had ended. "I've got to get going. It was very nice to meet you, Luella."

She held out her hand, and Luella took it. "Yeah, you too."

"Merry Christmas," said Cathy.

Luella forced a smile. "You too."

She watched Cathy walk out of the coffee shop with a pep in her step, wondering if it was because she was going home to her family for the holidays. At least that's what it looked like from where Luella sat, alone, at the tiny wooden table in a sea of strangers.

# three

Christmas Eve and she had nowhere to go. She sat alone at The Coffee Shack for a long time after Cathy left, trying to come up with any other idea besides the one Cathy wanted, but she came up short every time.

For a while, she just watched people coming and going out of the coffee shop, her mind replaying the events of the past two days. The meeting hadn't gone how she hoped. She was unemployed. And it was the holidays. She could go back to her apartment, but she'd be alone with her thoughts, and she knew where that would lead, especially at this time of year.

Instead, she walked down the street to the Tap Room Bar and Grill. She went there occasionally.

The musty smell of the bar hit her in the face as she pulled open the door. The warm air welcomed her as she stepped inside. The place was practically deserted. It was half-past noon, and there were only a few people sitting at tables and booths. Two men were in the middle of a heated game of pool in the corner of the room.

No one was sitting at the bar, so Luella walked over and took a seat atop one of the metal swivel stools. Christmas music echoed through the speakers overhead as a tall, blonde bartender walked over to her. She wore an elf's hat and looked less than thrilled to be there.

Luella didn't blame her.

"What can I get you?"

"I'll just take whatever festive drink you've got," Luella said. If she was going to be miserable on Christmas Eve, then she was going to at least have the company of a good drink.

The bartender nodded and walked back toward the kitchen. Luella's phone whistled, letting her know she had received a text. She pulled the phone out of her bag and saw a missed call and a message from Meggie asking how her meeting had gone. Luella didn't feel like letting her sour mood taint her best friend's Christmas Eve, so she ignored the message and set the phone down on the bar.

She pulled a notebook and a pen out of her bag. She was determined to come up with something. She began jotting down more potential ideas as George Bailey was about to jump into a frigid river on the television above the bar. She scribbled several ideas onto the notepad and scratched through each one after a few seconds.

*What's the point?*

She sighed as the bartender came back with a long-stemmed martini glass. "White chocolate peppermint martini," she said with a smile, setting the drink down proudly in front of Luella.

Broken peppermint pieces donned the rim of the glass. She took a sip of the white, milky liquid and scrunched her face up. It was strong. She nodded. "It's delicious."

The bartender smiled like she was pleased with herself. "Let me know if you need anything else," she said before slipping away again.

Luella's phone buzzed on the table. Benjamin. When she didn't answer, he called again. She rolled her eyes, gulped down the last of the martini, and set the empty glass down on the bar top. Her eyebrows furrowed as she wrote two words on the notepad, followed by a question mark.

*Chipley Creek?*

She stared at the name of the place she grew up. The population size was less than a thousand. It was all country roads, farmhouses, and nothing but pasture for miles. A vast difference from the city Luella now inhabited.

In Chipley, if you wanted groceries, you went to Bradley's. If you needed a prescription filled, you'd go to The Medicine Shoppe. There was no story there, despite what Cathy might have thought. Just a quiet life that ticked by at a snail's pace.

It wasn't necessarily the town that she disliked. It was the memories that it held.

Mainly the ones at 52 Palmetto Drive. That's where she grew up, down a gravel road on a little piece of land they called the farm. It wasn't an actual farm in the traditional sense of the word. They had chickens, horses, dogs, a slew of cats, and a duck that believed with all its heart it was a chicken.

A place like that soaks into you like gasoline on skin. It doesn't matter how many times you cleanse yourself of it, you'd still find the faint smell it left behind.

The day she turned eighteen, she took a bus one hundred and eighty miles to Atlanta and never looked back. That was eleven years ago.

She put Chipley Creek in the back of her mind and kept it there.

But when the city was quiet, or when she saw lovers walking hand in hand, she'd find it moving further and further to the forefront of her mind.

Like it did right then at the bar when a man walked through the door and strolled over to the two men playing pool. She couldn't see the front of his face. Only the side of it, the hard outline of his jaw attached to a head of light brown hair. She noticed his broad shoulders as he pulled off the jacket he wore. Her heart pounded.

It couldn't be him. Not here in the city.

The man turned, exposing his full face. Her heart sank right there at the bar. He caught her eye and smiled at her, but she didn't return it. Of course it wasn't him. It had been eleven and a half years since she last saw him. He was still a boy when she left. Who knew what he looked like now. But that didn't stop her from searching for him in the face of every man she passed on the streets of Atlanta.

She looked down, wrote another word, and then circled it.

*Paul.*

Six hours and three white chocolate peppermint martinis later, Luella staggered back toward her apartment. The city was covered in twinkling lights, and there were Santas on every corner ho-ho-ho-ing for change. Christmas was her favorite time of year, even if it made her a little sad.

As she neared a red light, she heard one of her favorite Christmas songs coming from a smooth, soulful voice. Something about city sidewalks and Christmas cheer. Her chest ached.

She looked over and found the man playing guitar on the corner, strumming and singing his cares away.

Luella stopped and listened to him. Her grandpa would play this song on his harmonica every Christmas when she was growing up. She let herself think about him and those Christmas mornings for just a few seconds before pushing them away.

But she loved this song.

She reached into her bag, pulled out the only cash she had, and staggered forward, placing a twenty in his guitar case. The man tipped his head to her in appreciation.

As she tottered back toward her apartment, her phone started ringing. She pulled it out of her back pocket to see who it was. The same phone number that had been calling her for days. This time, she answered. She didn't recognize the voice on the other end of the phone.

"Hello," said a woman. "Is this Luella McCrae? I've been trying to reach you for several days now. My name is Millie Beams."

A debt collector. Go figure. Which was the exact reason why Luella never answered phone numbers she didn't recognize. If it was important, they would leave a message.

"I'm sorry, you've got the wrong number," mumbled Luella. She was about to hang up, but what the woman said next stopped her.

"I'm calling on behalf of your grandmother, Helen."

Luella froze. A shiver ran through her. Despite the effects of the martinis, her mind sobered. "Is she dead?"

One second. Two seconds. They felt like an eternity. Her stomach clenched tight until the woman finally spoke again.

"No," said Mrs. Beams. "I'm calling regarding an offer your grandmother has put forth for you to consider. I'm sorry it's so late in the day, and on Christmas Eve, but there are matters to be solved, and I have been trying to get in touch with you for days."

When Luella didn't respond, the woman took it as a sign to keep going. "Mrs. McCrae is sick. She needs a caregiver for a while, as well as some help around the farm, and as you know, she has no living relatives—only you and your mother."

Luella took a deep breath. "Did you call my mother first? Let me guess, Mya can't be bothered."

"No, I didn't," said Mrs. Beams. "Helen explicitly requested I not call Mya. This offer is only available to you, per Helen's request. If you return to Chipley Creek and take over as her caregiver, then she'll write into her will that you are to inherit the deed to the farm, as well as all of her liquidated assets—around five hundred thousand, give or take."

Luella's mouth fell open. "Shut up."

"I beg your pardon?" said Mrs. Beams.

"Oh no, I didn't mean—I'm sorry. This is a lot to process."

"I understand, but like I said, this is a time-sensitive matter."

Luella was quiet for a moment, and then asked, "What happens if I don't accept?"

There was a pause, followed by a sigh. "Then, Mrs. McCrae will be moved to a care facility and all the assets will be liquidated and the sum total will be signed over to the Georgia Baptist Children's Home."

*Typical Helen*, thought Luella. She was an all-or-nothing kind of person. But half a million dollars was life-changing, especially for someone like Luella.

It came at a cost, though.

Helen knew how much Luella despised the farm and Chipley Creek. What was she playing at?

"I know it's a lot to take in," said Mrs. Beams. "You think it over and call me. I'll need your decision soon. Helen is in the hospital and is going to be released within the next few days. If you decide to do this, then we'll have to get this process moving along quickly."

"Why is she in the hospital?"

"She forbade me from saying. All I can say is that she's sick. I'll give you some time to think it over, but I'll be expecting to hear from you soon." Mrs. Beams wished her a Merry Christmas and then hung up the phone.

Luella looked at the screen to make sure that the conversation had actually happened.

Chipley Creek. Paul. Helen. It was too much to think about. Suddenly, her head was pounding. She walked the rest of the way to her apartment in sobering silence.

When she reached her door, Benjamin was sitting on the stairs, waiting for her. He got up and staggered toward her.

"Benjamin, what are you doing here?" she asked, opening the door to the apartment and stepping inside. He practically fell into the room behind her. She saw the flowers sitting on the entry table and remembered that when they parted ways this morning, he had said something about tonight. She wished she had paid more attention.

He stumbled forward and wrapped his arms around her. "I'm sorry about this morning . . . you drive me absolutely crazy, you know that?" He pressed his lips to hers and gave her a sloppy kiss. She could taste the Fireball Whiskey on his breath. The cinnamon flavor made her want to gag.

"You're drunk," she said, wriggling out of his embrace.

"And you're beautiful." He wrapped his arms around her waist and kissed her again. This time soft and slow.

Luella kissed him back, letting his desire for her silence all the noise inside her mind.

When their lips finally parted, she took a deep breath, re-grounding herself. "This can't happen," she said.

"Why not?" he asked, in between kisses up and down her neck.

"You know why," she said barely above a whisper. She closed her eyes—resenting the way she eased a little in his arms.

Sometimes it was easier for her to give in, more so when she needed to feel seen, validated, or loved. Even if it was just for a moment. There's only so much loneliness a person can take. If Benjamin could numb the ache in her chest, maybe she'd let him—just for tonight.

If it weren't for that phone call, and all the thoughts of Chipley Creek and Paul, she would have made him leave.

But instead, she pulled him toward her room, and toward her bed.

# four

At quarter to midnight, Luella woke to the sound of someone fumbling with the lock on the apartment door. Spooked, she grabbed Benjamin's button-up and threw it on. She grabbed the umbrella sitting by her dresser and held it up like a baseball bat as she sauntered toward the door. The lock clicked to the right, and the door opened. She swung the umbrella, barely missing.

Harper screamed, "It's me!"

Luella breathed a sigh of relief at the sight of her roommate and threw the umbrella down on the floor. She switched the light on.

"What is wrong with you?" asked Harper, visibly shaken.

"You weren't supposed to be here," said Luella. "I thought someone was breaking in."

"I was planning to go straight to Blue Ridge from the airport, but I was too tired to drive up there, so I figured I'd get a few hours of sleep here first. I'll head there in the morning." Harper looked Luella up and down, cocked an eyebrow, and smirked. "I can tell you weren't expecting me. I see you're not alone."

Luella's hands started sweating as she pulled the shirt tighter around her naked body. She tried her best to smile and shrug it off.

She turned around to hurry back to her room.

"Who are the flowers from?" asked Harper.

Luella turned toward her and smiled. "Benjamin." She started again for her room, but Harper continued.

"Oh my gosh, they're gorgeous," she said, fussing over the flowers. "But why would he send them here? He knew I wouldn't be back until after Christmas."

Just as Luella was about to take the last few steps to her room, Benjamin stepped out, wearing nothing but briefs.

"Everything okay?" he asked, his eyes landing on Harper as he did. His eyes widened like a deer caught in headlights.

Luella shut her eyes and waited for it.

"Benji?" said Harper in a high-pitched tone of disbelief.

And boom. Harper went off like a firecracker. She started yelling and screaming louder than Luella thought was physically possible. Luella's stomach tightened, and her mouth started watering like it always did before she threw up. She should have explained. But what was there to say? It was obvious what had happened. No way to sugar coat it.

Luella stepped quickly past Benjamin and shut the door to her room while he and Harper continued their lover's quarrel.

She pulled on a pair of jeans and slid her feet into her favorite worn-in Sauconys. Then, she pulled a sweatshirt over her head, grabbed her wallet and phone, and bolted toward the door.

Typical Luella. When it came to fight or flight, it was flight every time.

But she should have known better than to believe she could get away that easily. Benjamin and Harper were still screaming at each other in the living room as Luella reached for the doorknob. A coffee mug came soaring through the air, nearly hitting Luella before landing on the wall beside her. It shattered and fell to the floor. Luella snapped her head in Harper's direction. "Are you crazy?"

"I want you gone in the morning," said Harper.

Luella scoffed. "You don't even like him, you say it all the time. You're always talking about how you're going to break up with him."

"And that makes it okay for you?" asked Harper. She looked over at Benjamin. "It's a freaking code of ethics. You don't sleep with your girlfriend's roommate, and you don't sleep with your roommate's boyfriend."

Harper and Benjamin started yelling at each other again, both trying to be louder than the other. Luella wondered why she didn't feel bad, standing there in the middle of them. The truth was, all she really felt was numb—like her insides were frozen, just waiting for something to come along and thaw them out.

She twisted the doorknob and heard Harper yapping from behind about how Luella was dead to her. Luella looked at the time on her phone. 12:01.

*Merry freaking Christmas.*

Luella pulled her coat tight around her as the frigid midnight air bit at her skin. She hurried across the street to Mac's 24-Hour Diner. It was always open and welcome whenever she needed it. She couldn't stay in the apartment while Benjamin and Harper had their epic blowout. So, she did what she did best when confrontation arose—she left.

"Merry Christmas!" the two servers yelled in sing-song unison as Luella stepped inside.

She forced a smile and walked toward a small booth in the corner. Normally, she'd sit right up front where the servers and cooks were, talking to them while waiting to see Mac. But tonight, she preferred the solitude of a corner booth.

The electric pulse of Paul McCartney's "Wonderful Christmastime" started playing on the overhead speaker like a gift of mockery from the universe.

Luella knew the menu well, but she picked it up anyway. A server made her way over to the booth and took Luella's drink order. Coffee, black. It was probably a bad idea to have coffee at midnight, but she couldn't help herself. She looked out of the window at the city and felt so small against the backdrop of tall buildings.

When her coffee arrived, she thanked the server with a smile.

She looked out the window at her apartment building across the street. What a mess she had made. Sometimes she didn't know why she did the things she did. Helen used to tell her all the time how she didn't think about the consequences of her actions. She just did things as she pleased, paying no mind to how it may affect anyone else in her path.

Luella hated when Helen was right. Harper didn't deserve that. She had used Benjamin to numb the ache at Harper's expense. Luella sighed as she rubbed her forehead and then took a sip of her coffee.

If she hadn't received that phone call, none of this would have happened. Millie Beams had said Helen was sick. What did that mean? What if it was a trap? Helen lying to get her to come back to Chipley Creek. But why would she go through all the trouble? It made no sense.

Why now? After eleven years of silence.

Luella drank the last of her coffee as Mac stepped out from the back. His eyes landed on her, and she cocked her head to the side with a smile. He was never there that late. His big, grizzly face spread wide as he smiled from ear to ear.

"Luella!" he said with his thick Italian accent. "Merry Christmas!"

She couldn't help but smile. Mac had that effect. He changed the energy when he walked into a room. People relaxed around him. For Luella, coming to Mac's was like slipping on her favorite worn-in sweatshirt—comforting in all the best ways.

He walked over to her booth and slid into the other side, facing her. "What are you doing here so late?"

"I could ask you the same question," she said.

"We made some extra pans and dropped them off at the shelter off of MLK and the one on Ponce." He said it like it was no big deal. Like it was just any other day. Luella knew how hard he worked, though. He knew every one of his regular customers by name. He invested in people where other business owners would just reap the profits of their business and go about their lives. Not Mac.

"So, how did the meeting go? Did she like the story?" Mac asked.

Luella didn't want to tell him. The story was about him after all, but she couldn't lie to him, either. So, she told him the truth. She shrugged. "Not really. She said that I'm a talented writer, but there wasn't any fire in my words."

Mac nodded his head slowly, and Luella could tell he was trying to think of something encouraging to say. He'd try to find a silver lining in any situation. He had a knack for that. "Next time," he said with a softness in his voice that made Luella's chest warm and her throat go dry. His face perked up. "I've got something for you."

He got up from the booth and walked to the back.

When he was gone, Luella looked out of the window toward her apartment building. Benjamin was leaving. He had a small box in his hands, and something spilled out as he bounced down the steps. He bent to grab it, catching sight of Luella as he stood back up. They stared at each other for a moment too long. Luella's stomach tensed as a thickness formed in her throat. She looked away first. Their spat was over now. She knew Harper would still be awake, and she didn't want to deal with that tonight. She'd wait her out. When she looked out the window again, he was already gone.

Mac returned with a gift in one hand and a plate of pancakes in the other. Luella's stomach lurched in anticipation. Her mouth watered looking at the three perfectly stacked pancakes with butter and whipped cream on top. They were her favorite, and Mac knew it.

He set them down in front of her.

"I figured you could use these," he said, sliding back into the booth. He set the gift on the table. It was wrapped perfectly in brown kraft paper and tied around each side with a wide red burlap ribbon. The perfect rectangular shape of a book.

That was their thing. They had been exchanging books for years now. They liked to challenge each other with the other's suggested reading. Then, they'd talk about them at the diner.

But this one wasn't planned. He had caught her off guard. "Mac, I don't have anything for you," she said. "I can't accept that."

He brushed her statement off with a wave of his hand. "You will because this here is a Christmas gift." He smiled as he slid it across the table to her. She picked it up hesitantly and carefully unwrapped the bow and ripped at the paper, revealing a green hardback cover. There was no dust jacket, and it had visible signs of wear, which meant that it had been well-loved. Their favorite kind. The golden script on the front read *Anne of Green Gables.*

She looked up at him, her eyes wide. He smiled, pleased with his gift. "Mac," she said in a teasing tone. "I never pegged you as a big softy. You always pick epic adventures or true crime."

Mac's laughter erupted up from his belly in that big gusto sound that created smiles on the faces of anyone within earshot. Then, he took a deep breath, recollecting himself, and asked,

"Have you ever read it?"

Luella shook her head. Mac sighed and sat back against the booth. "My wife used to read it to our Gabriella. I'd listen from the other side of the room as they'd laugh and sometimes cry right along with Anne. It's a good one. I think you'll like it."

"Thanks, Mac," she said, running her fingers across the golden script. She cleared her throat. "Got big plans for Christmas?"

"Oh yeah," he said. "The whole family is coming to town the day after Christmas. It'll be a nice break from the daily diner grind." He smiled at her and then was silent for a few seconds, like he was deciding whether he should say whatever it was he wanted to say.

"What about you? You gonna go home for Christmas and see your family?"

He knew the answer. They had talked about her family on several occasions. He asked her anyway because to Mac, family was the most important thing. He would never give up trying to convince her of that.

"No," she said, eyes lowered to the book in her hands in the hopes of avoiding his eyes. But inevitably, she looked up to meet his gaze.

Mac smiled sadly. "Luella, I'm telling you . . . you need to call your family. Go see them. One day you're holding grudges, and the next day you won't ever get the chance to let go of them because the person is gone. Trust me, I know. Time is a thief, and you don't know that you've been robbed until it's too late."

Luella tried to shrug Mac's words off like they didn't bother her. But Mac wasn't everyone else, and she knew there was merit in his words. She tried to play it cool. Mac gave her a sympathetic look. She hated when he did that. When she couldn't stand it anymore, she shrugged and said, "I should go." She pulled out her wallet to pay him, but he put his hand up to stop her.

"It's on me tonight."

"Thanks, Mac," she said, placing her hand over his. He placed his other one on top and patted it. Luella smiled. "Merry Christmas to you and yours."

"Merry Christmas, kid," he said. He smiled at her, and it made her want to cry. If only Mac could be her family. He was easy to love.

When she opened the door to the apartment, the lights were off, and the silence was so loud it was ringing in her ears. She tiptoed into her room and shut the door as quietly as she could. Then, she fell onto the bed. It should have been easy to close her eyes and drift off to sleep, but her thoughts kept her awake.

That phone call had made her act irrationally. She still couldn't get past Mrs. Beams saying Helen was sick. If Luella knew anything about her grandma, it was that she was made of steel. Nothing got through her. Luella wondered what had finally done it.

She leaned over the bed and pulled out a plastic container from underneath. She opened it and pulled out a thick, faded purple journal. The pages were weathered from time and tears. She sat up on the bed and ran her hand over the top of it. Her most intimate thoughts were written inside its pages. She wrote in it the entire time she lived at the farm. She didn't write in it every day—only when it hurt. When the heaviness became too much, and she needed to pour it out and let it go. That's when she'd pick the journal up and write. Just like Helen had taught her.

She let the pages glide past her thumb like a deck of cards being shuffled. A folded-up picture fell out. Luella picked it up. A white line ran down the middle where time had weathered the image. She hardly recognized the kids in the picture. She and Meggie stood in front of the barn with their cheeks pressed together. Their lanky arms were thrown across each other's shoulders. There was someone else in the photo behind them.

Paul.

She fell asleep with the picture held tight against her chest.

# five

Several hours later, Luella woke up shivering. She got out of bed and pulled her chestnut brown hair up into a loose bun on top of her head. As she neared the door, she glimpsed her reflection in the mirror affixed to the dresser.

She barely recognized the woman staring back at her. She looked older than her twenty-nine years. Dark circles under her eyes. The vertical one-inch scar on her right cheek that she got from a stray dog when she was nine. The chapped lips and beginnings of crow's feet at the edges of her eyes.

She sighed, grabbing the ChapStick she kept in the glass decorative bowl on top of her dresser and slathered some on. Then, she grabbed the black fleece robe hanging on the back of her door and pulled it around her.

The apartment was dark, the only light seeped in through the windows from the dreary, overcast sky. The Christmas tree Harper had happily put up in between the windows after Thanksgiving was gone now. She must have torn it down in a rage while Luella was at Mac's. There wasn't even a dash of Christmas anywhere to be seen.

A rustling sound leaked through the crack at the bottom of

Harper's bedroom door. Luella wanted to apologize to her. To explain what happened. Tell her about Millie Beams and the phone call so that she might understand why Luella did what she did. But they weren't friends, and Luella couldn't make herself walk over to the door and knock. So, she waited instead.

Luella stood next to the kitchen counter with a mug of coffee in her hand when Harper came out of her bedroom dressed like she was going to meet the president. She had on black slacks, black high heels, and a red cashmere cowl neck sweater. Her blonde hair was perfectly curled and fell right below her busty chest. Her face was dolled up in full contoured makeup, complete with matching red lipstick. She looked like she stepped right out of a magazine. She stepped past Luella without saying a word.

Luella took a sip of her coffee. "It's freezing in here."

Harper stopped for a moment like she was deciding whether or not she wanted to respond, but she reached into the cabinet instead and pulled out a giant stainless-steel tumbler. She grabbed the carafe of coffee and emptied the rest of the pot into the tumbler, leaving none left for Luella.

*Touché.*

"I want you out by the time I get back from Blue Ridge," she said, twisting the top onto the tumbler. She turned around and looked Luella up and down like she was sizing her up. She tilted her chin up, and Luella knew Harper was thinking how much better she was than Luella.

"Can we just talk for a second?"

"I have nothing to say to you." Harper drew her shoulders back in opposition.

Luella took a deep breath and let it out. "I know . . . and I deserve that. He's your boyfriend, and I was wrong."

Harper stared back at Luella with disbelief in her eyes. She grabbed the tumbler full of coffee and made her way to the door. She turned around as she put a hand on her suitcase handle.

"You know, you've always been jealous of me. I'm too good for Ben anyway, but you were my roommate. There's an unspoken code there. I let you rent that room out of the goodness of my heart, and that's how you repay me?"

Luella felt her face getting hot, despite the frigid air in the apartment. "I mean, it wasn't out of the goodness of your heart." She took another sip of her coffee.

Harper took a step toward Luella. "Let's get one thing straight, sunshine. You are nothing compared to me. You'll always be like that little Podunk town you tried so hard to run away from. You can take the girl out of the gutter but can't take the gutter out of the girl."

Luella wanted to lash out at her. She wanted to hit her perfectly contoured cheekbone, but that was the last thing she needed, and it wasn't who Luella was, so she just stood there stone-faced as Harper walked toward the door.

Harper opened the door and turned around for one last dig.

"I cut the heat off since I'll be gone for a week." She shrugged a shoulder. "Save on the bill a little, since you'll be moving out. Not like you contributed much financially anyway. You were pretty much a charity case." Satisfied, Harper slammed the door shut behind her.

Luella spent the rest of the day watching *A Christmas Story* marathon on television. It was her favorite Christmas tradition—her *only* Christmas tradition. While most people enjoyed Christmas day opening presents with their families, eating casseroles, and laughing together around a warm fireplace, Luella spent her day with the Parkers.

It made her feel less alone, even if they were fictional.

She took several breaks from the movie and packed her things a little at a time. She didn't have much. The room came furnished. It wouldn't take her long to throw most of her belongings into a few bags.

She'd stop packing for the end of the movie every time it played. It was her favorite part.

Ralphie sitting with Old Man Parker and Mother Parker talking about the presents. Old Man Parker asks Ralphie if he got everything he wanted. *Almost*, he says. Then, Old Man Parker says *that's life*.

She always thought that was where the movie should end, because that really is life. Expectations hardly ever turn into reality or play out the way you think they will.

But that's also why Luella enjoyed the next part the most.

When Old Man Parker spots something beside the desk against the wall and tells Ralphie to go check it out. She loved the bewilderment on Ralphie's face. The joy on Old Man Parker's. And alas, Ralphie gets his BB gun.

The moment between father and son unravels like a tradition being passed down from one generation to the next.

A lump always formed in the back of Luella's throat, no matter how many times she had seen it and knew it was coming. She'd always wondered what that would feel like. What that kind of relationship would be like. She wiped a tear from her cheek as the credits began to roll.

She had lost the one person she shared that kind of connection with when she was fifteen. She would remember everything about that day. Little moments that played over and over in her memory like a montage.

~

The grass was still wet with dew as Luella went out to feed Boots, their palomino, before breakfast that morning. The morning was quiet as they sat around the table eating before work and school. The eggs were cold and bland, but Luella ate them anyway. Grandpa Fred winked at her before getting up to take his plate to the sink. The sink hose Helen used to rinse off the dishes. The kiss Grandpa Fred placed delicately on Helen's forehead.

"Alright," Helen said, grabbing a brown paper sack. "Off to work with you."

She handed it to him and nudged him gently toward the door. Luella swore she saw the remnants of a smile on Helen's face as she turned back toward the sink.

That afternoon, as the bus halted to a stop at the McCrae driveway, Luella knew something was wrong. There were too many cars at the house. Helen's old Jeep Wagoneer was normally the only one there when they got home. Walking up the driveway, they could see people coming in and out of the house, most of them visibly upset. As she and the others approached the porch, Helen's friend Vera got up out of the rickety old rocking chair and stepped toward them.

"Kids," she said, "I'm afraid I have some terrible news."

Luella had always loved the buttery, soft tone of Vera's voice. She could listen to her talk all day long, and she did whenever Vera came with her three sons to spend the day with Helen at the farm. But the words Vera said next would haunt Luella forever.

"Fred has passed away unexpectedly."

It hit Luella like a wave. She wasn't sure she heard her correctly. She asked her to say it again.

"Your grandpa has passed away, Luella."

Luella's legs were as heavy as cement columns. Her breath caught in her throat. Vera let out a small cry and then took a deep breath to steady herself again. She went on, and Luella heard the words she said but had a hard time processing them.

Grandpa Fred had gone to work at J.D.'s Automotive, like he had every morning for twenty-three years. He took his lunch break at 11:15 on the dot, opened his brown sack lunch, pulled out the turkey sandwich Helen had made for him, and suffered an aneurysm before the sandwich ever made it to his mouth. He was gone in a snap.

The entire house changed after Grandpa Fred's passing. The house was quieter. It felt deflated—like all the fun had been sucked out with a vacuum, and all that remained was a flattened, weakened version of what it was before.

That was what grief did.

~

Luella walked into her bedroom and looked at the suitcase laying open and empty atop the bed. She walked over to the dresser and pulled open each drawer one by one, placing the clothes into the same suitcase she packed them in the day she left the farm.

If Helen was sick, like Millie Beams had said, then Luella owed it to Grandpa Fred to go back to Chipley Creek and check on her. It didn't have to mean that she was doing it for Helen, and it didn't have to mean she would stay.

It could work in Luella's favor to go back, especially if she chose to write that story.

# six

She stepped onto a Greyhound on December 30th. Only two people boarded ahead of her, so she got the first pick of where to sit. She chose a spot in the front so she could get off the bus faster. It would also make her less likely to be bothered by anyone because most people preferred the back. Her leg bounced up and down as she waited for the others to board, stopping only when the bus started moving—the hum of the Greyhound a salve for her nerves. She leaned her head against the cold glass window and stared out of it as the world flew by.

Her mind drifted back to that first day in Chipley Creek, and back to the car ride with her mother.

It was a Tuesday.

She said it would only be for a little while. She promised. As they drove down the county highway, Luella knew in her bones that it wasn't true. She looked over at her mother. Her hair was a curly blonde mess around her face, and her eyes were hidden behind big brown tortoiseshell sunglasses. Luella knew there was a bruise below her left eye that she was trying to cover up. She watched as her mother blew her cigarette smoke out the rolled-down window.

Luella shifted uncomfortably in the seat. She had gotten in the way again. That's what Hank had told her mother. Whenever it happened, her mother would send her over to her friend Katie's for a night or two and let it blow over. This time was different. She made her pack a backpack full of her best things and said she was going to stay with her grandparents for a summer visit.

Luella liked the idea of grandparents. She couldn't remember hers; she only knew that their names were Fred and Helen McCrae, and they lived on a farm in the middle of Georgia in a small town called Chipley Creek. Whenever she asked her mother about them, that's all that she would say, so Luella never pushed. She was just happy to know that much.

The car shifted from concrete to gravel. Luella felt her stomach clench as they passed house after house until turning left onto a long gravel driveway. As they drove closer to the farmhouse, Luella realized it looked far different from the one she had imagined in her mind. There were cats roaming around, as well as a few dogs. She saw a horse behind a barbed wire fence next to a worn-down barn. But what surprised Luella was the children playing around the house. At least six of them. A few stopped to stare at their car as Mya shifted the gear into park.

On the porch, leaning against the wooden column, was a woman with short, black hair that fell just past her rounded cheeks. The same cheeks Mya had. And Luella. The woman wore cutoff jean shorts, with a short sleeve floral button-up shirt. Luella looked over at her mother, but she and the woman were in the middle of a stare-down. Luella looked between the two of them. It made her stomach twist, the way neither of them would relent. "Is that her? Is that my grandma?"

Her mother opened her mouth, but nothing came out. Then, she cleared her throat and said, "Yes."

Luella looked back at the woman on the porch, her arms now crossed like she was waiting for something. She wasn't at all what

Luella was expecting. When she thought of her grandma, she conjured up a vision of a plump woman with silver hair in a bun and glasses that rested on the bridge of her nose. She imagined meeting her for the first time. What that would feel like. Luella would run toward her, arms outstretched, ready to meet this ethereal being called Grandma.

But expectation hardly ever met reality.

Her mother broke first. She looked over at Luella. "Alright. Got your stuff?" She forced a smile, like everything happening was normal.

Luella searched her mother's eyes. "You're not getting out?"

Mya shook her head. Luella tried to protest but was cut off by Mya holding up her hand. "End of conversation," she said, her smile now replaced by the hard-set line of her lips.

Luella grabbed her backpack and opened the door to get out. Her mother wouldn't look at her; she just stared out the window. As Luella shut the door, she heard some of the kids snickering behind her. Luella didn't look at them, though. She couldn't peel her eyes away from her mother as she backed up the car. She hoped it was just a joke and her mother would roll down the window and tell her to hop back in the car. But she didn't. A tear fell down her cheek as she watched the back of her mother's blue Pontiac Bonneville make its way down the long driveway, leaving dust, and her, behind in its wake.

From the corner of her eye, she saw the woman from the porch—the one she now knew as her grandma, Helen, walking toward her. The woman stopped in front of her. Luella noticed the way the tops of her eyelids sagged down a little like puffy clouds above her eyes.

The woman looked her up and down, then she looked over at the children standing there staring. "Y'all go play before I make you sit at the table all day," she said.

The children scattered like ants, going this way or that to find something else to do. Luella wiped her face, her stomach twisting into a wad of knots, and looked up at her grandma.

There were no hugs. No introduction at all. No sympathy for the sadness that Luella felt. Just a stoic woman staring back at her like she had just walked up off the street. As if Luella was ages older than her almost seven years.

"Dry it up," said Helen, turning toward the house. "Follow me."

Once inside, her grandma led her to the back part of the farmhouse where there were two rooms. Inside each was a set of bunk beds, a futon, and two dressers. The rooms were practically identical. Her grandma led her to the room on the left.

"This bottom bunk is empty," she said. "You can take that one. Sarah and Florence stay in this room. Anna and Rebecca stay in the one next door. The boys' room is on the other side of the house. We just had a girl leave, so you'll take her bunk."

"I don't understand . . . who are all these kids?" asked Luella.

"We're a foster home," said Helen. "Your Grandpa Fred and I have been foster parents for a long time. Since your mother was young. You'll get used to the noise. I'm assuming you're here to stay? Your mother called and said she was bringing you, but I wasn't sure she'd go through with it."

"Mom said I was here for a summer visit," Luella said.

"Yeah, that sounds about right. She's always flown with the wind, expecting me to pick up her responsibilities. Figures she didn't have the gall to tell you the truth herself. I see nothing's changed. How old are you now?"

"Almost seven," said Luella.

Helen sighed. "Last time I saw you, you were about three months old. You look like her." She stood there for a moment like there was more she wanted to say, but she cleared her throat instead. "I'll let you get settled in, but then you wash up. Supper's almost ready. We eat at six o'clock on the dot, then bedtime and lights out at eight o'clock—even during the summer. Chores still have to get done at sun up." Then, she left the room.

Luella sat on the bottom bunk and let herself sink into the twin-sized mattress. A faded pink stuffed bunny was stuck between the mattress and the wall. Probably left behind by the other girl. Luella wondered if she'd miss it. She held it to her chest and pulled her knees up close like she did when she needed to feel safe. She willed herself not to cry, but she couldn't stop the tears as they ran down her cheeks.

She felt discarded in a place she didn't belong, with a woman who had no ounce of empathy. How would she ever feel like she could call this place her home?

# seven

Luella woke as the bus halted to a stop. She grabbed her things and stepped out onto the gravel lot. Only one other person got off the bus with her, which wasn't surprising. It was just a small stop right off the interstate on the way to anywhere else.

There was nothing off the exit besides the park and ride lot—not even a gas station. The bus squeaked and hissed as it pulled away, heading toward the interstate. Luella wished she was going with it, too.

A white minivan peeled into the small parking lot. Luella grinned, already knowing it was Meggie by the erratic driving. Some things never changed. But the minivan? That was a far cry from the convertible mustang she drove as a teenager. They would ride the roads over and over in that Mustang, top-down—even in the winter, blasting the heat and singing their hearts out to the radio.

That felt like a lifetime ago.

Luella smiled at the memory as Meggie shifted the van into park and hopped out, arms outstretched, squealing as she ran toward Luella. She was a tiny thing, always had been. Tiny and punchy. That was how anyone would describe her. Her unruly blonde hair and face sprinkled with freckles would fool you into believing she was the average girl next door. Until you made her mad.

"It's so good to see you." Meggie threw her arms around Luella's neck. Luella leaned into her hug. She wasn't an affectionate person by nature, but with Meggie, it was different—she was family. Meggie pulled back. "I can't believe you're here. I feel like I'm in the twilight zone."

They walked toward Meggie's van. Her driver's side door was still wide open, and the car was dinging from where she left the keys in the ignition.

"I can't believe you're a soccer mom now," Luella said with a laugh.

"Sweet ride, huh?" Meggie motioned toward the van like she was Vanna White.

They both hopped inside. Meggie cranked the van as Luella put her hands against the vent, waiting for the warm air to blow out.

"I can't believe you caved and got a van."

"You know, I can't believe it, either. But you try carting around two children who have soccer, ballet, gymnastics, and school. This van is a lifesaver."

"Said like a proper minivan mom," said Luella. They both laughed, and Luella felt her anxiousness melt away.

Conversation flowed between them. They didn't even turn the radio on. It had been almost two years since they had seen each other. It was hard for Meggie to get away from home, let alone make it to the city. And Luella didn't own a car, so she never offered to come to Chipley. Not that Meggie would ever ask her to. She knew how Luella felt about it.

They talked all the time through texts and phone calls and kept up with each other through social media. And that was enough. Theirs wasn't a friendship that required constant face-to-face contact in order to stay stable. No matter how long it had been, they'd pick up right where they left off.

They were just in different seasons of life. Meggie worked part-time, had two kids and a husband, and if that wasn't demanding enough, she also volunteered with the city's recreation department whenever they needed help with events. She had become everything they said they never would. But whenever Luella tried to give her heck about it, Meggie would always just smile and say, "You just wait."

Luella would shrug her shoulders and laugh it off, but deep down, she knew she'd never let anyone get close enough for that to happen to her. Meggie would talk about how when Luella got married, they'd go on double dates and family trips. Luella didn't want to put a damper on her excitement over those dreams. Even though that's all they'd ever be.

Meggie was the first friend she made in Chipley Creek. She met her on her first day of school. They rode the same bus. Luella boarded the bus with the other foster kids, but they quickly scattered to sit with their own friends. Luella had walked past each row, looking for an empty spot, until she reached Meggie sitting alone, slumped down, listening to her portable CD player. Her backpack was on the seat, probably hoping no one would try to sit next to her. Luella looked past her but didn't see any other options. Meggie looked up at Luella and assessed her before slinging her backpack onto the floor. Then, she smiled. The heaviness left Luella's chest, and she sat down before Meggie could change her mind.

"You're new," said Meggie, pushing herself upright.

Luella nodded. She knew they would be best friends when Meggie snapped her headphones in half and handed Luella one side. They listened to NSYNC the rest of the way to school.

Meggie's parents had money. She didn't have to ride the bus. Her mother stayed at home and drove her younger brother to school every day, but Meggie insisted she wanted to ride the bus. Luella thought that maybe life had thrown her a kindness by giving her Meggie. She had never stopped feeling that way, either.

"How's your mom?" Luella asked.

Meggie huffed. "She's fine. You wouldn't believe how she is as a gran. You remember our old nickname for her?"

Luella smiled and nodded. "Whirlybird."

They both laughed at the name. Meggie's mother Wren was the textbook definition of a helicopter parent. Meggie hated it. Luella loved it.

"She is the exact opposite with my girls. If they want three scoops of ice-cream, she'll give them four. Rules? What are those? They don't exist with Gran. Bedtime? Oh, that's no big deal."

Luella laughed, but she didn't miss the tone of annoyance in Meggie's voice. "Well, she raised her kids, so I guess now she gets to be the fun one."

"It drives me insane. It doesn't help when I'm trying to discipline them," Meggie said. And she went on. The longer she did, the more jealousy crept up from the pit of Luella's stomach. She wouldn't dare let it pass through her lips, though.

At least Meggie had a mother that wanted to be a part of her life. And her kids' lives. Even if it made Meggie's parenting a little harder. At least she had a mother that cared enough to make sure she knew how loved she was. One that hugged her, kissed her on the head, and said *I love you* daily. At least Meggie knew what that felt like.

As the conversation lulled, Meggie turned the radio on low in the background. She knew how much Luella hated the silence.

The closest hospital was in the neighboring town of Addison. As they drove, Luella felt her chest tighten a little more with every mile marker they passed.

The heat blew furiously through the vents. Luella shivered, even though she wasn't cold. She lifted her hand to the vent and held it there.

"What if she doesn't want to see me?"

As soon as the words left her mouth, she wished she hadn't said them. Even though Meggie was one of the few people Luella could be vulnerable with.

"She's the one who asked you to come," Meggie said.

"Yeah, but only because she needs someone. Must have been desperate to call me. That doesn't mean she actually *wants* to see me."

"She will," said Meggie with all the confidence in the world. "What grandmother doesn't want to see her granddaughter?"

Luella was silent after that, thinking what she didn't want to say out loud. The kind that doesn't contact her grandchild in eleven years, and when she finally does—has a lawyer call with an offer bribing her to come back, because there's no one else to do it.

Luella forced herself to stop thinking about it. No sense in ramping up her anxiety by playing out this scene six ways from Sunday. Luella closed her eyes to calm the noise inside her head. They'd be there soon enough.

# eight

The hospital parking lot was almost full by the time they arrived. Meggie pulled up to the front to drop Luella off, then looked over. "Do you want me to come in with you?"

"No. I'll be okay." Luella smiled and then stepped out of the van. She pulled her coat tighter around her as she looked up at the blue-gray sky. The news channel had said snow was possible in the forecast that morning. It hardly ever snowed in Georgia. She hoped they wouldn't get stuck at the hospital if it did. She also didn't want to keep Meggie away from her kids if it did. But Meggie insisted on waiting—she would go get some coffee and enjoy some time to herself while Luella went into the hospital.

The double doors opened automatically, welcoming her with a rush of warm air as she stepped through. The smell of antiseptic was thick as she made her way to the reception desk. She could almost taste the bitter aroma in the back of her throat.

The nurse behind the desk looked up. She was a pale woman with thick, platinum hair that made her almost blend in with the wall behind her. "Can I help you, dear?"

Luella hesitated for a moment and then cleared her throat. "I'm here to see Helen McCrae. I'm not sure which room she's in."

"Sure thing," said the woman. "Let me just look her up in the system."

Luella looked around while the woman pulled it up on her computer. There were several people sitting in the lobby, speaking in hushed tones. Hospitals had a heavy presence to them, like nothing good could come from walking into one. A TV hung in the corner playing old sitcom reruns.

"Room 317, sweetheart," said the woman. She pointed to the other side of the room. "The elevator's right over there."

Luella thanked her and walked over to it, her heart beating faster with every step. Through the glass windows, she could see tiny white flecks of snow starting to fall from the sky. When she stepped out of the elevator and onto the third floor, several nurses looked up from their station and smiled at her. She gave a pasted-on smile as she strolled past them, down the hallway in search of room 317.

Most of the doors were shut as she passed. Only a few were open, revealing families standing or sitting around with their loved ones. Luella looked away from those rooms quickly, not wanting them to feel as uncomfortable as she did.

She came up to room 317. The door was closed, but she could see through the long, rectangular glass window that the light was off. She bit her lip as she knocked twice, hoping someone would appear. When no one answered, she pressed the handle down and pushed the door, leaving it open as she walked into the room.

The shade in the window was pulled down over one side, casting a shadow over the top of the hospital bed. Light spilled in through the other side, illuminating the bottom half of the bed and the floor.

She held her breath as her eyes landed on Helen for the first time in eleven years.

If Luella hadn't known her room number, she wouldn't be sure that this woman was Helen at all. She didn't look like the Helen that Luella remembered. Back then, her hair was solid black, her body plumper, and her skin full of color. Now she was a tiny remnant of that woman—her bony frame barely visible beneath her hospital gown. Her hair was mostly gray, with strands of black peppered here and there. It was much shorter now, barely even touching her ears. Her skin was a milky white. And she was fast asleep. If it weren't for the slow rise and fall of her chest, Luella would have thought she wasn't breathing at all.

When Luella took a step closer, her foot caught, screeching across the hospital floor. Helen woke to the sound and looked around, adjusting her eyes. Then, they landed on Luella.

Their eyes locked, and neither said a word. The full weight of the years between them pressed down on Luella's shoulders, making it hard to breathe. She left Chipley Creek as a girl and was now a woman. But she didn't feel that way standing before her grandma. She felt like the same scared, abandoned, seven-year-old girl from that first day. What was Helen thinking? Luella wanted her to say something—anything. There was so much to say and yet neither knew what to say first.

There was a knock on the hospital door. Luella broke first and stepped back from the bed as a doctor walked into the room holding a clipboard in his hand. He smiled at them. "Everything is looking good, Helen," he said, eyes scanning the clipboard. "You'll be able to go home in the morning."

"The morning? I don't want to stay here another night." Her voice came out like a hiss.

*There she is.*

"It's the best I can do," he said. "I know it's not what you were hoping for, but we just want to monitor you one more night before we send you home."

Luella looked over at Helen. "Why? What happened?"

But Helen wouldn't look at her; her eyes were fixed on the doctor. When he opened his mouth to answer, Helen cut him off.

"Dehydration," she said. "Nothing fluids and a little rest can't fix, right, Doc?"

He cleared his throat and shot Helen a look that said he would not lie. Clearly, there was more to be said, but he didn't say it. "I have another patient I need to see next door. I'll see you again in the morning before you leave."

Helen nodded. "Thanks, Doc."

Once he was gone, she kept her eyes straight in front of her like Luella wasn't there at all. Luella gritted her teeth and pressed her lips tight.

After a moment, Helen blew out a heavy breath. "I can't believe you actually came." Her tone went up at the end like it was a joke.

Heat rose in Luella's cheeks. She almost let out the snippy response she wanted to make. But she knew better. She had danced that dance with Helen many times, and she never won. Instead, she took a deep breath in and let it out slowly. "You asked me to come," she said, finally.

Helen scoffed. "No. I arranged for you to come."

"What does that even mean?" Luella snapped. "It's the same thing."

"It's not. They wouldn't let me leave unless I had someone around to help. I just needed the doctor to see your face. You're not obligated to stay. And besides, I didn't think you would accept."

*Typical. Asks for help and then balks when it arrives.* "Well, here I am."

"Yes, you are," said Helen. She looked over at Luella then, her eyes scanning up and down as if she could see inside of her. As if she could see the complacency of Luella's life in the city and the mess she had made with Harper. Like she could see her getting fired from *Scandalanta* and her failure of a meeting with Cathy. Like she could tell from one look that she was exactly the same girl that left.

Helen looked away. "You don't need to stay here with me. I'm fine. You can go on to the farm and use the Wagoneer to pick me up in the morning. The key is under the—"

"Flowerpot by the porch."

"Yes," she said. "The keys are—"

"On the hook," Luella finished.

Helen looked up at her then, but looked away quickly. She nodded her head just once.

"Alright, then I'll see you in the morning. I'll be here by nine," said Luella.

Helen laid her head back on the pillow and closed her eyes, letting her know the conversation was over.

Luella stepped out into the chilly December air and moved quickly toward Meggie's van. The snow had picked up, lightly dusting the ground. Before long, it would blanket the entirety of Chipley Creek.

When she reached the van, she knocked on the passenger side window. Meggie jumped as her eyes landed on Luella. She unlocked the door with a click.

"You scared me," she said, as Luella stepped inside. "You weren't in there very long."

Luella pulled the door shut and looked over at Meggie, pressing her lips into a thin line.

Meggie scrunched her nose up. "How'd it go?"

"Oh, you know how Helen is. She said I should go on to the farm. That she didn't need me here with her. They're releasing her in the morning."

The sun was beginning its descent behind the trees. Soon, the temperature would fall, and the roads would be covered in ice.

"Come home with me instead," said Meggie. "Stay with me tonight. It's been years since we've had a sleep-over, and I can use it as an excuse to make Will put the girls to bed." She smiled at Luella deviously and lifted her eyebrows in excitement.

"I don't want to intrude," Luella said. She had only met Will once, and now he and Meggie had two young kids. She didn't want to impede on whatever routine they had. But a part of her also hoped Meggie would insist because she didn't feel like facing anymore of her past today.

"Oh please—you're not intruding. It would be a treat. It's decided. You're coming home with me."

She eased back into the seat and tried not to think about how horrible it had gone seeing Helen again, or how she'd possibly get through any more of that same tension. She wasn't sure what she was expecting to happen. She hadn't really thought about it at all. Hadn't planned on coming back, especially given how she left. She only knew one thing for sure. There was more to Helen's diagnosis than dehydration.

# nine

Meggie, it's gorgeous." Luella said, marveling over the house as they drove up the long driveway toward it.

It was dark outside, but the colonial-style home was lit up like a beacon in the night. Trees and lights lined the length of the driveway on the way up, like the place belonged to royalty.

"Is it too much?" Meggie asked, crinkling her nose up. "Mom went a little overboard designing it."

It was a lot to take in, but Luella would never tell Meggie that. She knew how much Meggie hated anything that flaunted her wealth, so it was a surprise to Luella that Meggie let her mother design it. "No, no. It's beautiful."

And it was. It looked like one of those homes that donned the pages of *Southern Living*. Bright white Christmas lights adorned the rooftop top and wrapped around the columns on the porch. The white house blended in against the backdrop of the snow-covered yard.

Meggie's parents had deeded her a couple of acres of their land. Probably to ensure that she stayed in Chipley and close to them.

As soon as Meggie parked the van, the door to the house opened and out came two little girls. Meggie's mother, Wren, stood in the doorway yelling for them to come back inside, that they were going to freeze. Meggie opened the car door and laughed. "Are y'all crazy?" she said, scooping them up into her arms.

"We were too excited to wait for you to come in," said Livvy, the youngest.

Isla shivered and chimed in, "Let's go inside. We made pizza!"

Meggie wrangled them out of the car as Luella grabbed her bag and got out. She walked up to the porch, and Wren smiled at her.

"I almost forgot what you looked like," Wren said, pulling her in for a hug. "Oh, it's good to see you." Luella sank into her embrace. Meggie and the girls walked past them and into the house. Wren pulled back with her arms still on Luella's shoulders, and looked Luella in the face with furrowed brows. "I'm sorry about Helen."

Luella wondered how much Wren knew. If she knew more than Luella did. She wanted to ask but couldn't bring herself to do it. She thanked Wren instead and pulled her lips into a tight line. Wren must have known how Luella felt about Helen. Especially after her years of friendship with Meggie. Wren never let on if she did, and Luella was thankful for that. In her eyes, Wren was exactly what a mother should be. Strict but loving. Hard but soft. The perfect balance of love and discipline.

Luella spent many nights and weekends over the years at the Caldwell house. She was comfortable there in a way that she wasn't at the farm. Maybe it's because it was quieter in their house, and she had some privacy. Helen didn't let her spend the night there often, but when she did, Luella would stay as long as possible soaking up every second with the Caldwells. Meggie even cleaned out a drawer for Luella to use whenever she came over. She knew Luella had to share her space with the other girls in her room, and she wanted her to have something that was just hers. Wren agreed and even bought Luella some things she could keep in the drawer—like pajamas and toys or knick-knacks as they got older. Luella used to close her eyes and pretend she was a part of the Caldwell family. But that daydream was always shattered when Helen would call for her to come back to the farm.

"Let's get inside where it's warm," Wren said, cupping Luella's cheek in her hand.

Luella blinked back the tears forming in her eyes. They walked into the house.

Will walked up to Luella and hugged her. "It's good to see you, Luella."

"You too," she said, smiling at Meggie, who rolled her eyes.

Then, the girls were at her side, each one tugging on a different arm, begging her to follow them into their playroom so they could show her their toys. Luella's eyes widened at their shrill excitement. Meggie jumped in to save her.

"You girls finish getting dinner ready. I'm going to show Luella to the guest room. Let her relax for a minute. She's had a long day."

The girls' collective sounds of disappointment made Luella feel guilty, but before long, they were running around playing again, and suddenly, Luella was old news. Meggie showed her to the guest room and told her to come down whenever she was ready.

At the dinner table, the girls said the blessing in unison before they ate—a nightly tradition Luella knew came from Wren. Luella listened to the ease of their conversation and watched the monotony of their lives unfold before her. It was so different from her own. It made Luella feel like she was sitting back at the Caldwell's dinner table all those years ago. She smiled over at Meggie, who smiled back knowingly.

~

After dinner, Will offered to put the girls to bed so Meggie and Luella could have some time together. Luella tried to put the dishes away and clean up the kitchen, but Meggie wouldn't let her. She was a guest, Meggie kept saying. So, Luella sat on the floor in front of the roaring fire Will started for them. When Meggie was finished, she walked over with two glasses of wine and sat down beside her.

"So," she said. "Tell me all about your meeting with Aunt Cathy."

Luella took the wineglass from her and shrugged. "It didn't go how I hoped it would." She took a sip of the wine.

"Oh, no. What did she say?"

Luella sighed. "She said that I was a good writer, but the story wasn't good enough. So basically, just that I have potential."

"Ouch. I'm sorry. I knew she wouldn't do you any favors just because you're my best friend. Aunt Cathy is all business. I'm just glad she agreed to meet with you at all. I didn't even think she would do that much."

They were quiet for a moment, sipping wine as the fire crackled. Then, Luella spoke. "She said I should think about writing about Chipley Creek . . . about growing up on the farm in a foster home since it was a non-traditional upbringing."

Meggie eyed her cautiously and slowly shrugged her shoulders. "It's not a bad idea."

"Really," said Luella in disbelief. "Not you, too."

Meggie set her empty wine glass on the rock hearth of the fireplace. "It's just that you have so many stories. And it could promote conversations around foster care. It's a win-win situation if you look at it that way. You publish a story, maybe a family opens their home for a child after reading it. Did you know that there are fourteen thousand kids in foster care in Georgia?"

Luella shook her head.

Meggie nodded sadly. "I did some research," she said. "Will and I thought about fostering. I know how you feel about Helen, but she did some good at least."

Luella considered it. "I wonder when she stopped."

"About seven years ago," Meggie said. When Luella looked at her with no response, Meggie shrugged. "Small town, remember? And besides, I asked her about it when we were considering it. I ran into her in town."

Luella blew out a breath, feeling out of the loop.

Will jogged down the stairs and walked over to them. "Rugrats are in bed. I'm following suit. I made up the guest bed and put fresh towels in the bathroom."

"You're a good man, William Burns," Meggie said, lifting her face up for a kiss. Luella watched as Will kissed Meggie on the lips. She felt her cheeks flush and she looked away quickly.

"Goodnight," he said to them before walking back up the stairs.

When he was gone, Luella smiled at Meggie. "You have a beautiful family . . . I'm so happy for you. You got a good one. And the two sweetest girls. I can't believe you have two kids. You've got a good life here."

Meggie laughed. "It's funny how life works out, huh? I always said I never wanted kids. Remember that? I couldn't even process the idea of being a mother. Will and I barely talked about it before we got married. Neither of us was sure we were cut out for parenthood. But then surprise—four months in and here came Isla. We never even stood a chance."

Luella's smile faded. "It's funny how it works out," she said, though she didn't find it funny at all. Because it didn't work out anything like she thought it would.

While she didn't see herself having a family like Meggie's, she thought by now she'd be happier than she was. But she had been so fueled by her desire to get out of Chipley Creek and away from the farm that she severed a little piece of her heart by leaving. Or rather, a big part of it. She had been grieving the loss of that relationship ever since.

"How's Paul?" she asked, looking at the fire.

Meggie was quiet for a moment. Then, she sighed. "You said you never wanted me to bring him up. That you didn't want to know."

"I know," said Luella. She grabbed a pillow off the floor and started picking at the fringe.

"But I'm bringing it up. You're not breaking any promises to me. I'm the one who asked."

Meggie looked like she wasn't sure whether she should say anything, so Luella pushed. "It's just being back here, I guess. I have no right to know, really. I just want to know if he's good . . . if he's happy."

Meggie smiled sadly. "He's good. He's really good."

Luella wasn't sure what she had expected Meggie to say. That he was miserable? Would that have made her feel better? He said he could never live without her, and now Meggie says he's doing just fine. She didn't want her voice to betray her, so she simply said, "I'm glad."

They sat by the fire for another hour, trading stories from the past. After that, they both ended up in the guest bed, talking more in the darkness.

"Are you going to be alright going back there?" asked Meggie.

"I don't really have much choice," said Luella. "I screwed things up back in the city, so I can't go back there even if I wanted to."

"Why? What happened?" asked Meggie, her voice full of surprise.

"I don't want to talk about it. I'm here now. I'll just have to deal with it as it comes. It'll be fine."

She wasn't sure if she was answering Meggie or trying to convince herself. It was quiet for a few moments and then Meggie asked, barely above a whisper in the safety of darkness, "Do you still love him?"

Goosebumps covered Luella's arms. She made herself believe it was because of the cold radiating from the window. A few minutes later, she took a deep breath and let it out.

"I don't think I ever stopped."

Paul was the first boy she ever loved. He was there on the worst day of her life, and all the ones after that. She could still close her eyes and see his pudgy nine-year-old face across from her at the dinner table that first night on the farm. It took her some time to warm up to him. To trust him. But eventually, they were hand and glove.

There came a day when her feelings for him shifted into something else. Something that made her heart beat faster and her stomach flutter whenever he was around. Feelings that eventually came at a cost.

When Luella looked over at Meggie, her eyes were closed. The wine had caught up with her. Luella was glad Meggie hadn't heard what she dared to admit out loud. She watched the slow rise and fall of Meggie's chest. How had they gotten here? Most days she still felt like that scared, lonely child. Only she wasn't a child anymore, and time seemed to tick by at a much faster rate than it did then. She was thankful Meggie invited her over for the night. Going straight to the farm may have sent her over the edge and running again. Meggie knew that. She always knew what Luella was thinking without her even having to say it.

Luella thought about waking Meggie up to go back to her own bed but decided to be selfish instead. It had been a long time since she slept in the bed next to someone she loved. She had forgotten how comforting that felt. A tear fell from her cheek. She brushed it away with her hand. The quiet night was deafening. She pulled the covers up over her ears, closed her eyes and sank further into the memory foam mattress.

# ten

Luella's stomach had been in knots from the moment she woke up. One of Meggie's girls came up behind her, and Luella practically jumped through the roof.

She never expected to return to Chipley Creek. Never wanted to step foot back on the McCrae farm. It made sense that she'd be a little on edge. Not to mention the two giant cups of coffee she practically inhaled while waiting for Meggie to get ready for work.

As they pulled into the gravel driveway, Luella's heart thumped against her chest. Memories flooded her mind as the house came into view. Most of them as cold as the snow on the ground.

Mya leaving her.

Vera crying on the front porch.

Paul, the day he was sent away.

The farmhouse had aged since she last saw it. The grey wood now weathered by time. The gutter dangled from the side of the house. A window in the front was boarded up. A lump formed in the back of Luella's throat, surprising her. She swallowed against it.

Meggie stopped just in front of the concrete stones that led to the front porch. She looked over at Luella, her face full of concern. "Are you going to be okay?"

Luella nodded. "I'll be fine." Meggie raised an eyebrow in question. Luella rolled her eyes and laughed it off. "Really, I'm gonna be fine."

Meggie blew out a breath and leaned over for a hug. Luella wrapped her arms around her best friend and held tight.

"See you later, alligator," Meggie said.

Luella smiled at the old, familiar phrase. "See you soon, baboon."

It was their tradition any time they had to say goodbye to each other. Meggie started it as a way of making Luella smile when she knew she wanted to cry.

Luella watched as Meggie drove away—an all too familiar feeling. Then, she turned back toward the house, took a deep breath, and made her way to the front porch. The brick steps were slick as she stepped up each one. She bent down and lifted the yellow flowerpot and grabbed the key from underneath. The metal was cold against her warm hand. She put the key in the lock and twisted it to the right. She pushed, but the old door wouldn't budge. It didn't give until she rammed her side into it, sending it flying open with a groan.

Luella stepped into the house. Her eyes scanned the space that was once her home.

Though the outside was different, the inside hadn't changed at all. It was eerie, the way it looked preserved in time, everything in the same place as before. The dated furniture. The floor-to-ceiling shelves crammed full of books. The raggedy throw pillows. The musty scent that filled the air—the result of having never used the central heat and air. The feel of the old floorboards under her feet, and the comforting way they creaked in all the same places.

She half expected her younger self to go zipping by at any second. The only noticeable difference was the silence. That was what she couldn't get past. If a house could talk, what would it say? If a house had feelings, how would it feel?

The house was never quiet before. Noise came from every corner of every room. That was one of the vivid things Luella remembered about her first day there. She didn't have time to wallow in her sadness because the house was loud and distracting. It was the one thing she liked about it. Feet were constantly slamming against the hardwood floors. Inside and out, kids were laughing, and sometimes fighting, but were always audible.

The only time it was quiet was at night, while everyone slept.

She strolled through the rooms in the house, remembering what it felt like to live within its walls. Suffocating was how she'd describe it. How she hated always having an audience wherever she went, never having too much time to herself.

Just before the girls' side of the house was Helen and Grandpa Fred's room. Luella had only been inside of it a handful of times. Helen and Grandpa Fred were adamant about no one going into their room. They opened their home to as many kids as they could, but their bedroom was sacred—just for them. Luella stepped over the threshold and looked back like she was being watched. It was silly; she knew no one was there, but the fear of getting caught crept up from her chest and warmed her face.

She looked around the small room. The bed was made. The nightstand was free of the junk that one would usually find strewn about on top. Luella walked over to the window. Even the blinds were free of dust. Everything was perfectly clean. It wasn't until she turned to leave that she saw them laying on the floor on his side of the bed. It felt like a punch in the gut. Her Grandpa Fred's favorite navy and red flannel pajama bottoms were laying in a pile on the floor like he had simply stepped out of them, and they were just waiting for him to come back.

Fifteen years. That's how long it had been since he passed, and Helen had never moved them. Grief can make you do funny things. Her throat went dry, and her eyes welled up. She reached out to grab the bedpost for support and took a couple of deep breaths. This was too close, too intimate. She didn't know Helen like this. She left the room in a rush.

She walked past the tiny bathroom in the hall between the girls' bedrooms. She flipped the light on. When she did, it was like switching on another memory.

In the mornings, the girls would wake up when the rooster crowed and scramble to be the first one in the bathroom. There was no sense of privacy in the McCrae house. The girls came in and out of the bathroom at will—despite if someone was sitting on the toilet or bathing in the shower. Sometimes, the girls even took showers two at a time. It took a while for Luella to get used to. She switched the bathroom light off and moved to the next room.

The door was shut. She twisted the knob and pushed it open. Exactly the same. She leaned against the doorway, staring into her old bedroom as though there was an invisible barrier keeping her from walking inside.

She shared the room with two other girls. Nothing looked like it had been touched.

Unlike Helen's room, this one had collected a fair amount of dust. She wondered when the last time was that Helen had walked inside of it. She imagined Helen walking into the room looking for her the day she left, to scold her for missing the bus, only to find an empty bunk.

She walked over and pushed the rug aside that laid in front of the bunk on top of the hardwood floor. She finagled one of the wooden boards until the side finally popped up. Then, she moved the piece of wood to the side and stuck her hand down into the hole, feeling around in the dark for the small tin box she had hidden there. When her hand finally landed on it, she pulled it out and wiped the dust off the top.

One Christmas, Grandpa Fred had given her a small tin box full of cookies that were just for her. He said she didn't have to share them. So, she found somewhere to hide the box when no one was looking. It became her favorite hiding hole. She opened the tin box that contained the letters her mother had written her during the twelve years she spent at the farm. She had forgotten to grab them before she left. There were only five. Each one was the same baby blue envelope with matching baby blue and white striped paper, with a bird in the middle of a floral crest at the top.

She took out an envelope and pulled out its letter. The handwriting had faded, but the words still had the same effect.

*Dear Luella,*

*I hope you had a wonderful first day of school. I'm sorry that I haven't called lately. I'm thinking of you and will see you so soon.*

*All my love,*
*Mama*

She stared at the words for several seconds before folding it back up and putting it in the envelope. Her mother never called. She never came to see her. The letters were all she got.

Until she turned seventeen. Mya showed up out of the blue one day, there to take Luella back home with her.

Luella had been out at the barn doing her afternoon chores when she heard the ruckus coming from the driveway. As she got closer, she could see Mya and Helen arguing. Her heart beat picked up at the sight of her mother. Luella ran toward them.

"Mama," she called out when she reached them.

Luella looked at her mother. Her hair was a disheveled mess, and she was sweating profusely. Mya could hardly stand up straight, but that didn't matter because she was actually there. Luella could reach out and touch her.

"What are you doing here?" Luella asked, looking over at Helen, who stood stoically with her arms crossed over her chest.

"She was just leaving," said Helen.

Luella's heart sank as she stammered out, "But she just got here."

"You need to go wash up for dinner," said Helen.

"But she *just* got here," Luella said, trying to control her words along with her tone. She knew what would happen if she got an attitude with Helen. She had only done it once before, and it didn't work out in her favor.

"Luella, go inside," said Helen.

"She's *my* kid. I can take her back if I want to," snapped Mya. She took a step toward Luella, but faltered and almost fell down.

"Look at you," Helen spat. "You can't even take care of yourself."

Luella wanted to argue, she wanted to stay outside where her mother was. But she did as she was told and went inside. She wouldn't even look at Helen as she walked past her.

A few minutes later, Luella heard the hum of Mya's car engine. She watched through the window as her mother once again drove away from her. That was when she decided she would leave the farm the day she turned eighteen. It was only a few months away.

She didn't speak to Helen much at all after that. She never forgave her for it, either.

# eleven

Luella walked as fast as she could into the hospital. She told Helen she'd be there by nine, but there she was, hustling through the hospital doors at nine-thirty. She had taken too long a stroll down memory lane at the farm.

She couldn't move her feet fast enough. Her shoe caught, shrieking against the linoleum. The woman behind the desk looked up and gave her a sympathetic smile—the one that most people give in a place like this. The overwhelming feeling of dread was suffocating. It gave Luella a sense of déjà vu as she walked over and pressed the button between the two elevator doors.

There was no doubt in Luella's mind that Helen would be furious over her being late. Helen prided herself on punctuality. She couldn't stand to be late anywhere—always arrived fifteen minutes before she needed to be somewhere. Luella wasn't ready for the argument that was sure to happen the minute she stepped inside Helen's hospital room. She needed a buffer.

Gum. That would help. It was Luella's solution whenever she felt anxious.

As she waited for the elevator, she fished a hand around the inside of her bag, searching for the pack of Orbit Wintergreen she had tossed in there a week ago. But she couldn't find it. She opened the bag wider, scanning the bottom with her eyes as the elevator doors opened.

Through her peripheral vision, she saw two people step out before her, heard their hushed tones and clunky footsteps as she stepped into the elevator, pressed the button, and began her search again.

Then, she heard a voice from the past.

"Lue?"

She froze—her eyes locked on the bottom of her bag. There was only one person who ever called her that. She wondered for a second if her mind was playing tricks on her like it did that day in the bar. She looked up just as the elevator doors began to close.

And there he was. Her mind wasn't deceiving her this time. It really was Paul. Her heart thumped wildly against her chest. She couldn't move. She just stood there staring at the boy she left behind.

Only he wasn't a boy anymore, and the intensity of his gaze made her shift uncomfortably where she stood. But she couldn't pry her eyes away him. Paul didn't move, either. He stared at her like he was trying to figure out if she too, was real.

The elevator doors closed, separating them again.

Luella let out a deep breath as her heart hammered against her chest. She pressed a hand against the side of the elevator to steady herself.

When she thought of what it would be like to see him again, she never thought it would be like that. Unexpected and cut short. She didn't have enough time to take in the sight of him. What was it she saw in his face? Anger? Confusion? Probably a little of both. Was he happy to see her?

The ride up to the third floor felt like an eternity, the way car rides did when she was a kid. But when the doors opened, there he was again. Only now his cheeks were red, and he was a little out of breath. His hand rested on his hip like he had just finished a marathon. She stood there so long that the doors started to close again. Paul leapt forward this time and reached his hand out to stop them.

Luella stepped out of the elevator. "How'd you—"

"I ran up the stairs," he said.

"But how did you know which—"

"I'm assuming you're here to see Helen," he said. "Figured it would take something as serious as this to drag you back."

The bitterness in his tone stung, but she deserved whatever anger he was going to throw at her.

They stood there, not knowing what to say to each other after so much time apart. She looked up at him, letting her gaze linger. Taking in all the ways he had changed in the past eleven years. He had grown into his broad shoulders, and his boyish face was now covered with a short beard. There were creases at the corners of his eyes, but they suited him well.

Heat rose in Luella's cheeks when her eyes drifted up and realized his were perusing over her as well. It sent a wave of electricity coursing through her body. She couldn't help but wonder what he was thinking. Did he like who she had become? Did any part of him still feel the same way? Or were they simply strangers now?

He wore a navy uniform with a black belt. On his right shoulder, the word PARAMEDIC was embroidered in white.

The corners of her mouth lifted as she remembered a conversation they had years earlier.

~

They had only talked about it once. Paul was seventeen and months away from aging out of the system. He had become Luella's best friend, aside from Meggie. Luella asked him one day what he was going to do after he turned eighteen. She was scared everything was going to change.

"I don't know. Dad's teaching me about mechanic work. Maybe I could do that. I could go work at J.D.'s with him . . . or I could join the Marines. I haven't really thought about it yet."

Paul and Grandpa Fred had been restoring an old Firebird that Paul had gotten from Old Man Stanton down the road as payment for a summer's work of lawn care. It didn't run, but Old Man Stanton said Fred could probably help him get it running. Luella knew he liked the one-on-one time he got with her grandpa but also knew that Paul didn't really love mechanic work. It wasn't his forte. She could tell from his eyes that he was nervous about it all, even though he tried his best to hide it from her.

"What about EMT school?" Luella knew how much Paul loved helping people.

Whether it was through a good deed or in a crisis, he enjoyed being the guy that swooped in to save the day. That's what he had always done for her. It was in his nature. She asked Grandpa Fred once how Paul had found his way to the farm. Grandpa Fred's face turned serious. Then, he took a deep breath and told her.

Paul was found inside a double-wide trailer doing chest compressions on his mother. She had overdosed and was long gone by the time firefighters and ambulances arrived. The police officer on the scene said Paul must have been doing those compressions for hours. He was trying to save her. He had seen it on the television, and it had worked then, but six-year-old Paul couldn't understand why his mother wasn't waking up like the woman on the television did.

Paul tried to be everyone's rescuer after that.

~

And there he was, standing in front of her in his uniform. He had followed through. She smiled proudly. "You're a paramedic."

He ran his teeth across his bottom lip, the way he always did when he was nervous and nodded.

Luella rocked on her feet nervously, waiting for him to say something else. When he didn't, she spoke up instead. "How are you?"

He opened his mouth to answer but was interrupted by the beep of his radio, followed by the sound of his partner's voice coming through the speaker, letting him know he had the ambulance out front waiting.

"It's okay," she said. "I've got to go anyway. I'm already late. Helen's gonna be furious."

He nodded his head. "I'll see ya."

"Yeah," said Luella, expecting him to turn and leave, but he lingered instead. Luella wanted nothing more than to throw her arms around him and sink into his chest. But she resisted the urge. They didn't know each other anymore. Which was another feeling altogether that she couldn't deal with at the current moment. "I'll see you around," she said, and then she stepped past him.

She made it halfway down the hall before she turned to see if he was still standing there. But he wasn't. She walked the rest of the way to Helen's room.

The door was open, so she stepped inside without knocking. Helen sat at the end of the bed with the remote in her hand, flipping through the channels on the television.

"You're late," she said without looking over at Luella.

Luella clenched her jaw, wishing she had found that stick of gum. "Sorry," she said.

"Lucky for you, they haven't discharged me yet. I'm still waiting for the nurse that was supposed to be here an hour ago." Helen clicked the remote furiously.

Luella took a seat beside the window. She looked over at Helen sitting on the end of the bed and noted that her color looked much better today, even though she still looked frail. Helen didn't speak, and Luella was thankful for the sound of the television being a buffer between them.

Twenty minutes later, a nurse finally came in with a wheelchair and a handful of papers.

"Took you long enough," Helen said, clicking the television off. She threw the remote onto the bed.

The nurse pressed her lips into a thin line, and Luella suppressed the urge to laugh. Clearly, the nurse had had her fill with Helen. "I'm sorry, Mrs. McCrae. We're a bit short-staffed this morning. I apologize for the inconvenience. I have your discharge papers right here. I just need to go over them with you."

She started to show Helen the papers, but Helen held a hand up, silencing her. The nurse looked confused as Helen looked over at Luella and cleared her throat.

Both the nurse and Helen stared at Luella. "Oh . . . right," Luella said, getting to her feet. "I'll be right outside."

She shut the door as she stepped out but left it cracked just enough. The hallway was empty. No nurses or visitors in sight. She leaned as close to the crack as she could and listened. Their voices were quiet, but she could make out a word or sentence here and there. The nurse told Helen to follow up with her regular doctor to go over her plan for care. Luella heard the shuffling of papers, and the rest was muffled except for two words that she heard clear as day.

*Palliative care.*

She stepped away from the door as thoughts swirled in her mind. Palliative care? All she knew about that was that it was for people living with a serious illness. Ricky's dad had chosen palliative care when his cancer came back for the third time. Ricky used to talk about how tough it was watching him go through it.

But what did it mean for Helen?

Luella was lost in thought as the nurse wheeled Helen out of the hospital room and looked over at Luella, who stood there in a trance.

"Don't mind her," said Helen. "Just wheel me to the parking lot. She'll follow eventually. She's running a bit behind today."

Luella rolled her eyes but bit her tongue so she wouldn't say anything snarky in front of the nurse, who clearly felt uncomfortable by the look on her face. Luella forced a tight-lipped smile to ease the tension. Then, she began to walk toward the elevator as the nurse wheeled Helen, her mind going back to those two words and what they meant.

# twelve

Helen stared out the window like an angry child as they drove in silence toward the farm. Luella didn't have the energy to argue, so she just kept her eyes on the road and her thoughts to herself. She looked over just once and saw Helen gripping the seatbelt as if she might go flying out of the car at any given moment. Luella suppressed the urge to ask her if she was okay.

When they finally pulled into the gravel driveway, she noticed Helen's entire body relax. Luella parked the Wagoneer in its usual spot beside the pathway to the porch and cut off the engine. Still buckled, she looked over at Helen.

"Are you dying?"

Helen looked her in the eyes for the first time. "Not today." She unbuckled her seatbelt and got out of the car like it was the most natural response in the world. Luella sat there for a moment, taking in her words.

When she finally opened the car door to get out, a yippee little chihuahua-mix barked angrily at her feet. It hadn't been at the house before when she arrived, but stray dogs often came and went. The dog was tiny and fluffy, except for its tail, which seemed to have suffered a great hair loss. The dog followed Luella to the front door, where it ran in before Luella could catch it. Helen had never allowed animals in the house before, even though the farm had an abundance of them. Luella looked around for the dog, trying to catch it, and put it back out before Helen could see it.

She walked into the living room and heard the dog yap again, only this time it was perched atop Helen's lap. Luella's eyes went wide.

"Hush, Gus," Helen said. She patted the old dog's head to reassure it, but Luella could still hear the dog growling softly.

"You have a dog . . . in the house." It came out more like a question than a statement.

"This is Gus. His bark is bigger than his bite." She stroked the dog's fluffy mane. "Gus, this is Luella." As if on cue, the dog looked up at her, then back at Helen.

Luella stood there for a moment, not knowing what to do next. She wasn't sure what Helen expected or how she could help.

A knock on the door gave her an excuse to walk away. "I'll get it," she said.

She pulled open the old oak door, and there stood a woman with short, fiery red hair and a fidgety young girl.

"Who are you?" asked the young girl curiously. The woman shushed her and looked back at Luella.

"Hello, is Helen home?" the woman asked, trying to peer past her.

As if summoned, Helen appeared at the door. "Come on in. It's cold out there."

The young girl stepped through first and wrapped her arms around Helen. "We were so worried. We're so glad that you're home."

Helen patted the girl on the back. Gus started barking again at Helen's feet. The young girl didn't even hesitate to pick the dog up and take off into the living room with him.

The red-headed woman stepped inside and smiled as she pulled Helen into an embrace and then pulled back suddenly. "I told myself I would not hug you. I don't want to give you any germs, but I can't help it." The woman looked over at Luella as though she had suddenly remembered her standing there.

"This is my granddaughter, Luella," Helen said, taking a step back.

The woman's eyebrows went up, and a surprised smile crept across her face. "Well, it's so nice to meet you. I'm Cheryl and that's my granddaughter, Taylor. We live two houses down."

Luella resented the way bitterness bubbled up inside of her at the surprise on Cheryl's face when Helen introduced her. Like she had never mentioned she had a granddaughter before.

"In the Stanton's old house?" Luella asked.

Cheryl nodded. "I bought it from them nine years ago now."

There was an awkward silence that followed as the three of them stood in the foyer. Finally, Cheryl lifted the basket in her hands and looked at Helen. "We brought you New Year's Eve lunch," she said excitedly.

Luella hadn't even remembered that it was New Year's Eve. Cheryl looked into the living room at Taylor and shook her head as the girl let Gus lick every corner of her face. Cheryl looked back at Helen and Luella. "I've told more times than I care to count not to let dogs lick her in the face. They have so many germs. So many."

"Ah, they're just boosting her immune system," said Helen.

Cheryl scoffed. "That's rich coming from you. The person who should be a bit more concerned about germs right now."

In true Helen fashion, she barreled right past the comment and right past Cheryl and Luella into the kitchen. Cheryl sighed and told Taylor to come and eat some lunch. Luella followed.

In the kitchen, Cheryl took out the contents of the basket while

Helen got out the plates and Taylor set out the forks. It was obvious they did this a lot. It was rhythmic. Luella stood there feeling like an intruder until Taylor tugged on her sleeve and told her to sit. She explained where each of them usually sat and that it was nice to have the last seat occupied at the little round table in the kitchen.

Cheryl uncovered the casserole dish full of lasagna and scooped out a portion onto a plate and handed it to Luella with a smile.

"Lasagna for lunch?" asked Helen, as Luella took the plate.

"You'll have leftovers," said Cheryl.

Luella breathed in the savory smell. Her stomach lurched. She was starving. She couldn't remember the last time she had a home-cooked meal.

When Cheryl went to scoop out Helen's portion, Helen interjected. "Just a small scoop. I still don't have much of an appetite."

"But it's your favorite," said Cheryl. "And you need some strength."

Cheryl placed a heaping scoop onto the plate, but Helen didn't protest. Taylor reached for a piece of bread, but Cheryl popped her hand away.

"Not until you wash those grimy hands," she said. "Might as well wash your face, too. I saw Gus licking all over it."

Taylor giggled but obeyed. The three of them started eating without her. After a few minutes of silence, Cheryl looked at Luella.

"So, how long are you here for?"

Luella looked over at Helen for some clue of what to say. She wasn't sure how to answer or what Helen wanted her to say. But Helen didn't offer any help, just took another bite of her lasagna.

"I'm not really sure," said Luella, a bit hesitantly. "Helen's doctor seems to think that she could use some help . . ." Helen side-eyed her then. "With the farm, I mean."

"Oh, honey," said Cheryl. "I've been saying that for years. That she needed to either hire some help or get married again."

"Not happening," said Helen, without even a hint of amusement in her voice.

Cheryl laughed. "Which one?"

"Neither," said Helen. They both laughed at that. Taylor rejoined them at the table with freshly washed hands and a clean face.

"What did I miss?" she asked. Cheryl and Helen laughed again.

Luella forced a smile. It was weird seeing Helen like that, in such a laid-back fashion, laughing with her closest friend. Luella had never sat at this table before. She had only ever sat at the big ten-foot table with the children. It was an odd feeling, being on the other end of childhood—like being given a bigger lens to look through. She wasn't sure how to feel about it.

After lunch, they made their way into the living room. Luella mostly listened to Helen and Cheryl's conversation while the wood stove warmed the room. Taylor played with Gus the whole time, or rather, she pestered him. But he was a good sport about it, obviously used to having her around.

Eventually, Cheryl turned to Luella. "What do you do for work?"

Luella could feel Helen's eyes on her. "I'm in between jobs, but I'm a writer. I used to work for a news blog in Atlanta."

She wouldn't dare say it was a gossip blog in front of Helen. Cheryl smiled and nodded, but Helen remained silent. She didn't ask about the jobs or what Luella was doing next, which irritated Luella more than if Helen had shown an interest in her life. Helen changed the subject, but Luella wasn't ready to move on. She interrupted Helen mid-sentence.

"I'm actually doing some freelance work now. I'm working on a story about what it was like growing up here at the farm."

"Oh," Cheryl said, smiling again. This time a bit too big. Luella could sense Cheryl's discomfort with the tension. Helen didn't make a remark about her statement this time, either, and her stare gave nothing away.

After that, Luella said nothing else. She only listened.

Before they left, Taylor fed all the animals so that Luella and Helen didn't have to worry about it that afternoon. Luella could see how Taylor had wiggled her way into Helen's heart.

When it was finally just the two of them alone in the living room, Helen picked up the remote and turned on the television, breaking the silence with the sound of a newscaster giving weather updates on the snow. They sat that way for almost two hours before Helen said that she was tired and wanted to go to bed. Luella wanted to mention the fact that Helen hadn't eaten dinner, but she bit her tongue as Helen disappeared into her room for the night.

Luella switched off the TV so the sound wouldn't disturb Helen. Then, she went into the kitchen and heated a plate of Cheryl's lasagna. She sat alone at the table as she ate, her mind going over every detail of the day. Why had she come? Why in the world would she have agreed to this? She could have found somewhere to live and another job. She had done it before. Being back in Chipley, around Helen, only magnified the desolate feeling in the pit of her stomach.

But seeing Paul again had sparked something that she hadn't felt in such a long time. She pulled her phone out of the pocket of her cardigan and sent Meggie a text: Ran into Paul today . . .

Her phone chimed back immediately: No way! You okay?

Luella typed back: Yeah. A little in my head about it, but it was good to see his face.

Meggie sent back a line of heart emojis, followed by another text: Call you tomorrow for all the deets.

Luella set her phone on the table and got up to wash her bowl. So much ran through her mind. How did she really feel about seeing him? It was such a jumbled-up mess of emotions that she didn't know how to process it.

She set the dish in the drying rack and grabbed her laptop as she strolled to the opposite side of the house—to the boys' old bedroom.

It was the room Josh and Paul shared for years. Until Josh left, and Gee replaced him. It was like its own little oasis on the far side of the house. She used to get so jealous of their seclusion when she was growing up.

She pushed open the door and smiled when she saw the two twin sized metal beds sitting side by side. The one by the window was Paul's. She walked over and sat down on it. The room smelled a little musty, as though the door had been shut for years and the windows never opened. But Luella didn't mind. It made her feel closer to Paul. The Paul she knew back then. The one that was her best friend.

Even after he left the farm, his bed was never given to anyone else.

She pushed herself further up on the mattress and crossed her legs. Then, she opened her laptop on the pillow in front of her.

A blank document was already open. The cursor blinked in front of her in anticipation. She wanted to write. Wanted to feel like she was doing something productive. But every time she began typing, she'd get too inside of her own head and delete what she had written.

There was too much noise in her head for her to think clearly. Too many emotions to think openly. So, she did the only thing she knew to do. The only thing that worked.

She began typing everything she felt. Just like Helen taught her to do.

~

After Luella's mother had dumped her at the farm, she had a lot of anger built up inside of her. Once, she let that anger out when one of the girls said something spiteful to her. Luella threw herself at the girl, and they ended up in a tangled mess on the ground with the other kids crowding around them watching.

Helen yanked them apart. Then, she got on to Luella, but not the other girl, which infuriated Luella. She screamed at Helen how much she hated her.

The next day was a Saturday. Therefore, as punishment, Luella had to sit at the table all day long. That was all their punishments whenever they got into trouble. Neither Helen nor Grandpa Fred ever laid hands on any of them.

That day, Luella sat at the long wooden table for hours with no one saying a word to her, not even Helen. She would have rather been yelled at. Grandpa Fred didn't say a word, either, which broke Luella's heart the most.

After lunch, while the other kids were outside playing, Helen came over to the table with a piece of paper and a pencil in one hand and a glass mason jar in the other. She sat down beside Luella and slid the jar in front of her, then set the paper and pencil on the table beside it.

"I think you've got a lot of feelings bound up inside of you that're just bursting to get out," said Helen. "At least, it seemed that way last night. Look, I understand you're upset you're here instead of with your mom. It's not what you want—I get it. But holding all of that in is doing nothing but eating you up inside. It's making you as bitter as a grapefruit."

Luella's mouth went dry and a lump formed in the back of her throat. Her eyes stung as tears welled up, but she just looked at the table in front of her. She would not cry in front of Helen.

"I want you to write everything you feel on that sheet of paper," said Helen. "Everything you think you hate. Everything you want to say to me, to your mom, and to anyone else. Cover that paper with all your angry and sad feelings. Then, I want you to put it in that jar and take it outside and bury it. And I never want to hear about them again."

She stood up like she was going to leave but stopped and sighed.

"I know you think you've been dealt a bad hand here," she said. "But believe me, it could be worse. I'm sure every kid in this house wishes they had your life . . . the shovel is in the barn when you're done."

After that, whenever the noise in her head got too loud, she'd sit down and write all her emotions onto the page. It always made her feel better.

Luella typed page after page until eventually, she fell asleep on Paul's bed.

# thirteen

A rooster crowed outside, jarring Luella from sleep. She groaned as she looked over at the window. Daylight was breaking through the darkness. The light of a new year. Luella usually loved the beginning of a new year. She'd buy a new planner, set new goals, and bask in all the possibilities a new year presented.

She didn't feel that excitement this time.

The house was so quiet that the silence was ringing in her ears. The back porch's screen door creaked open and then slammed shut. Luella heard footsteps on the hardwood floor.

Helen. She always woke up before the sunrise—like it was a competition between her and the sun.

Luella got out of the bed and pulled on her oversized cardigan, wrapping it tight around her chest and walked into the kitchen.

Helen was taking off her jacket and hanging it on the coat rack in the corner. She turned around and saw Luella standing in the doorway. "You're still here," she said with feigned surprise. "I thought you'd sneak out and leave . . . wouldn't be the first time."

Luella rolled her eyes. "Happy New Year to you, too. I fell asleep in Paul's old room. I was up late writing."

Helen walked past her to the coffee machine. She grabbed the carafe, stuck it under the sink faucet, and turned the water on.

"I can do the morning chores," said Luella. "You really shouldn't be—"

"I don't need help." Helen dumped the water in the back of the coffee machine and slapped the top down.

*Clearly.*

She clenched her jaw and took a deep breath. *One. Two. Three.* Then, she released it. "I'm here because you asked me to come here. Just let me help. It doesn't have to mean that you need it, just that since I'm here anyway, I can help."

Helen didn't turn around as she scooped coffee and dumped the spoonful of it into the filter. Luella was about to walk away when she heard Helen say, "Boots still needs to be fed. His feed is outside by the front door . . . and I didn't ask you to be here. I needed to be able to say that I had help—someone else in the house so they'd leave me alone."

"They?" asked Luella.

"Yes, they. Doctors. Friends. Church peers." Helen stood with her back toward Luella as she waited for the coffee to brew.

Luella put on the jacket she left hanging on the rack, shoved her feet inside a pair of rain boots, because they were the only boots she had, and went to the front porch to grab the feed. She let the door slam shut behind her, hoping it irritated Helen.

She bent to grab the bag leaning against the rail, but it was heavy. Her anger gave her more determination this time. She bent again and snatched it up.

She clutched the bag as she made her way down to the barn. The snow had melted, but the ground was still frozen. The grass crunched under her feet with every step she took. As she walked, she noticed just how many things around the farm needed fixing. There were broken boards along the side of the house. The chicken coop was destroyed, which left the chickens roaming around the yard at will. There were piles of miscellaneous junk that needed hauling off.

And cats. *So many cats.*

As she neared the barn, she couldn't stop the smile forming on her face. The sight of it warmed her heart. Just like the farmhouse, the barn had also been weathered by time. But it didn't matter because it was her favorite place.

It was *their* place. Her and Paul's.

When she needed to escape, she would find her way down to the barn and hide out. Most of the time, Paul would always find her there. Eventually, it became their spot. But that wasn't until after her favorite memory that involved the barn. Her second kiss.

~

It happened the same day as her first, not even an hour in between. She was fifteen. Paul was seventeen. His senior year started with a bang. He came down with the flu and missed the entire first week of school. Rebecca, one of the foster children—a girl who was rude to Luella for no real reason, took great pride in bringing home his missed work for him since they were in the same grade. Luella could tell that Rebecca was trying her best to hold it over Luella's head and make her jealous. But Luella wouldn't give her the satisfaction, and besides, she couldn't think about Paul like that. It was off limits. Helen and Grandpa Fred had strict rules about it, which was why the boys were on the other side of the house.

Meggie was out of school that first Friday of the school year, and Luella found herself alone in their usual seat on the bus.

Tyler, a senior who sat in the back of the bus with the other popular kids, came up to her seat and asked to sit with her. Luella had always had a tiny crush on Tyler—after all, he was the star quarterback, so she slid over and let him sit down beside her with no questions asked.

His buddies Cameron and Joel came up and sat in the seat in front of them, but turned around to face them. Luella wasn't used to so much attention from boys. She had matured a lot from fourteen to fifteen. The pudgy cheeks she had all throughout her adolescence had thinned out just enough to define her cheekbones. Her wavy brown hair was halfway down her back. She didn't think of herself as pretty, especially compared to Rebecca and her friends. But she felt like one of the popular girls sitting beside Tyler.

She was so lost in thought that she wasn't even paying attention to what any of them were saying. Tyler twirled a strand of Luella's hair with his finger. "A little birdie told me you've never been kissed," he said.

Cameron and Joel smiled deviously.

Joel chimed in, "Yeah, how do you make it through middle school without kissing someone?"

Luella felt her cheeks get hot. She had a feeling of who was the giver of this information—whether true or not. When she looked to the back of the bus, there was Rebecca watching with her posse of popular girls.

"I've kissed boys," said Luella defensively. "A lot of boys."

"Prove it," said Tyler. He looked her square in the eye. "I dare you to give me a kiss on the cheek then." He looked over at Joel and Cameron and smirked.

Luella's heart thumped against her chest. Her stomach had that fluttery feeling—not the good kind. But it was just a kiss on the cheek, right? Where was the harm in that? "Fine."

Tyler leaned in, turning his face to the side so that his cheek was facing her. Luella hesitated, but she wasn't about to let Rebecca win. She leaned over to kiss his cheek, but Tyler turned his head at the last second, and their lips smacked together. And then Tyler's tongue was in Luella's mouth. She tried to pull away, but he grabbed her arm, holding her in place as he kissed her. Finally, she shoved him off. Cameron and Joel laughed in the seat in front of her.

"No wonder you haven't kissed anyone," said Tyler. "That was like kissing a deranged cat." He made a disgusted face to Joel and Cameron, and they all laughed and got up to move to the back of the bus.

Luella wouldn't turn to look because she already knew that Rebecca and everyone else was laughing at her. She could hear them. Luella sank down in her seat and pulled her book bag closer to her chest.

When it was finally her stop, she shot up and bolted off the bus. She ran all the way down the driveway with tears streaming down her cheeks. Paul was sitting outside at the picnic table working on his missed assignments when he saw her coming and smiled.

"Look who's feeling better," he said with a fist pump to the air. But Luella ran past him and went straight down to the barn. Paul found her there, slumped down against the wall.

"Lue," he said, stepping toward her. "What's wrong?"

"Just go away. I want to be alone."

She looked up at him, revealing the splotchy red spots all over her face and neck. It happened whenever she was in distress; it didn't matter whether she was nervous, mad, or upset.

Paul normally teased her about it, but he didn't then. He leaned against the wall and slid down to sit beside her.

"Paul, I'm serious. Just leave me alone."

"No," he said. "I'm gonna sit here until you tell me what's wrong."

She sniffed and wiped her nose with the back of her hand. Then, she looked over at him.

"Tyler," she said, noticing the way Paul stiffened at the name. He knew what kind of guy Tyler was. "Meggie was out today, so it was just me in the row. Tyler, Cameron, and Joel came up. Tyler sat down beside me and said he'd heard that I had never kissed anyone before."

She rolled her eyes and then went on, embarrassed. "They were being nice, so I didn't think anything about it. But then Tyler dared me to give him a kiss on the cheek . . ."

"You didn't," said Paul with a look of disbelief.

"He turned his face at the last minute. Then, he stuck his tongue down my throat, and when he wouldn't stop, I pushed him off me."

"I'll kill him," Paul said. It was a typical teenage boy threat, but it made Luella feel better knowing that someone cared. He knocked his shoulder into hers, and she smiled up at him.

"There we go," he said. "That's better."

They sat there for a few minutes listening to Boots chomp on hay, and then Paul asked hesitantly, "Was it, though? Your first kiss, I mean."

Her heart started pounding. She could feel the heat in her cheeks again. She didn't want to tell him, wasn't sure what he'd think of her, but she nodded anyway. Paul's eyes scanned her face, but Luella couldn't tell what he was thinking. He stood up and held his hands out to her. She grabbed them, and he helped pull her up. He stared at her for a moment, like he was trying to decide whether he should say whatever he was thinking. Finally, he told her to close her eyes.

Her heart hammered inside her chest as she did. Then, she felt Paul's hands on the sides of her face. He stroked her cheek with his thumb, and chills ran down her arms and spine. He brushed his lips against hers lightly, waiting for her to protest. When she didn't, he pressed them softly against hers. An electrifying wave passed over her.

She had dreamed of what her first kiss would be like, but never imagined it would feel like that.

When he pulled back, Luella opened her eyes. Paul's face was flushed, but his eyes were still on her lips. Before she knew it, she was leaning forward to kiss him again. His lips were warm and soft. What was she doing? It was Paul. She knew she should stop, *had* to stop, but his lips were hot against hers, and it felt too good to stop. When he pulled back, Luella tried to steady her breathing. He placed one last gentle kiss on her lips.

"Paul," she said breathlessly.

"I'm sorry. I know I shouldn't have . . . I just wanted you to have a real first kiss."

"Thank you," she said and then immediately regretted it. Who says thank you after a kiss like that? Paul brushed her hair behind her ear with his hand and smiled. Then, he walked back toward the house. Luella would relive that kiss over and over in her mind—each time spurring a tingling sensation through her body.

That's when her feelings for Paul shifted into something more than friendship.

~

The frosty air bit at her skin, pulling her out of the past and back to reality. Seeing him had brought up old feelings that she thought had settled a long time ago.

Boots came around the corner toward her.

She smiled. "Hey, old friend. It's been a while, huh?" He neighed at her. She stroked the soft spot between his nose and eyes, and he bobbed his head in protest.

"Alright, alright," she said. She tore open the bag of feed and poured some into the bucket. She dumped it into the bin inside of his stall. He ate right away. She leaned against the wooden rail and noted that his stall needed mucking badly.

As she walked back toward the house, she looked around the yard at all the worn-down things that seemed so magical as a child. Things that every kid that passed through the house had enjoyed. Things that made the long, hot days of summer more bearable.

The basketball post cemented in the ground. The net hung on by a thread, its loops worn and stretched from years of kids throwing balls through the hoop.

The old plastic riding horse on springs. Its brown color had been bleached by the sun into a warm white with specks of brown here and there. The metal frame it was attached to now rusted, where it had once been a shiny black.

The tire swing Grandpa Fred made for them out of a long metal chain and an old truck tire. It hung from a beautiful, tall oak tree. The leaves were gone. The bitter winter had stripped it bare. A slight breeze made the branches sway ever so gently, as if it was waving and wishing for someone to remember it. How many children had swung beneath its branches?

This house and land had been a place of refuge for so many kids. Hundreds of children had moved in and out of it. This place had become a home for them. Why couldn't she see it that way? All she saw when she looked around was the abandonment she felt as a child.

She opened the back door and stepped inside, letting the door slam in the face of all the ghosts from her past.

# fourteen

There was a knock on the door two days later as Luella stood in the kitchen, heating some potato soup. She turned the stove's eye on low and walked out of the kitchen toward the front door. Luella could see an older man standing on the other side through the three glass panes on the wooden door. She peered into the living room where Helen sat in front of the TV with a crocheted blanket thrown over her. Her eyes were closed. She looked too peaceful to bother.

Luella reached for the door and pulled it open. The man smiled at her, and it reached all the way up to his eyes, making his wrinkles more pronounced.

"Hello there," he said, dragging out the *lo* in hello. "My name's Percy."

He was a tiny little man, probably as tall as Luella, which wasn't very tall. Five foot three at most. He wore dark jeans with a flannel button up and what looked like a suit jacket. His arm was wrapped around a potted orchid plant. He extended his free hand. Luella took it in hers and shook it delicately, afraid she might break it.

"I'm Luella, Helen's granddaughter. She's resting right now. Do you want me to wake her?"

He shook his head. "No, no. Don't wake her. I just wanted to drop this off. It's an orchid," he said, leaning forward. He smiled, pleased with himself. "I know she loathes flowers, but I don't think this counts because it's technically a plant." He smiled wide, like he had hoodwinked Helen.

Luella couldn't help but smile back. She liked Percy.

"Please tell her I came by and that we miss her at Friendship," he said.

"Of course. I'll let her know."

Percy handed over the orchid. Luella cradled it in her arm, just like he had. Percy held his hand out again, and Luella looked at it, a little unsure. His eyes were gentle and expectant, so she placed her hand in his. He lifted her hand to his mouth and placed a kiss on it. Luella's eyebrows went up, surprised by his chivalry.

"Thank you," he said. "It was lovely to meet you, Miss Luella." He let her hand go and turned to leave. Luella smirked as she watched him walk slowly back to his Buick.

She shut the door behind her and peered into the living room again. Helen was still asleep. She set the orchid on the small round table in the kitchen. *Friendship*, he had said. Luella stirred the soup in the pot as she mulled over the name of the church she grew up going to. Helen drove them up the road to Friendship Baptist on Sundays. When she was a teenager, Helen would take them to Youth Group on Wednesdays as well. She even let them attend camp sometimes. They didn't get to do much other than that, but Helen said church was good for them, so she let them go there whenever they could. Luella didn't like church much—the families always reminded her of what she didn't have. But it was an escape from the farm, so she went anyway.

Helen never missed a Sunday, except for three consecutive Sundays after Grandpa Fred passed away. It was like she was having a standoff with God. Protesting him taking Grandpa Fred too soon. Luella had always wondered what she did with that alone time while all the kids were in church and she was by herself. Maybe she was out there arguing with God.

After three weeks, she gave in and walked back through the church doors. She didn't speak about it, and no one asked. They knew Helen would come back eventually. She just needed time to find God again.

Grandpa Fred always used to say that God would find you where you were. You didn't have to go to church to be with him. He was in everything. The trees. The rays of the sun. The wind.

Luella always thought that was a lie because she didn't feel him anywhere. Despite that, she believed Grandpa Fred. Because she had watched the way he closed his eyes against the warmth of the sun in the afternoons and smiled—like God had reached out and cupped his cheek.

Sometimes she'd close her eyes, too, but she never felt it. She wondered if she ever would.

Helen made her way into the kitchen, pulling Luella from her thoughts. She watched out of the corner of her eye as Helen reached out and grabbed whatever was in front of her for support along the way. Helen was a hard woman. She was strong. Luella had never seen her look so weak. It sent an odd sort of fear down her spine to see how frail she had become. Luella looked over at her and watched as she made her way to the table in the kitchen. When Helen's eyes landed on hers, Luella looked away fast. Helen didn't like an audience.

"Soup's done," Luella said over her shoulder as she reached into the cabinet for two bowls. "I hope potato soup is fine because it's all you had. I can pick up some more soup and some groceries from the store tomorrow if you just make me a list of what you want."

"Paul usually brings groceries once a week, but he didn't get to last week and then I landed in the hospital . . ."

"Paul?" Luella asked.

Helen didn't elaborate further. She simply nodded.

Luella took a deep breath and let it out. "That orchid is for you. A man named Percy dropped it off a little while ago." She tried her best to sound nonchalant about it.

Helen stared at it as she ran her fingers down the stem.

"Who is he?"

"Just a friend from church. His name is Percy Webster. We're in the same Sunday school class. He tried to come by the hospital, but I said I didn't want visitors. This is probably from all of them."

"He didn't say that," Luella said, setting the two bowls of soup on the table. "He was dressed pretty fancy just to drop off a plant. I think he likes you."

Helen scoffed and waved her hand in the air, dismissing the statement. "I am too old to worry myself with matters of like and love. Besides . . . my soulmate died years ago." She lifted a spoonful of soup to her mouth.

"I think Grandpa Fred would want you to be happy."

It slipped out before she realized what she was saying. Helen's eyes flicked up, making Luella regret the words instantly. Now wasn't the time to egg on an argument. Luella looked away and lifted the spoon to her mouth. It really wasn't her business. Percy seemed nice, though, and Luella liked the idea of having a distraction for Helen. Something to take the magnifying glass off her own life so that Helen wouldn't scrutinize it. But so far, Helen hadn't even asked anything about her life now.

Growing up, she stayed out of Luella's business. She just demanded three things: good grades, good behavior, and pulling her weight on the farm. Luella had managed most of those, and Helen never really asked about anything else, like boys or friends. That is, until she found out about Paul.

But Luella couldn't think about that right now, or she'd pack her bags and leave, regardless of how much Helen needed her help.

# fifteen

Waking up became a competition. Luella began setting alarms to ensure she would wake up first, but somehow, Helen was always faster.

It took her nearly two weeks, but she finally did it.

Luella was so determined to win just once that she woke up thirty minutes before her alarm went off. She went out to feed the animals while Helen slept, hoping it would surprise her when she got up and it was already done.

Luella had been trying to check her email all morning. She had to use her cell phone because Helen didn't have internet; she didn't even have cable TV. Luella wasn't expecting anything in her inbox, but it would just feel nice to be connected to the rest of the world.

She gave up after several failed attempts, made a pot of coffee instead, and sat down at the little round table in the kitchen. The hot cup felt good against her icy hands. They never used the central heating and air, so in the winter months, there was always a fire in the wood stove and electric blankets for their rooms. In those months, they slept with the doors open so the heat from the wood stove would drift in. There was a small electric heater in the corner of the kitchen, which Luella promptly turned on as soon as she got up. She could hear Helen shuffling around a few minutes later. She had slept later than usual, but Luella brushed it off. When Helen finally came into the kitchen, she was fully dressed and ready for the day. Her eyes betrayed her, though. They looked tired and her body frail.

"Morning," she grumbled, making her way over to the coffeepot.

"Good morning. I fed the animals," Luella said, holding her phone up in the air like it would grant her better reception.

Helen grabbed a mug from the cabinet and poured the steamy hot coffee from the carafe into the cup. She looked back at Luella waving her upheld phone around in the air.

"Your generation wouldn't know what to do without those things. They've become a permanent part of your body."

Luella rolled her eyes. "Well, this is the world now. You gotta be tech savvy to do anything these days. Especially if you want to be a writer. Is there nowhere on this farm that gets decent service? I've been trying to check my email for two hours."

"I thought you were *between jobs*?" Helen asked, pouring cream into her coffee mug and stirring it with the ornate teaspoon she always kept by the pot.

Luella took a deep breath to center herself before responding. It was too early to argue; she hadn't even finished her first cup of coffee. "I am." Helen stared at her, waiting for more. Before Luella could stop herself, she said the first thing that came to her mind. "But I'm working on a story that will hopefully put me in *The Georgian* and help me get a foot in the door. But that requires the use of the internet. Which you don't seem to think is very important."

"Never had any need for it," said Helen.

"How do you pay your bills? You call them in?"

"Mostly pay them in person."

"You've got to be kidding me."

Helen shrugged and took a sip of coffee. "You can pick up the neighbor's Wi-Fi on the back porch. That's what Taylor says. We also have a perfectly good, under-used facility in town with excellent internet and fully stocked computers . . . It's called a library."

Luella stood up, pressed her lips in a tight line. "Thanks for the tip," she said, heading toward the back porch.

~

She sat on the back porch swing, waiting for the Wi-Fi on her phone to connect. She watched at least a dozen chickadees chirping happily while feasting among Helen's many bird feeders.

It was more peaceful than she remembered.

Tires rolled down the long gravel driveway, echoing around the corner of the house to the back porch. They weren't expecting anyone. At least, she didn't think they were. Luella got up from the swing to walk around to the front. The screen door slammed shut behind her.

A black Chevy Silverado parked beside the path to the front porch. The driver's side door opened and out stepped Paul.

Luella stopped walking and watched as he leaned into the cab to grab several bags. With his hands full, he used his boot to slam the door shut behind him. He looked up then, and their eyes met. They stood there like it was a standoff. A few seconds of silence that felt like eternity.

Luella couldn't take it anymore. "What?"

Paul shook his head. "I just figured you'd be gone by now."

Luella scoffed. Was that why he hadn't come by before now? Because he expected her to be gone before he came over? She thought he may have come within a few days of seeing her at the hospital. "Well, I'm still here," she said, crossing her arms over her chest.

"I can see that." He stepped past her and walked toward the front porch. He fumbled, trying to open the door with the bags in his arms. Luella stepped forward and grabbed the screen door, opening it for him.

"Thanks," he said, pushing the front door open with his back. He stepped into the house and walked into the kitchen to set the bags down on the counter. Then he stood there for a moment, staring out the kitchen window. Luella took a step closer. The floor creaked beneath her.

Paul looked over his shoulder at her. "Why are you *really* still here?"

The words stung. Luella cleared her throat. "I'm here to help Helen."

She always knew if they ever saw each other again face to face that he'd probably be angry with her. How could she blame him? She left. She left *him*. But she didn't realize how much it would affect her.

He turned around to face her. "She called you?"

She contemplated her answer. She didn't want to lie, but she also didn't want him to know that Millie Beams had been the one to call her, not Helen. "Is that so hard to believe?"

"Yeah, it really is," he said, meeting her eyes this time. She noted the way his body stiffened around her like she was the enemy. It broke her heart, but she understood. She deserved it. "I'm gonna go say hey to her."

She listened as he walked into the living room where Helen sat. Their muffled voices echoed as she took the groceries out of the bag and set them down on the counter.

Paul came to the farm when he was six years old. Most kids stay in foster homes for a couple of months and sometimes a few years. Paul had lived at the farm until a few months before aging out of the system. He was just three months shy of his eighteenth birthday.

Helen and Fred were the only parents he ever had.

He walked back into the kitchen as she grabbed the last item out of the bag. "She said she's gonna read in her room and maybe take a nap."

Luella nodded. After a few awkward moments, she asked, "How bad is it?"

Paul looked over at her, his eyes scanning her face. "It's not good," he said with eyes full of sadness.

She wanted to ask more, but she wasn't sure she wanted to know the severity of it. Helen obviously didn't want her to, but it was also hard for a woman like Helen to show weakness or vulnerability. She had two emotions: anger and indifference. At least, that's how Luella had always seen it. She had only seen Helen cry once.

It was after Grandpa Fred died.

She didn't cry at the funeral. She stood stone faced as people came by to pay their respects before it started. During the service her eyes stared forward like she was concentrating on the cross, just above the baptismal pool. Even after the service, at the gravesite, Helen stood stoic as they lowered Grandpa Fred into the ground. Luella hated her for it. She wanted her to express the same grief that she was feeling. Hadn't he been the love of her life? She stood there watching as the casket went lower and lower, her eyes bone dry.

It wasn't until they got back home that night that she broke.

Dozens of people stopped by after the funeral. Food lined every inch and crevice of counter and refrigerator space they had. After everyone had left and the kids were in bed, Helen went into her and Grandpa Fred's room and only then did she crack.

Paul, the oldest, and now the man of the house, went to check on her and found her crumpled on the floor sobbing so hard she could barely breathe. The rest of the kids stayed frozen in their beds, some too new to understand, and others too wrecked from their own grief.

Luella tiptoed into the hallway. The door wasn't shut all the way, and she could see Paul and Helen through the open crack. She watched the way Paul held Helen in his arms, comforting her. His eyes flicked up and landed on Luella. They stared at each other with quiet understanding.

"It's good that you're home," said Paul.

Luella looked up at him. "This place was never my home."

Paul leaned back against the counter like she had struck him. "Well, it was the only one that I ever had." He started putting the groceries where they went in the cabinet and the refrigerator as Luella stood there watching him, feeling guilty for having said it. He turned his head to the side, as though he could sense her gaze. "I can't stay. I was just dropping some groceries off and checking on Helen."

"I can get the rest of that," she said, motioning toward the groceries. He checked to make sure all the cold things were put up and then turned around to face her. He stared at her—his eyes hard to read. For a second, she felt like she was fifteen again and unsure of his feelings for her or what she should or shouldn't say. Only now she was almost thirty years old. He won this time. She looked away first.

"Walk me out?" he asked.

They walked quietly toward his truck. Luella with her arms crossed against her chest, and Paul with his hands shoved into the front pockets of his jeans. He stopped in front of the driver side door. She wasn't sure what she was expecting, finally seeing him again face to face.

She had played it out a thousand times in her head, but those were just fantasies.

Staring at him now, she felt the years between them. The boyish face she loved was now replaced by a man's. Lines by his eyes. A fresh scar above his eyebrow. Years of going through things that she didn't know about—evidence that they didn't know each other anymore.

Paul fiddled with his pocket like he was looking for something, before finally pulling his hand out. His thumb and index finger grasped a flattened copper penny. He held it out to her.

She gasped. "My lucky penny."

Railroad tracks ran through the back side of the property. They used to sneak back there when they were young and leave coins on the track for the train to flatten. Luella's favorite was a penny that Grandpa Fred had given her that had her birth year on it. It wasn't much, but it was the most thoughtful gift she had ever been given. She carried that flattened penny everywhere, like a tiny sign of rebellion that only she and Paul knew about. A tiny memory that reminded her of both Grandpa Fred and Paul. She gave it to him two months before she left, to bring him good luck in an interview he had at the Sales Barn on Hixon Street. But she had left Chipley Creek and never gotten it back.

He held the penny out for her to grab. She took it. "You've had it all this time?"

He nodded. "I always thought if I kept it close, maybe it would bring you back home."

He smiled and shook his head, as if it was a childish thing to believe. His face grew serious then.

"Look Lue, life doesn't give you many second chances, and when it does, you gotta grab it with both hands and hold on, even if it hurts."

Luella looked over at him, leaning against his truck with his hands shoved into his pockets. Her heart hammered against her chest just like it did that day in the barn when she was fifteen years old. "I shouldn't have left you like that," she said. She meant it with all of her heart. Her leaving was never supposed to cost her Paul. Would she still have gone if she'd known it would?

He looked down at his boots. "I don't mean us. I mean you and her. You and Helen. There is so much between you that you need to figure out. All that static. You never could with your mom, but that doesn't matter. She left you. Helen didn't."

"How can you say that after what she did?"

He was quiet for a moment, like he was thinking it over, and then he said, "Because it's the truth."

She scoffed at that. "Saint Helen, is it?"

"You know I'm right," he said, looking her right in the eyes.

"I know you think you're right . . . it was good to see you," she said before storming off toward the house.

"You always had a bad temper," he yelled behind her. But she didn't slow down, she just kept walking. She let the porch door slam shut behind her, hoping it felt like a slap in the face.

# sixteen

It took two Sundays for Helen to feel good enough to go back to church.

Luella was sitting in the kitchen nursing a cup of coffee when Helen walked in wearing her best khaki pants and solid blue button up blouse. She had fixed her hair and put on just a touch of makeup.

"Why are you all dolled up?" Luella asked, eying her suspiciously.

Helen didn't respond. She just poured herself a cup of coffee. She turned around and stared at Luella when she was done. "I take it you haven't stepped in a church on a Sunday morning in eleven years then." She lifted the mug of coffee to her mouth.

Luella pressed her lips together. Of course it was a Sunday. The days seemed to bleed together in their monotony, but Helen was right. It had been quite a while since she stepped inside of a church. Helen stared at her expectantly.

"You want me to go, too?" Luella asked.

"If you're staying in this house, it's church on Sunday mornings. Non-negotiable. Besides, I'm still feeling a bit too weak to drive."

Luella blew out a breath. She slid the chair back and stood. "I'll go get dressed."

~

Twenty minutes later, they were driving down the road to Friendship Baptist. Helen preferred the early service at nine o'clock because she said it was quieter. They pulled into the church parking lot. It didn't look quieter to Luella. There was a parking lot full of people, but it was also a small parking lot. People made their way toward the building. It seemed like mostly older people attended the first service. The men dressed in suits and the women in various dresses with pantyhose and short heels.

As they approached the building, several people stood outside the church doors talking while the ushers held the doors open for those coming inside. An organ playing an old familiar hymn echoed out through the doors, welcoming them.

Pastor Wynn also stood at the door of the church, ushering his congregation inside. His face lit up as they walked up the stairs. He hugged Helen and said, "It's so good to see you, Mrs. McCrae. We sure have missed you and hope you're doing well now."

Helen patted him on the back twice and then pulled back and motioned toward Luella. "You remember my granddaughter Luella, don't you?"

Pastor Wynn looked over at Luella with bright eyes and a smile as wide as the ocean. "Of course," he said, extending his hand. Luella shook it. "It's good to have you back here at Friendship."

Luella thanked him as she walked over the threshold of the church.

In the sanctuary, the pews lined both sides of the room with a walkway right down the middle. Luella hoped Helen would sit toward the back so she could have an easy exit should she find she needed one. But Helen walked right past those last few pews and up toward the front.

*Of course she sits right up front.*

Helen stopped at the third row, but before she could sit, a plump little woman with white hair pinned up in a bun in the back came strolling toward them. Luella heard Helen's intake of breath and saw the way her body stiffened as the woman came strolling up.

"Helen, honey, it is so good to see you back at Friendship," she said. "When Percy told us you were in the hospital, we were so scared." She held a service program in one hand and her Bible in the other. She clutched her purse under her arm.

"No need to worry. It was just a minor operation . . . I'm doing much better now."

Luella's eyebrows went up. She knew Helen was a private person, but how did she plan to fool the entire town?

The woman noticed Luella standing there awkwardly at the end of the pew.

"Well, who is this?" she asked in a sing-song voice, looking between Helen and Luella.

"This is my granddaughter, Luella," said Helen.

The woman's eyebrows shot up, and she smiled. "I'm Estelle," said the woman. She extended her hand. Luella shook it. "So, what brings you to town, Luella? Are you single?" The woman stepped closer, inspecting her—as if doing so would release all of Luella's secrets.

Luella took a step back.

"Leave her alone, Telle. She's in town helping me around the farm for a bit," said Helen.

"I didn't think you needed much help around the farm," Estelle said teasingly before looking over at Luella. "I tried to get Helen to hire my grandson Troy as a farmhand, but she said she didn't need no help, and if she did, it certainly wouldn't be from a man."

"Alright, that's enough. Church is about to start," said Helen, walking further down the pew, cutting Estelle off. She sat down with a thud.

Estelle made a disapproving sound. "You're no fun, Helen." She reached her hand out and touched Luella's arm. "If you need anything while you're here, you can give me a call. I know everything about everyone and can get you an answer faster than a google search ever could." She smiled, and Luella felt pressed to smile back. The woman had a suffocating personality, and Luella wanted nothing more than to move past her and sit down in the pew beside Helen.

"It was nice to meet you," Luella said, stepping around her and walking down the pew to where Helen sat. When Luella looked back, the woman had already stopped some other poor soul, giving them an earful. Luella took a deep breath and let it out.

Helen leaned over, trying to be quiet. "We call her Telle because she will *tell* all of your business to anyone who will listen. Careful with that one."

Luella nodded to let Helen know she understood. She pressed her lips tight to keep from laughing. Small town antics were more amusing than she remembered. Especially among the older crowd.

Pastor Wynn walked out and stood before the podium, welcoming everyone. The choir stood, and the church followed. Helen grabbed a hymnal from the back of the pew in front of them. She turned it to the hymn they were singing and handed it over to Luella, who took it and held it while everyone around her sang the verses. Every time the song changed, Helen would flip through the hymnal and find that one, until finally the singing portion of service was over and Pastor Wynn took his place at the podium. Luella caught herself nodding off several times during Pastor Wynn's sermon. Each time she did, Helen would nudge her with her elbow, which made Luella snap her eyes open and lift her head. Not that she wasn't listening to what Pastor Wynn was saying, it was just that he had a monotonous way of speaking and dragging out his words that seemed to lull her and several others in the congregation to sleep. He rarely got heated in his preaching. He didn't yell or smack the podium like she had seen some pastors do.

After the service was over, Helen rushed Luella out of the pew, out of the church, and toward the parking lot.

Percy Webster stopped them when they were just a few feet away from the Wagoneer. Luella suppressed the wide grin she wanted to show and settled for a smirk so that Helen wouldn't scold her for it later. She thought Percy was precious in his suit and bowtie, stumbling around his words as he asked Helen how she was doing and if he could do anything for her. It seemed like Percy could tell there was something more serious going on with Helen, but she kept his suspicions at bay with her quick answers and brief encounters. She politely cut him off and told him they had somewhere to be. Then, she wished him a good Sunday and walked past him to the car.

"It was nice to see you again, Percy," said Luella, hoping it would soothe some of Helen's rudeness. His face turned a darker shade of pink, and he smiled and said it was nice to see her as well and told her goodbye.

Luella got into the Wagoneer and shut the door behind her. She looked over at Helen and raised a brow. "Where exactly do we have to be so quickly that you couldn't talk to that sweet man?"

Helen didn't answer. She buckled her seatbelt in silence.

"That's what I thought," Luella said and turned the key in the ignition.

"I do not have the energy for it today," Helen said, staring out of the window, pretending to watch the people getting into their vehicles.

"Well, you could have been a little nicer at least, instead of being an ice queen," Luella said, surprising herself. But Helen didn't say a word, so she backed the Wagoneer out of the parking spot and drove toward home. She looked over at Helen but her eyes were cast out the window and the corners of her mouth drawn downward as if she was depleted of all the happiness she could possibly possess.

"I just don't see the point," said Helen.

The melancholic way she said it made Luella's heart break a little, and she decided to let it go. They rode the rest of the way in silence.

## seventeen

Three weeks into her stay, Luella found the house oddly quiet. She hadn't seen Helen come out of her bedroom all morning, and she started to worry.

When she looked in Helen's bedroom, it was empty. The sheets were pushed back, and the bed unmade, which was very unlike Helen. The door on the other side of the room was open. That's when Luella saw the bathroom door shut in the hallway outside of Helen's room. She tapped lightly on the door.

"What is it?" Helen asked.

"Just wanted to check on you. I haven't seen you all morning."

"I'm fine," Helen said in a weakened voice. Her usual snippy tone was watered down.

Luella didn't like the way she sounded. "Are you sure?" she asked, putting her hand on the door, twisting the knob against her better judgment.

"Don't open the door!" Helen yelled.

Luella let go of the knob quickly and stepped back.

But she stayed in the hallway, listening. It was quiet for several seconds and then she heard Helen vomiting through the door. She had seen people throw up many times, but this one hit differently. This wasn't from a hangover or food poisoning. Her heart started racing, and she felt that panicky feeling inside her chest.

And then it dawned on her. Helen had never followed up with her doctor. Luella felt a sense of guilt for not pushing her about it. "Let me help," she said.

"No, I don't need—" and then Helen was retching again. Luella didn't know what to do. She started looking around frantically, like the rooms or the walls were going to give her an answer. Finally, she picked the phone up off the receiver and hit the speed dial button to call Cheryl.

She was at the house in a snap. She came through the door, ready to tackle the task at hand. Taylor slinked in behind her. "Where is she?" Cheryl asked.

"The back bathroom. I don't know how long she's been like this. I hadn't seen her all morning and got worried. That's when I found her locked in the bathroom."

Cheryl nodded, like she understood. "Stubborn as a mule, that one. I'm glad you called. It'll be alright. I've got this. You take Taylor outside, and y'all just give us a bit of privacy for a little while."

Luella nodded helplessly. Wasn't that what she was here for? She was the one who came back to take care of Helen, and here she was, paralyzed when needed. She was envious of the ease with which Cheryl came in, ready to help, knowing exactly what to do without being asked.

Outside, Taylor and Luella walked down to the grassy area where the rusted old basketball hoop stood. The tall swing set sat beside it. They each sat on a wooden swing, Luella staring into space, and Taylor pumping her little legs to go higher in the air. The metal chain squeaked in protest every time she'd go flying backwards.

Luella looked up at the sky. The sun was completely overhead, heating the ground and the air. It was the end of January, but it was nearing sixty degrees. That was Georgia weather, though—always unpredictable, no matter what the meteorologist said. You could experience all four seasons in the same week, sometimes in the same day. Luella closed her eyes against the warmth of the sun, but it didn't make her feel better. She couldn't feel it. That thing that Grandpa Fred seemed to feel.

Taylor's swinging slowed down. She pushed her feet into the dirt to stop herself. Then, she looked over at Luella. "Mimi will help. She's good at taking care of people."

Tears welled up in Luella's eyes, stinging the edges. She blinked back against them and sniffed, smiling at Taylor. Luella wondered why adults couldn't be more like children. They have all the confidence in the world without an ounce of doubt. Probably because adults shield them from the harsh realities of the world. At least most do. Some are not so fortunate, and experience those harsh realities for themselves. Like Luella and most of the children that passed through the farm.

"Mimi says she and Helen are kindred spirits," Taylor said, as she twirled her foot around in the dirt.

"What?"

Taylor pointed to the book that Luella was holding in her hands. "Anne of Green Gables," she said.

Luella looked down at the book. She hadn't even realized that she grabbed it on her way out.

"You've read it?"

Taylor nodded. "Me and Mimi read it last year. She says every girl should read it, and she wished she had a daughter to read it with. But now she has me, so we read it together."

"I bet that's nice," said Luella, looking out across the dormant field. "I would have loved for my mother to read a book with me."

She wouldn't have cared if it was the newspaper or even the

dictionary. Luella would have relished every word and every line, savoring the attention that a daughter craves from a mother. She wished more than anything she could have had that.

"What happened to her?" asked Taylor, as if she could read Luella's mind.

It was a loaded question with such a complicated answer. Who was Luella to tell a young girl about the harsh truths that she'll inevitably come to learn? It wasn't her place. And she refused to be the one to break that magical childhood point of view. She wished for Taylor's sake that she would keep it as long as possible.

"Nothing. She's still around somewhere. She just left when I was little. So, I grew up here."

"Oh," Taylor said, like it made all the sense in the world for a mother to leave her daughter. Taylor started swinging again until she was soaring higher and higher. The sun shined off her long, dirty blonde hair as she swung back and forth, her eyes closed against the sun and the breeze.

In that moment, silly as it may be, she wished with all her heart that she could trade places with Taylor. To momentarily feel the unburdening of her heart and swing freely into the unknown.

~

A little while later, Cheryl walked toward them. Her face was grim and her eyes heavy.

"Mimi! Watch me," yelled Taylor, pumping her legs harder as she sent the swing higher. She jumped as it soared forward, landing on her feet.

Cheryl clapped and smiled and gushed. "That was so brave . . . but also dangerous. Don't do that again."

"Okay," said Taylor with a giggle. "I'm going to find Gus." Then, she was off hunting for the tiny Pomeranian mix, leaving Cheryl and Luella alone. Cheryl sat down in Taylor's empty swing.

"How's she doing?" Luella asked.

"She's alright. She's resting now."

Luella nodded.

"Is this the first episode she's had like this?" asked Cheryl. When Luella didn't answer, she went on. "I know it's not my business. Helen is very private."

"It's the first one that I've seen," said Luella. "She naps a lot these days. She rests, and she doesn't overdo it, but yeah . . . this is the first one like this."

Cheryl nodded this time. "I don't want to scare you; I just want you to be prepared. It may only get worse from here."

A sinking feeling took over Luella's chest. Heaviness—like she was just realizing what it meant to agree to come home and help Helen. She wasn't prepared for it. She got fired, then kicked out of her home. It was logical to say yes, but she didn't realize everything it would entail.

"Luella?" Cheryl said a bit too loud, like she had been trying to get her attention.

Luella looked over at her. "Yeah?" she asked, her voice barely above a whisper.

"Are you okay, hon?"

This time Luella didn't fight back the tears. She wasn't even sure what they meant. She could only feel the warmth as they ran down her cheeks. Suddenly embarrassed, she wiped them away with her hand. "She wouldn't let me help. I asked her to let me in. To let me help. But she wouldn't."

"It's okay," said Cheryl. She leaned over and patted Luella's leg, comforting her.

"She was supposed to follow up with her doctor, and she never did. I never made her, either . . . I should have. Maybe she wouldn't have—"

"Don't do that," said Cheryl. "This isn't your fault. If Helen had wanted to see her doctor, she would have. That was her decision." She took a breath and blew it out slow. "I'm just down the road. You call me if you need me. I'll be here in a jiff. We're gonna go now, but I mean it—you call if you need to."

Then, she was up out of the swing and walking toward the front of the house, looking for Taylor. Luella went inside a little while later and found Helen resting in her usual spot on the couch.

Luella's heart ached at the sight of her—tiny and frail underneath a quilt twice her size. But a small part of her was also filled with anger.

Anger from being called here to help, but when the time came for it—Helen pushed her out instead of letting her in.

"Why am I here?"

Helen looked over, but her gaze didn't linger. Her eyes drifted back toward the television.

The volume was barely audible. When Helen didn't answer her, Luella sat down on the loveseat beside the couch.

"What's wrong with you?" she asked, her tone a bit harsher.

Helen stared at the television. She wouldn't look over and even acknowledge Luella's question.

Luella sighed, feeling defeated with the conversation. She stood up to leave, and that's when Helen spoke.

"Stage four non-Hodgkin's lymphoma."

Luella sank down onto the loveseat, swallowing against the dryness in her throat. "When did you find out?"

Helen looked over at her then. "Seven years ago."

Luella's breath hitched and her body tensed. Seven years? Meggie said that was when she quit fostering. It all made sense now. That must have been why she stopped. Luella was astonished that Helen had been carrying this around for seven years—while all that Luella had been carrying was resentment, which paled in comparison.

"But what about treatment? Can't you—"

Helen raised a hand to stop her. "I've done treatments. Some of them worked for a while. But each time it came back more aggressive than before. And I'm tired . . ."

Luella wanted to protest. She wanted to drag Helen to see a doctor right then and there.

Force her to take medicine. She couldn't wrap her mind around the fact that Helen didn't want to fight anymore.

But it was Helen's life, and Helen's choice.

Helen turned the volume up on the television, and the two of them sat in silence as an episode of *Jeopardy* came on.

# eighteen

It had been almost six weeks since Luella arrived back in Chipley Creek.

Their days became methodical. Luella got up every morning to feed the animals, and if Helen was feeling up to it, she cooked a small breakfast. She napped most days. She didn't have another episode like the one in the bathroom. In fact, Helen didn't seem to be getting sicker at all, but then she also didn't seem to get better, either. She was just coasting along.

Luella didn't push the doctor issue. Besides, it didn't seem like Helen needed much help. Sometimes Luella wondered why she was even there at all.

Cheryl and Taylor came by at least once a week with a meal, but Luella knew it was really just so Cheryl could check on Helen.

Still no Paul. He stayed away. Didn't bring any more weekly groceries now that Luella was in town. He must have known she'd take over where he left off. His absence bothered Luella more than she cared to admit.

~

One Friday morning, Helen woke up with a pep in her step and more color in her face than Luella had seen since she arrived. Helen was even a little chipper—which was highly unusual.

Luella stood in the kitchen clutching her coffee mug when Helen came breezing in. She poured herself a cup, then turned around to face Luella. She leaned against the counter. "I was thinking we could ride to town in a bit. I need to go by the pharmacy and pick up a prescription." Luella nodded so Helen would know she was paying attention. "Then, we'll have to come back so I can start dinner. I invited Cheryl and Taylor over . . . Paul, too."

Luella almost choked on her coffee. "You invited Paul?"

"Is that a problem?"

What could Luella say? She didn't want Helen to think it was or wasn't. "No. Not at all. I'm just surprised to be honest."

"Paul has been a big help around here these past few months," said Helen.

"So, the two of you get along now?"

Helen took a long sip of her coffee. "Paul forgave me years ago. It's only you who still holds a grudge. I did what I did for the well-being of both of you. Not to mention that I had to."

Luella gripped her mug harder, clamping her jaw tight to stop her from saying something to Helen that she'd regret. She took a deep breath and poured her coffee into the sink. She rinsed the mug and stuck it on the wooden drying rack beside the sink. "I'll be ready to go in a little while."

~

When they returned from town that afternoon, Cheryl and Taylor were already inside. Luella looked over at Helen in the passenger seat with confusion on her face. "They went in without you here?"

"Cheryl has a key."

It hurt Luella's feelings a little because she didn't even have one. Only the spare that was beneath the plant on the porch. They got out of the Wagoneer and went inside. Cheryl was hard at work in the kitchen. Helen walked over to her and started harping about how she was the guest and not the cook. They bickered back and forth, and Luella walked into the living room to find Taylor playing checkers by herself on a little wooden table.

"Need an opponent?" Luella asked. Taylor looked up excitedly before moving the pieces back to their starting positions. Luella grabbed a pillow off the couch and threw it on the floor to sit on. Taylor went first. She was relentless in the game, and she was actually really good at it. Luella was having a hard time beating her.

"You're great at this," she said.

Taylor shrugged. "I like games." A couple of moves later, Taylor said, "Paul's coming you know." She didn't look up to meet Luella's eye.

Luella took her turn, sliding her red checker piece diagonally to the end of the spaces. "I knew that. King me."

Taylor bounced two of her checkers and took them off the board. She looked up at Luella and smiled.

Luella was deciding what move to make next when someone knocked on the door. Her heart thumped faster. She knew who it was.

Taylor also knew and laughed. "Why are you so nervous?" she teased.

"I'm not nervous."

"You're acting weird." Taylor said, as Paul came through the door.

"No I'm not." She said it more defensively than intended.

They listened as he walked into the kitchen to greet Helen and Cheryl. He must have tried to hug Cheryl, because she gasped and said, "You still have your uniform on. There's no telling what kind of germs are on it."

Luella and Taylor looked at each other and laughed quietly.

"Where's Lue?" he asked Helen, and she felt her heart drop right into her stomach.

"She and Taylor are playing checkers in the living room," Cheryl said.

"I'm the checker champion in this house," he said, making his way into the living room where they were.

"Good luck beating her," Luella said. "She's good at this game. Might even be better than you." Luella looked up at him, and their eyes locked. He smiled at her. She felt like that same jittery teenager who had just realized her feelings for him.

"We'll just see about that," he said, tousling Taylor's hair.

She swatted his hand away. "You're on," she said.

Luella scooted over so he could sit down. Taylor giggled as he struggled to cross his long legs on the floor. Taylor moved the pieces back to their starting positions again. Paul bumped Luella's leg with his, and she smiled. He was so ruggedly handsome, and she loved it. It was the best kind of handsome, in her opinion. The scruff on his face. The bump on his nose from where he broke it when they were kids. The smile that reached his eyes with the dimples that made her defensiveness melt like butter. Her shoulders relaxed and her body eased as they sat next to each other on the floor, his knee resting against hers. She'd give anything to stay right there forever.

They played four more games before dinner was ready. For once, they ate at the big ten-foot wooden table in the dining room of the house. It was the first time they had a meal there since Luella had been back. The little round table in the kitchen seated four, and that was always enough, even if Cheryl and Taylor came by for dinner.

The big table had seats at the ends, with long wooden benches on the sides. It was practical when they had a house full of kids and people. Much easier than chairs. They used to squish in, leaving not an ounce of room on those benches. Luella smiled to herself as she thought about it. Paul sat across from her. She looked up at him, and he smiled knowingly. He kicked the bottom of her shoe with his, just like he did when they were kids, which made her laugh.

Cheryl and Helen set the table with food, plates, napkins, and utensils. The middle of the table was lined with green bean casserole, homemade mac and cheese, rolls, and a ham that Helen and Luella had picked up in town. It was a proper southern meal. Luella's mouth watered just looking at the food. Cheryl made each of them wash their hands before sitting down. Taylor grabbed a roll and took a bite. Cheryl swatted at her hand.

"Lucky you didn't choke," she scolded. "We haven't said the blessing yet."

Luella and Paul smiled at each other. Even Helen smiled a little. Taylor rolled her eyes, put the roll down, and closed her eyes. Helen said the blessing. The conversation flowed, and everyone seemed to enjoy themselves. Luella felt happy at that moment, for the first time in a long time.

After dinner, Helen and Cheryl retreated into the living room to sit by the warmth of the woodburning stove. Luella and Paul volunteered to clean the aftermath of their dinner. Taylor lingered after Helen and Cheryl had already headed into the living room, but Cheryl called after her to follow. She was a little annoyed about it, but Luella was grateful that she'd be left alone with Paul. They emptied the leftovers into containers and piled the dishes into the sink. Paul turned on the old radio that sat on the counter in the corner. When Luella heard what station it was, she laughed.

Paul looked over at her with amusement in his eyes. "Can you believe we used to hate this station as kids, and now it plays all of our music from back then? That's how you know we're getting really old."

She shook her head at him. "I know. It's crazy."

They fell into a peaceful rhythm: Paul washed dishes and Luella dried them and put them up. They never had a dishwasher, so this was what they were used to. *Just like old times.* When they did it together, it never felt like a chore.

She was expecting him to leave when they finished, but he crossed his arms against his chest and leaned back against the counter instead. He stared at her for a moment, like he was contemplating something.

"You want dessert? I brought a pie." His eyebrows went up with a smile.

She couldn't help but smile back. Those dimples got her every time. She nodded.

"Sweet." He walked over to the microwave. He pulled out the pie as Luella opened the cabinet to grab two plates. She hesitated for a moment, wondering if she should also grab three more for Cheryl, Taylor, and Helen, but decided against it because she was enjoying having Paul to herself.

He cut a slice for each of them and then put the pie back.

"Is this Helen's chocolate chip pie recipe?"

Paul nodded proudly.

"No way," said Luella. "You didn't make this."

"I did too. You know it was my favorite, so I had to learn how to make it."

She took a bite. "Mmm," she said. "This might be better than Helen's."

Paul looked pleased. They sat at the round wooden table and ate the rest together, neither one saying a word. Paul smiled when Luella looked up at him. She noticed the way it reached his eyes this time. She smiled back.

"You have chocolate on your face," he said.

She wiped at it but must have missed because Paul leaned over and drug his thumb gently across the side of her mouth. And just like that, there in the pit of her stomach were the butterflies only he could create. She hadn't felt them since she left Chipley Creek. No one had made her feel the way he did. After years without something, it only takes a moment of feeling it again to make you want it more than anything else in the world.

Paul got up and rinsed his dishes and put them on the drying rack. He grabbed Luella's and did the same. She was sure he'd leave now.

"Wanna go sit on the back porch?" he asked.

She looked up, surprised. "It's cold out there."

"Come on. Chicken."

She jumped up. "I'm not a chicken. Let's go."

"Atta girl," he said.

They went out to the back porch. The chilly night air seeped in through the screen. Paul put on his big Carhartt jacket, and Luella wrapped herself in one of Helen's soft plush blankets. They sat down on the swing. Paul rocked them backwards with his foot and then they were swaying.

The chain creaked every time they sailed forward.

"So . . ." he said. "What's your life like now?"

She shrugged, unsure of how she wanted to answer his question. How much she wanted him to know. "I worked for a popular blog in the city, writing stories about prominent people in Atlanta."

"Worked?" he asked.

"Yeah . . . It didn't work out. But that was never my endgame anyway. I want to write for *The Georgian*. I want to write stories that matter. Meggie got me a meeting with her Aunt Cathy who works there. She wants me to write a story about growing up here at the farm."

"Yeah?" He seemed intrigued.

Luella shrugged. "I wasn't going to, but being back here brings up all kinds of memories and emotions . . ."

Paul considered her words. He stood and walked over to the side of the porch and stared out into the dark yard.

Luella watched him looking out into the night. Crickets chirped while everything else stood completely still. "It's quiet out here. It's nice."

He looked over at her, the corners of his mouth turning up. "You don't mean that. You hate the quiet. It's one of the reasons you left this place."

"That's not true," she said.

"Yes, it is," he said with a laugh. "You've always wanted the BBD."

"The what?"

"Bigger Better Deal. You've never been content with what you have. You've always wanted more. That includes this place."

She was taken aback by his comment. Did he really think that of her? "That's not fair," she snapped.

"It may not be fair, but it's true, and you know it," he said. She could hear the hurt in his voice.

"What's wrong with wanting more?"

He shoved his hands in the front pockets of his uniform pants and sighed. "It's okay to want more. You're ambitious. You always have been. I've never been able to keep up with your momentum. I understand why you left."

"Paul, if I could go back—"

He shook his head to stop her. "But you can't. Besides, it's all water under the bridge now."

Her throat went dry, and she found it hard to swallow. She wanted to tell him how she thought about him every day since she stepped onto that bus. She willed the words up from within, but she couldn't force them out. He deserved more than she could ever give him. She had already let him down once.

"Lue," he said, pulling her back from the pitfall of her mind. They stared at each other for a moment and then he walked back over to the swing and sat down beside her. He put his arm around her and pulled her close. Luella leaned into him, resting her head on the space between his neck and shoulder. The spot she felt was meant only for her. Her eyes closed as she breathed him in, smiling at the familiar scent. Woodsy and heavy. She always loved the way it smelled on him.

She looked up at him. His honey-colored eyes stared back at her, scanning her face like he was trying to work out the years that stood between them. His gaze softened, and in that moment, the years between them ceased to exist. They were the same two teenagers, drunk off lust and love. Luella leaned forward and placed her lips delicately on his.

Waiting. Asking. Begging.

It took three agonizing seconds and then he cupped her face with his hands and kissed her like he was making up for all the years lost.

But then he pulled away suddenly. Luella had to catch herself so that she didn't fall off the swing. He turned away from her. "Dang it, Luella."

She sat up straight, like she was being scolded. Her shoulders stiffened. "Guess that means you've got someone?" She couldn't bring herself to look at him. To think of him being with someone else.

He ran his hands over his face and breathed deep. "Sort of. Something like that. It's complicated."

"Who is she?"

"You don't know her. She's not from here. She landed here by accident."

"Sounds like fate," she said, trying to hide the tone of jealousy in her voice.

"She's a travel nurse. We've been off and on for a couple of years."

"Years? Wow," she said under her breath.

Luella tried to read his face for what he wouldn't say out loud. She hesitated, but then finally spoke up and asked the question that might hurt her the most. "Do you love her?"

Paul ran a hand through his hair. He sighed. "I care about her . . . and a part of me does love her. Or loved her. But I'm not sure I could say I'm still in love with her."

His eyes met hers then. The look in them begged for forgiveness. But what did she have to forgive him for? She was the one who had done the leaving.

"She wants me to take a traveling job. They take EMTs, too. She's been on my case about it for a while."

"What do you want to do?"

"I don't know. All I've ever known is this town. Maybe I should just try it out and get out of here for a while."

Luella's heart sank. She had finally come back, and now he might be leaving. It bothered her more than she cared to admit. She looped her arm through his, and he pushed off the ground, sending them swinging backward once again. She looked out into the night and saw the old basketball goal down by the tire swing and smiled.

"You remember when we were little, and we'd play Spotlight after dark? You'd be my partner every time—always found the best places to hide . . . and you were so fast. We always won."

Paul laughed. "You remember Gee? That lanky kid that stayed here for about a year. Remember the time he hid in the tree and fell asleep before making it back to the goal? He slept outside all night and woke up sunburnt and hating life."

They both laughed then.

"Things were simpler back then, weren't they?" she asked.

"Man, it feels like yesterday. Dear old yesterday."

Luella smiled. "Yeah, it does." She took a deep breath and

watched Paul's face as they swung back and forth across the old, weathered porch. It had been so long since she felt that comforting sensation of feeling safe with a person. They sat there swinging until Helen called for them to come inside and tell Taylor and Cheryl goodbye. It felt like hours, but also didn't feel like long enough.

As soon as he left, Luella pulled her phone out and texted Meggie: I kissed Paul . . .

Her phone immediately started ringing.

"Tell me everything," Meggie said, as soon as Luella picked up.

So, she did. She recounted every single detail to her best friend, feeling just like a teenager again.

# nineteen

The next week, she arrived back from the feed store one morning to Helen and Cheryl in the kitchen talking at the little round table. The thick smell of coffee wafted through the air. She laid the bags on the big table and walked into the kitchen. The women paused their conversation.

Luella poured herself a cup of coffee and turned around, facing them. She leaned against the counter and took a sip.

"Did they have Gus's food this time?" asked Helen.

"Yep. I got two bags just in case."

"Good."

Cheryl smiled at Luella as she pulled the chair next to her out a bit. "Sit," she said. "Have coffee with us."

Luella eyed Helen for a cue whether it was okay if she did, but Helen simply took another sip of her coffee. Luella sat down anyway. She had spent enough time by herself lately and wouldn't admit it out loud, but she was hungry for social interaction.

"We were just talking about Taylor's dad," said Cheryl. "He's trying to contest my adopting her when he was the one who left her with me to begin with. He said he wouldn't bother us again. But here I am, trying to make it official that he can't, and he goes and makes it complicated."

"Is he your son?" asked Luella.

"Not biologically. He was my stepson. But we lost touch after his father passed away. He came back into my life after Taylor was born. It was fine for a while, but then he started skipping out on Taylor. He would leave her with me for days at a time, then weeks, and eventually months. I never minded; I love Taylor like she's my own."

"That's terrible," said Luella. "How much does Taylor know?"

"I try to spare her the muddy details, but she knows enough to know that it's going to get sticky before it gets better."

"She's a strong girl," said Helen. "She'll be alright."

Luella scoffed. Something about the way Helen said it infuriated her. Sometimes she thought Helen saw all children as little soldiers instead of the vulnerable spirits they were.

"She's eleven . . . she shouldn't have to be strong. She should just be able to be a kid without having to worry about things like that."

"Yes, but life isn't really like that, is it?" said Helen. Cheryl looked cautiously between the two of them. "Life is intrinsically complex. Nothing is ever *really* just black or white, it's a multitude of gray. And we shade in the picture of our life for ourselves. We get to decide which areas are darker than others."

Luella suppressed an eye roll. *Always a lesson with Helen.* Though she wouldn't say it, she believed things were distinctly black or they were white. The gray area is just where they bleed together a bit. Yes, Cheryl may have taken better care of Taylor, but he was her dad. Luella's heart stung for the young girl.

"Does she get a say in any of it?" Luella asked, directing her question at Cheryl. She didn't give her enough time to answer, though. "It should matter what she thinks and how she feels. She might be young, but that doesn't make her feelings any less important."

"At least she has someone like Cheryl to look out for her best interest," said Helen, her voice raised slightly as she slammed her mug onto the table.

Luella had struck a nerve, and even she knew it was time to relent. She nodded in agreement.

Cheryl tried to smooth the conversation. "The judge said he'll take it into consideration. But he has a reputation for placing children back with their parents because he thinks that's best."

"Where's her mom?" asked Luella.

Cheryl's face filled with sadness. "She died a few weeks after giving birth to Taylor."

"Oh. I'm so sorry."

"It's okay. We talk about her a lot. I think it's important. She was the sweetest person I've ever known—nothing but pure sunshine. You wanted to just bask in her warmth. There aren't too many people like that these days. I see a lot of her in Taylor. I'm glad, too. It's like her spirit lives on."

Luella smiled sadly. Cheryl blinked back against her watery eyes. Luella understood why Helen and Cheryl were so close, being that they were neighbors and all. But they were nothing alike, in her opinion. The most drastic difference being that Cheryl was much softer than Helen. She was happy about that, for Taylor's sake. Taylor seemed like a well-rounded, carefree kid—despite what she was having to go through.

Luella zoned out on the conversation and checked back in when she heard Helen say, "Well, sometimes it's better that a child is not with their biological parent."

"You're talking about Mya, aren't you?" Luella said defiantly.

Helen looked over at her. "No," she said. "Though, I wouldn't disagree in that regard, either. I'm talking about my own mother. Now, she was a real piece of work, and she hated me. Told me on as many occasions as she could. She hated that motherhood stopped her from doing all the things she wanted to do instead. Said that she'd be an actress in Hollywood if it weren't for me. But most of all, she hated that my daddy loved me more than he loved her. If it ever came down to the two of us, he'd pick me every time. And he did—until she forbid him from coming around. That woman had more meanness in her than anyone I've ever met. Not even children could bring her happiness."

All three of them were silent for a moment, not knowing how to follow that. Helen took a sip of her coffee.

"I didn't know that. You've never talked about that before," said Luella.

"You never asked."

Luella felt a pang of guilt. All the years she had lived with Helen, and it just occurred to her she didn't even know that much about her. She had always pictured Helen exactly as she was when Luella was a child, like that was where her life began.

But Helen had been a child, just like Luella had. Helen had experiences outside of being a foster parent and a grandma. But she had been a daughter and a wife, too, and Luella had never taken that into consideration. Never thought to ask about Helen's life *before*.

She never really questioned why her mother and Helen didn't get along or barely spoke. After meeting Helen, she assumed it was because of her hard exterior and sternness. But maybe it was because of something else. Defenses Helen put up to keep her heart safe.

Luella took another sip of coffee. Helen and Cheryl started talking about something else. It only took a few seconds before a wave of nausea hit her hard. Her skin got hot and clammy, yet cold at the same time.

She stood up and practically ran over to the bathroom beside the kitchen. Everything she had eaten, along with the coffee she drank, came rocketing back up in her throat. She opened the toilet lid just in time.

When she was done, she sank to the floor and grabbed a towel off the wooden cabinet beside her. She wiped her mouth with the back of her hand and leaned her head back against the glass door of the shower. It had been years since she had thrown up.

A knock on the door pulled her out of her thoughts.

"Luella honey?" asked Cheryl, muffled by the barrier of the door. "Are you alright?"

"I'm fine," said Luella, getting to her feet. She turned the water on and wet the cloth in her hand. She wiped her face off and then took a swig of mouthwash. The cool mint taste burned in her mouth. She spit it out quickly, afraid it might make her sick again. Then she gargled with a handful of water and spit into the sink. She watched it disappear down the drain. What had made her sick? It was probably the biscuit she had eaten from Smallwoods that morning before she went to the feed store. Who knew how long they kept those out under a heat lamp. She turned the water off and opened the door. Helen and Cheryl had stopped their conversation.

"Something turn your stomach?" asked Helen.

Luella nodded. "I got a biscuit from Smallwoods this morning. Probably that."

"There's a stomach flu going around, too," Cheryl offered. "Taylor's teacher sent a note home about it. I hope she didn't bring something over to you, or to Helen. Lord, that would be awful. Do you have any Lysol, Helen? We need to spray." Cheryl got up and opened the cabinet under the sink.

Luella shook her head. "I'm fine. I really think it was just some bad food. The coffee didn't help, either. I'm going to lie down for a minute."

Cheryl walked toward the bathroom clutching a can of Lysol. Helen sat at the table staring at Luella with suspicious eyes that made Luella uncomfortable. Cheryl broke the silence by over-spraying the bathroom. Luella turned to leave the room.

As she walked away, she heard Helen from behind her. "Pregnancy can do that, too, you know."

Luella froze.

When was the last time she had a cycle? She hadn't really thought about it. It didn't even cross her mind. But she had been there two months already and hadn't had one since. The last one she remembered was before Christmas. *No, no, no.* She did the math quickly in her head. Eight weeks since she last had one.

How could that much time pass without her realizing? She tried to calm her breathing. It could just be from the stress of coming back to Chipley . . . of taking care of Helen . . . of seeing Paul again. Or she got sick from the biscuit. Yes, that was it. A combination of all those things, stressing her body out.

She turned back to Helen. "I'm sure it was just the biscuit."

But as she walked toward the back of the house, she wasn't sure at all.

# twenty

It seemed silly. Surely she would know if she was pregnant. Her body would go through all kinds of changes, making her aware that there was another life growing inside of her. Wouldn't it?

She stood in the aisle at Bradley's, looking left and right constantly to make sure she didn't see anyone she knew as she tried to decide which test to buy.

Why were there so many options? They couldn't make it easy and just have one type of pregnancy test to grab and go for occasions such as this? There was the digital kind, the rapid detection kind, early response kind, ones with the little strips. It was overwhelming. Especially for someone who had never even looked at them before. Never expected to have a reason to.

Add in the uneasiness she felt, and it was enough to make her nauseous. Or was that because she was pregnant? *No. It's just anxiety.* Had to be.

She grabbed one quickly off the shelf and threw it in the basket. On her way up the aisle, she grabbed a few more items to conceal the small rectangular box that she desperately wanted to keep hidden.

There was no line. She had gotten there right as they opened at eight. A lanky, freckled face girl stood behind the register chewing bubble gum like she was bored out of her mind. She looked fresh out of high school, which reminded Luella of the reason she had left Chipley at eighteen. She wanted more than this little town had to offer. She didn't want to get stuck in a job she hated with nowhere else to go.

Luella set the basket on the conveyor belt and stood in front of the card machine as the girl picked up one item and after another and scanned them in no particular hurry. Luella looked around the store nervously. When the girl lifted the box out of the basket to scan it, her eyes roamed over Luella—inspecting her. Luella noticed the way the girl's eyes immediately went to her left hand, no doubt looking for a wedding ring. She put the box in the bag and hit a button on the cash register.

"Twenty-six dollars and eighty cents."

Luella swiped her card and entered her pin number. She could feel the girl's eyes on her as they both waited for the machine to ding. When it finally did, the girl ripped off the receipt and handed it to Luella.

"Have a nice day," she said.

"Yeah, you too," said Luella, as she grabbed the bag and hastily made her way toward the doors.

She took a deep breath once she was safe inside the Wagoneer. She pulled the box out of the bag and ripped it open, pulling out the instructions. Her eyes scanned over them three times.

She looked up. How was she going to do this? She didn't want to chance Helen interrupting her or questioning her while she was taking the test. But where else could she go? Her eyes landed on the Hardware store across the street. Even if they were busy, the store was usually full of men, and men minded their own business.

Luella drove across the street and parked in front of the building. She grabbed the pregnancy test from the box and slid it inside her sleeve.

The man behind the counter smiled at her as she stepped inside the store.

"Where are your restrooms?" she asked with a pasted on smile.

"Back left corner," he said, his attention now back on the newspaper in his hands.

Luella made her way to the restroom and locked the door behind her. Thank goodness it was a single bathroom. She couldn't imagine having to do this in a stall. She ripped open the packaging and took off the cap, squatted over the toilet, and held the test exactly how the instructions said to. Five seconds in the urine stream.

When she finished, she put the plastic cap back on it and set the test face down on top of the toilet paper dispenser. *Now to wait.* She threw the box and wrapper in the trash can. She set a timer on her phone and paced the tiny bathroom as she waited. That one minute stretched into an eternity.

Her phone vibrated when the timer ran out, and she shoved the phone in her back pocket, and took a deep breath. *Please be negative.*

She flipped the test over.

Two dark blue lines met in a perfect cross. They weren't faded or weak. Her answer was so blatantly clear that her breath caught in her throat. She picked up the test to inspect it further. In case her eyes were playing tricks on her. But they weren't. There was no denying those lines.

*No, no, no. This cannot be happening.*

Her body felt hot and cold simultaneously, making her face and hands clammy. She shoved the test back up her sleeve and then washed her hands without looking up at her reflection in the mirror. She couldn't face the fear that was sure to be visible all over her face.

She rushed out of the bathroom, intending to head straight for the door—until a voice caught her by surprise.

"Luella? Is that you, dear?"

She froze at the sound of her name, only five feet from the door.

*So close.* She turned around to find Estelle standing at the end of an aisle. *Of all places.* Of course Estelle was in the hardware store. "Yes, hi."

Estelle made a smacking sound with her lips and inched her way forward. "Well, what are you doing in the hardware store? Don't tell me Helen has you doing all the man's work around that farm?"

Luella looked around for an out, but there wasn't much for her to grab. No excuses she could easily find. She spotted a pack of nails at the end of the counter, grabbed them quickly, and slid them over to the register.

"Nails," she said, glancing at Estelle. "There are some spots on the porch that need nailing down, and the ones in the shed are ancient."

One of Estelle's eyebrows went up—like she wasn't buying Luella's story. Truth was, Luella knew it sounded ridiculous, but it came out faster than she could stop it. Luella took a few deep breaths to calm her racing heart. There was no way Estelle knew what she had done in the bathroom. She dropped her hand to her side, and the test slid past the end of her sleeve. She caught it in her hand at the last minute and pushed it back up.

The man scanned the nails as Estelle watched through curious eyes. "That'll be ten fifty-two," he said.

It was then that she remembered she didn't bring her wallet inside the store with her. *Wonderful.* "I left my wallet in the car. If you just give me a second to grab it . . ."

"Sure thing," said the man, picking his newspaper back up.

Luella turned to leave but spun around again. "On second thought, I'll just come back later. I think I probably need a few more things anyway."

"Alright," said the man, drawling out the beginning of the word.

Estelle stared at her with a look of concern on her face. Concern or Curiosity, Luella couldn't tell which. She'd assume the latter though. "It was nice to see you again, Estelle," she said.

Then, she whirled around and practically ran out of the door. No doubt all of Chipley Creek would hear about Estelle's strange encounter with Helen's granddaughter in the hardware store.

~

Luella paced the floor of her bedroom. She knew she needed to make a doctor's appointment to confirm the pregnancy. Helen was taking a late morning nap, so Luella tiptoed into the kitchen to call and schedule an appointment with the health clinic in the next town over.

Helen still had a house phone she kept by the entryway, along with a calendar and a slot for her mail. Luella walked over to the table in search of a phone book. The weather was still chilly, and she didn't feel like spending forty-five minutes using the neighbors spotty Wi-Fi on the porch to look up the local clinic's number. She knew Meggie was busy with the recreation department, and truthfully, she wasn't ready to tell her. She didn't want to tell anyone. So, that left using the old school method of looking it up via phone book. She looked around the table but didn't see one, so she pulled open the drawer and found it sitting inside. She grabbed it and walked to the side of the house that was farthest away from Helen. The line rang and rang. Finally, a woman picked up that sounded about as cheerful as Luella felt.

Luella told her she'd like to set up an appointment but was hesitant when the woman asked what type. "I might be pregnant," she said. "I got a positive test this morning, but it was probably a false positive. You know how finicky those tests can be."

She didn't know—only hoped that the woman would agree. But all the woman did was ask Luella a series of questions resulting in her scheduling her for the earliest appointment she had, which was for the following Wednesday.

Luella thanked her and hung up fast. She opened the drawer to put the phone book back, and scanned for something to write down the appointment details on so she wouldn't forget.

A sticky note was attached to the drawer underneath where the phone book had been laying. It had Mya's name scrawled on it with a number underneath. She pulled it off and stared at it. The number was different. Luella used to know Mya's number by heart. She would call it often from the farm whenever she could, with no one knowing. When she moved to the city, she tried it a couple times to no avail. All she wanted was to talk to her mother. She thought maybe it would be different since she was an adult. She wouldn't get in the way. They could start over. Then one day, she called, and the number had been disconnected. She stopped trying to contact her after that.

But now she held a different phone number in her hand. One that would probably work.

She wanted to put it back in the drawer like she had never seen it, but she just couldn't. It was like Pandora's Box. It couldn't be unseen. She started dialing the number before she even realized what she was doing. She looked back toward Helen's room but didn't hear a peep.

The line rang twice and then she heard her mother's same raspy voice saying hello.

Her heart thumped wildly inside of her chest—a mix of anger and longing.

"Mom?" she said into the phone. Mya was quiet, but Luella could hear rustling around on the other end, so she knew she was still there. "It's Luella."

"I know who it is. I thought I told you not to call me that. It's just Mya."

The hurt Luella felt by her remark was rivaled only by the anger she also felt. She cleared her throat. "Helen's sick."

"Okay," said Mya.

"She has stage four lymphoma . . ." When Mya didn't say anything, Luella went on. "It's changed her. She's tiny, gets tired easily. She's napping a lot. I just think you should come."

Mya scoffed. "She'll be alright. She always is. Besides, it looks like she's got you there to take care of her. I'd just be in the way."

"Did you hear anything I just said to you?" Luella asked, her voice a little louder.

"Look, Luella . . . your grandma and I have nothing left to say to each other."

She heard Mya sigh on the other end of the phone. Luella had nothing left to say to her and didn't want to give Mya the benefit of the doubt anymore. She hung up the phone and put it back on the receiver. She wished she hadn't even bothered calling her. It was obvious nothing had changed.

Except for Luella. She had changed.

She was no longer that little girl that used to yearn for a phone call or a visit from her mother. In the twenty-two years since Mya had left her, all she had were the five letters that Mya wrote to her. Five letters in twelve years. Luella could hardly stand the wait between the letters when she was young. How naïve she had been.

It's hard to come to terms with the idea of being better off without someone you thought you needed as much as breath or air. To realize that life ticks on just fine without them. Even tougher to realize that maybe you're better off in their absence and that they weren't the sun you thought you needed in order to grow.

She walked into the living room and found Helen awake, sitting on the couch beneath a blanket. She hoped she hadn't overheard Luella's conversation with Mya. Or with the doctor's office. If she had, she didn't give it away in the slightest. The news played quietly on the television. Helen's eyes were closed, but she opened them every few seconds. The fire in the wood stove had warmed the room to an almost unbearable temperature, and still Luella thought she could see Helen shivering beneath her blanket.

"Was it a good nap?"

Helen's eyes snapped open at the sound of Luella's voice. She nodded. "I just can't seem to wake back up."

"Probably the weather," Luella offered. They both knew it wasn't the weather, though.

Helen nodded again and closed her eyes.

Luella couldn't help but notice how small Helen looked in the big, empty house. She had spent most of her life raising children in that farmhouse. Years of chatter, laughter, and footsteps echoed through a house that was now a shell of what it once was. She wondered if Helen felt that way, too. Years of raising other people's children, only to find herself alone in the stillness after it was over.

For the first time, she was glad that she was there.

Luella knew one thing. If she really was pregnant—the best thing she could do for the baby was give it to a family that would love and welcome it with unconditional love. She wasn't sure she was capable of such a thing. Babies were meant for people who wanted them. She knew she was selfish; she didn't deny that.

The truth of it was that she didn't want to add another McCrae to an already broken family.

She wouldn't do it.

# twenty-one

Luella could hardly handle the week-long wait for her appointment. She told Helen she was meeting Meggie for a late lunch so she wouldn't ask too many questions. If she told her she was out running errands, then she'd ask what kind and why and offer all kinds of unsolicited advice on how to best use one's time, and Luella didn't need a lecture today of all days.

She pulled the Wagoneer into the parking lot of the Women's Clinic and parked in a space close to the front. The lot was fuller than she expected, and she said a silent prayer that she wouldn't see anyone she knew. She cut off the engine and looked in the mirror. She ran her hands through her hair and took a deep breath. "It's gonna be fine," she said to her frazzled, anxiety ridden reflection.

Inside, several women sat in the waiting room—all of them with varying sizes of protruding bellies that made Luella feel a wave of nausea. A blonde in the corner looked up at her and smiled as she cradled her belly. Luella forced a smile as she made her way to the reception area.

The woman behind the desk didn't look up, but simply told her to sign in on the clipboard. After doing so, the woman took the clipboard and typed her information into the computer.

"Insurance card?" she asked.

"I don't have insurance."

"Alright . . ." The woman didn't even try to hide the irritation in her voice. She grabbed a clipboard from the bin beside her and handed it to Luella. "I just need you to fill this out and bring it back to me so I can get your information in our system."

Luella grabbed a peppermint from a glass bowl on the desk. Only then did the woman look up at her. Luella took her time unwrapping the mint before popping it into her mouth. She grabbed the clipboard and pen. "Thanks."

Thirty minutes later, and it was finally her turn. A tall, older woman opened the door and called out her name. Luella got up and rushed through the door as the woman held it open for her. She introduced herself as Tammy, the ultrasound technician, as she guided Luella back to the room.

"Ultrasound?" Luella asked, hoping the woman couldn't hear the shakiness in her voice. She realized she had stopped walking. Tammy turned around and noticed, too. She smiled as she told her it was normal procedure when someone suspected they were this far along. Luella wasn't prepared for an ultrasound. She thought she would simply pee in a cup and see a doctor. It was too much, too fast. *Breathe. It's just stress. They won't find anything. It was just a false positive.* She didn't know if she was trying to reassure herself or speak it into existence.

Tammy gave her a gown and sheet and stepped out so Luella could undress. When she came back in, she turned off the light and sat down beside Luella in front of the screen. She explained what she was going to do to ease Luella's nerves, but it didn't work. She shifted uncomfortably against the wand and kept her eyes glued to the spackled ceiling tiles above her. Tammy apologized for the discomfort. Luella fought back tears. It felt like Tammy could see everything she was feeling inside, and not just her uterus.

After a few seconds, the silence was broken by a *womp-womp-womp* sound that filled the room.

"Yep," said Tammy. "There it is. You're definitely pregnant."

Luella looked over at the screen with widened eyes. There in the middle of the black circle was indeed a tiny little baby. It looked more like an alien than a human to Luella, but what did she know? Its head was bigger than its body, but you could see its hands and feet, and it was moving all around.

It was the most amazing thing she had ever seen.

"You're measuring around nine and a half weeks," she said. She looked over at Luella then.

"You didn't have the slightest idea that you were pregnant?"

Luella shook her head, but she couldn't shake the way Tammy was making her feel—like she was already failing as a mother. She didn't even have the slightest clue she was growing a human inside of her body. She couldn't do this. Her body got hot and cold again, like it did in the hardware store the day she found out she was pregnant.

"Is it hot in here to you?" she asked Tammy, fanning her face.

Tammy looked over, concerned. "Are you alright? Do you need me to get you some water?"

"I . . . I just . . . how much longer do you think this will take?"

"I just have a few more measurements to get and then we'll be done. Do you think you can sit through that?"

Luella nodded as she scrunched the sheet beneath her hands, holding on for dear life. The next few minutes felt like an eternity. After Tammy finished, she told Luella she could get dressed and come out whenever she was ready.

Luella sat there for a minute, taking it all in as Tammy left the room. She hesitantly placed her hand on her belly for just a few seconds before getting dressed.

When she opened the door, a different woman stood smiling in front of her. She was younger than Tammy, and Luella guessed that they were probably around the same age.

"I'm Claire," she said with a cheery smile as she held a cup of water.

Her short hair was cut into the perfect bob and the prettiest shade of strawberry blonde that Luella had ever seen. She had an air of positivity surrounding her that Luella couldn't quite match. Claire handed her the cup.

"Here. Tammy said you needed this." She held the cup out to Luella, who took it and immediately downed the entire thing. Claire smiled. "I'll be getting you ready to see Dr. Irving. If you'll just follow me."

She had Luella pee in a cup in the bathroom before stepping on a scale. Then, she led her to the room the doctor would see her in. Luella climbed up onto the table. The light felt too bright as Claire took her blood pressure. She must have sensed Luella's unease because she asked her if she was alright. Luella wasn't sure how to respond, so she just nodded instead.

"Is this your first?" asked Claire. Luella nodded again, and Claire smiled sympathetically.

"It's okay. The ultrasound makes it even more real, huh?

"Yeah, it really does. I wasn't expecting to have that done today and certainly not right when I walked in. I thought for sure that I had gotten a false positive, given that I've had zero symptoms except for one bout of morning sickness. Things have been a bit crazy the past few weeks, but still . . ."

Claire put her hand on Luella's leg to calm her. "Deep breath," she said. Luella did as she said and took a deep breath and focused only on Claire as she exhaled. "Good. Dr. Irving will be in soon. I'll be right outside if you need anything."

Luella nodded. Claire closed the door, and Luella took one deep breath after another as she waited on Dr. Irving.

~

After the appointment, Luella sat in the car staring down at the black and white ultrasound picture that Dr. Irving gave to her. She didn't want the picture, but she couldn't say so when he held it out for her. What kind of mother doesn't want their baby's first ultrasound picture?

He'd said he'd see her in a few weeks for a follow-up appointment. Luella's head was spinning. She tucked the picture into the pocket of her wallet before throwing the wallet back in her bag. What was she going to do? She wanted to ask what her options were, but in a town like Chipley Creek—you didn't ask those kinds of questions. It was already bad enough that she wasn't married. Even worse, that she was single.

She would start showing soon. Helen was going to find out eventually . . . and Paul. Oh no, Paul. How was she going to tell him? She couldn't face him. This messed up everything.

Whatever spark she might have felt between them at the farm wasn't possible now. How could it be? How did she screw up every single chance she got?

And Benjamin. Did she need to tell him? Did it matter now? She wasn't even sure how to get in touch with him, and she didn't think it would be a very good idea to call up Harper and ask for his number. That bridge had been more than burned.

But worse, how would she manage a pregnancy while caring for Helen . . . or even just being around Helen? She knew as soon as Helen found out that there would be all kinds of judgment and told-you-so innuendos. She didn't want to give Helen the satisfaction. At least she was twenty-nine. At least she was an adult. Even though she didn't feel like one. At least she had a job . . . wait, no, she didn't. She didn't even have a vehicle. She borrowed the Wagoneer when she needed to. How in the world did she think she could raise a baby?

She squeezed her eyes shut and clenched her jaw. It was too much. The appointment had been stressful enough, and she had already been gone longer than she had hoped. Certainly longer than a lunch date. Luella decided she would swing by the diner and grab Helen a chicken salad croissant to coincide with her story. Hopefully that would distract Helen from asking questions, and she could just let all the overwhelming information from the day settle.

She had to figure out what she was going to do. About the baby. About her life. All of it.

# twenty-two

The beginning of March was cold. Cold enough to keep Luella in baggy clothing, but not cold enough to keep her stuck inside with Helen. Luella had been throwing any energy she had into work around the farm.

Pulling up weeds. Mucking Boots' stall. Cleaning all the animals' water bowls. Mowing grass—only because Helen had a riding lawn mower, and there was certainly a learning curve.

The list went on. So many small things that added up to a full day's work of maintenance around the farm. No wonder it had looked so neglected when she returned. Helen couldn't possibly handle the upkeep on her own, even if she wasn't sick. But Helen would never ask for help.

After completing the day's chores, Luella stepped inside the house and took off her tennis shoes. The house was quiet. Helen was probably reading or napping. She walked into the kitchen but found it empty. She peeked into the living room, but Helen wasn't in her usual spot.

The floor creaked above her, followed by a loud clunk of something falling to the ground.

"Helen?" Luella called out for her.

When Helen didn't respond, Luella walked over to the stairs leading to the attic. She heard Helen murmuring. Slowly, Luella made her way up the rickety wooden steps, wondering if it was safe to even be on them at all.

When she reached the top, Helen was on the floor beside piles and piles of pictures. They were scattered everywhere. Helen was trying to gather them up. Luella saw the broken cardboard box on the floor. They must have fallen and made the sound she heard.

"What are you doing up here? I don't think it's very safe. These boards are worn out," Luella said.

Helen let out a laugh that erupted up from deep down in her stomach. It felt foreign to Luella's ears. She just stared at Helen, like she was witnessing a breakdown. Helen never laughed.

"Not as worn out as me," she said, and then laughed again.

"You're in a chipper mood today." Luella said, bending down and gathering up a few pictures in her hand.

"Sometimes you just have to let go and say to hell with it."

Luella's eyebrows shot up at her comment. She sat down on the cold wooden floor as she picked up more pictures. "I didn't realize you had all these," she said.

Helen sat back against the wall and flipped through the few she held in her hand. "I documented everything. When I was younger, I had a camera in my hand at all times. Snapping pictures of whatever I could. Knowing one day that I'd want these. It used to drive your Grandpa Fred crazy."

Luella's heart sank. It was the first time that Helen had brought him up. She held out a photograph for Luella. It was a black-and-white picture of Helen and Grandpa Fred when they were young on a beach somewhere. Helen was just a tiny little thing in her two-piece bikini, standing beside a young Grandpa Fred as he scowled at the camera—his caterpillar eyebrows furrowed. She smiled at the memory she held in her hands. She had never seen him young before.

Luella looked up and handed the picture back to Helen. "You remember all those trips we'd take to Fort Morgan? We'd pile in the Wagoneer on a Friday, and Grandpa Fred would drive all night, and we'd wake up at the beach, spend all day Saturday and then drive right back home that night."

Helen smiled. "Fred was crazy like that. When he got the itch to go, nothing could stop him." She sighed. "I'd give anything to be on that beach again. To feel the sand between my toes. Hear the waves crashing against the shore. It's been too long."

Their beach trips stopped after Grandpa Fred passed away.

They sat in silence for several minutes, both stacking memories from the past, until Luella came across one photograph that she couldn't quite place. It was a baby in the arms of a man that she didn't recognize. "Who is this?" she asked, handing the photograph over to Helen.

Luella noticed the way her jaw stiffened as she looked at the picture. Her eyes flicked up at Luella and then back down at the picture. "That's my first husband," she said. "Mya's biological father."

Luella's jaw fell open. She was unsure she heard her correctly. "I'm sorry—what?"

Helen took a deep breath and set the picture on the ground as she stretched her legs out in front of her, crossing them at the ankles. She brushed her thighs off with her hand, took a deep breath, and then began.

"I got married when I was seventeen. His name was Arthur. He used to come around our house a lot. My mother was smitten with him. When he started showing me attention, she encouraged it. She forced me to marry Art, even though I didn't want to. I didn't want to be married. I wanted to see the world, wanted to travel."

Helen sighed, and Luella felt sad for her. For what she had lost. Her youth, the dreams she had for herself. If Luella had been forced to marry someone she didn't love, she'd be bitter, too.

Helen went on, "We got married. I had your mother three years later. I was just twenty years old, but most of my friends already had two or three kids by twenty. That was common in those days. It took me a while to get pregnant. Art wasn't happy that it was a girl. He wanted a boy—someone to carry on his family name. He wanted to try again as soon as possible, but I was a new mom and in the throes of postpartum, so I said no. That I wasn't ready for another baby. Well, he didn't like that answer, so he held me down and . . . went on with it."

Luella's mouth fell open again. Helen wouldn't meet her eyes. "You didn't tell anybody? That was rape. He raped you. I don't care if he was your husband."

"People don't like messy," said Helen. "It would have been my fault."

"What did you do?"

"That night, after he fell asleep, I pointed a rifle in his face and tapped it on his forehead. His eyes flew open, but he didn't move an inch. I told him to leave and never come back, and he did. I haven't seen him since."

Luella's mind was reeling from everything Helen had said. How could she never have known? Never had an inkling that Grandpa Fred wasn't hers by blood, like she always thought he was. And how could she never have thought about what Helen might have been through in her life to make her the way she was. Luella had thought her bitter and mean. But seeing it now, she couldn't blame her for being a bit emotionally cut off.

"And Grandpa Fred?" asked Luella.

Helen smiled. "I bumped into him one day on the street when your mother was about five years old. I ran right into him. He dropped the groceries he had in his hands, and we bumped heads as we both bent down to pick them up. He smiled, and I fell in love with him right there. We got to talking, and when your mother got antsy, he bought her an ice cream so we could stand there and talk a little longer. It was like I'd known him my entire life. I missed him the instant he left. He called the next day, and we were inseparable after that for the next twenty-seven years."

Luella smiled sadly. "I miss him." She picked up a picture of him off the floor and held it to her chest.

"Me too. Every single day."

Luella looked at the pictures on the floor. It was still a bit of a mess, but at least they were now in piles.

"What made you want to come up here and look at all these?" Luella asked.

Helen sighed and looked at the pictures. "When you get as old as I am, and you realize that your hourglass has more sand in the bottom than it does at the top, you panic a little. You want to remember everything. You want to look back on your life and see all the ways you got to where you are. You wonder . . . did I get it right? What could I have done differently? And looking back at it all, you realize how precious time really is."

Luella thought about it as she looked over at Helen. She was so much different now than Luella remembered. So much older than the girl and woman in the pictures that lay spread out on the floor before them. It caused an ache in her chest for Helen unlike any she had ever felt before. An ache that she resented. She had thought herself indifferent when it came to Helen. But now she was finally getting to know her, and she couldn't quiet the panicky feeling in her heart.

The one that told her they were running out of time.

Luella looked down and saw a picture of her and Paul as kids. She picked it up and studied the faces smiling back at her. She couldn't have been more than nine, which meant he was about twelve.

"You two were always drawn to each other. Practically attached at the hip after you got here."

Luella clenched her jaw and looked up at Helen. "Until you sent him away," she said without an ounce of conviction in her voice.

And as quickly as her empathy for Helen came, so did the resentment she felt toward her.

Helen was the reason Paul left.

All because of a lie. A misunderstanding of the truth. Luella couldn't make Helen see that.

Helen never took her side. Never even tried.

Rebecca was also in love with Paul. The entire house knew it. Or rather, she was infatuated—because what do fifteen-year-olds really know about love? Rebecca had been watching Paul and Luella, like she could sense the shift that happened between them after Paul kissed her down at the barn. It made Rebecca spiteful.

Grandpa Fred's passing only made Luella and Paul closer. They both loved him immensely and found comfort in grieving together.

Add in their budding romance.

They'd sneak down to the barn for kisses. Their feelings for each other a secret just between the two of them, until it wasn't anymore.

One day, while they were in the middle of a heated make-out session, Luella looked up to find Rebecca standing by the barn door, watching them with all the fiery jealousy her eyes could hold.

When Luella gasped, Paul looked over and spotted her, too. Luella's heart sank as she watched a spiteful grin slowly emerge across Rebecca's face. She darted back toward the house. Luella was quick on her heels, pleading.

Rebecca ran inside and told Helen exactly what she'd seen. Only, she stretched the truth. She told Helen that she had caught Luella and Paul having sex in the barn. By the time Paul made it back up to the house, Helen was already on the phone with Paul's caseworker.

Luella tried through tears to explain that Rebecca was lying, and it was just a kiss, but Helen wouldn't look at her or Paul.

Paul didn't try to change Helen's mind. He packed a bag and sat on the front porch until the caseworker arrived.

It was only two months until he turned eighteen. Just two short months until he aged out of the system.

But Helen had him moved anyway. She practically shunned him after that. It was devastating for Luella. She could only imagine how Paul must have felt.

"I did what I had to do," said Helen, her voice pulling Luella out of the past and back to the present. "If I hadn't, then I would have lost my certification to foster. And I couldn't let that happen. Especially with Fred gone."

Luella scoffed. "This was the only home he ever had."

"It killed me to do what I did," she said, gathering up the piles of pictures again. "Me and Paul have put it behind us. I'm not gonna chew on it all over again with you."

The way she dismissed the conversation sent heat flushing through Luella's body. She wasn't finished talking about it. She couldn't hold it in anymore. "This isn't just about Paul," she snapped—her heart pounding against her chest. "This is about how you took her side . . . how you always took everyone else's side but mine."

"I don't know what you're talking about," said Helen.

Luella laughed derisively. "I'm talking about how you never treated me like a granddaughter. How I was just another boarder in your house. Just another mouth at your table," she spat out—louder than intended. Helen's face looked taken aback. Luella had surprised herself, too. She didn't intend for it to come out the way it did. But years of pushing that resentment down gave it a force like no other. Hot tears stung at her eyes.

Helen sat back, and her shoulders hit the wall—like Luella had slapped her. She recovered instantly and tightened her eyes until they were nothing but slits. "When are you gonna stop feeling sorry for yourself? For the hand that you've been dealt? It's time to grow up, Luella."

Helen tried to push herself up off the floor, but she struggled. When she finally got to her feet, she made her way to the stairs and then turned back around to face Luella. "You're holding on so tight to the past that you're letting the future breeze right on by because you're too stubborn to let the past go. What a shame."

Luella watched Helen make her way down the stairs, each one cracking beneath her with every step.

~

They didn't speak to each other for the rest of the day. Helen didn't sit on the couch that night in her usual spot and watch *Golden Girls* reruns before bed. After she made dinner, she went into her bedroom and shut the door.

Luella wanted a reason for why she never treated her like a granddaughter should be treated. But Helen wouldn't give it to her. Which only infuriated Luella more. Was she not even worth an explanation?

She grabbed her laptop and took it outside to the porch. She sat on the step and typed word after word about her life at the farm, growing up in a foster home, and the grandmother who never loved her like a grandchild. She channeled her anger, and the words came fast and abundantly.

She read it back, feeling it all over again.

When she finished her read through, she wiped the tears from her cheeks and attached the document in an email addressed to Cathy.

She took a deep breath, her finger hovering over the touchpad. Then, she let her breath out and saved the email to her drafts instead.

# twenty-three

She made a list.

*Mow grass. Muck Boots' stall. Clean water basins. Fix chicken coop.*

It was a beautiful day, and she planned to be outside for all of it. She told herself it was because of the sunny weather, but really, it was so she didn't have another run in with Helen.

Three days later, and they still weren't speaking to each other.

Luella worked on cleaning the water basins first. After she finished that, she started toward the barn but stopped when she heard the familiar rumble of Paul's truck coming down the driveway.

She wasn't expecting him to come over but found herself excited that he had. Her heart thumped faster at the sight of him stepping out of his truck.

"Fancy seeing you today," she called out.

He grinned as he walked toward her. He wore a black short-sleeved tee, brown work boots with a pair of worn-out faded jeans. And he wore them well.

"I'm off today. Figured since it's warming up, I'd come help around the farm. See what needs to be done."

She laughed. They used to be like this—brains on the same wavelength. "Well, you're in luck. That's what I'm doing today. See, I made a list." She pulled the list out of her back pocket and held it out for him. He grabbed it and scanned over it with his eyes. "I just finished the water basins."

"Dibbs on mowing the grass," he said.

She rolled her eyes.

"Guess that means you're mucking Boots' stall." He scrunched his nose up and then smiled.

She scoffed playfully. "I can work on the chicken coop without your help."

His eyebrows went up, and sarcastic smile appeared on his face like he didn't believe her.

"Alright fine," she said. "I'll muck the stall."

When she finished, she went inside to make them some lemonade. Helen sat in the living room, but she didn't say a word as Luella walked into the kitchen.

Luella waited for him on the picnic table outside, admiring him from afar as he finished mowing the pasture up and down in vertical lines like Grandpa Fred had taught him. When he finished, he parked the mower back in the shed and walked over to the picnic table. Luella couldn't stop the smile that spread across her face.

"Why are you smiling?" asked Paul.

"Just because," she said.

Because he was there, working on the farm with her. It made her feel like a kid again. It also made the farm feel like *home*. For the first time, she didn't have the urge to leave. She was happy exactly where she was. Paul smiled like he knew exactly what she was thinking. Maybe he felt it, too. But he didn't say it out loud, either.

"What's wrong with the chicken coop?"

"Needs a new run."

"Alright, let's get to it then."

~

Paul ran to the hardware store. Luella didn't want to leave Helen alone, despite their fight. And besides, she wasn't exactly itching to go the hardware store again, considering her last visit.

Once Paul returned, they were hauling supplies to the chicken coop. Paul went to work framing it out with new boards. Luella watched, supplying tools and a helping hand when needed.

She mostly enjoyed watching Paul work. The way he bit his bottom lip when concentrating made her pulse race. And when his hand brushed hers as she handed him a different tool, it sent an electric jolt through her body. She wondered if Paul felt it, too. The look he gave her the next time it happened answered her question. Their eyes locked and heat rose in her cheeks. She looked away first.

It was a new, yet familiar feeling.

When the framing was finished, they began laying out the welded wire fencing horizontally around the run.

"We need to skirt the bottom edge," Paul said.

"Why?"

"To deter digging predators," he said as he laid the fencing on top of the ground outside of the run. "Or you know—little girls with a vendetta."

He lost her there. "What does that mean? Are you talking about Taylor?" "I'm talking about *you*," he said with a chuckle.

Her brows furrowed as she tried to work out what he meant. He looked over, seeing her confusion, and stood up in front of her.

"Helen made you mad because she wouldn't let you go on that vacation with Meggie's family and you came out here and ripped up the run—letting all the chickens out as you did.

Then, you blamed it on a fox." He chuckled at the memory like it was replaying in his head.

"Lucky for you, she believed it."

Luella's mouth fell open as it came back to her. It was one of the few times she did something that defiant. She was too scared of getting caught. Too scared someone might snitch on her if they saw. But Paul never would.

"I can't believe you remember that."

Paul's face grew serious then, his jaw tensing. His eyes found hers. He leaned forward, his mouth just beside her ear. "I remember everything," he said, barely above a whisper.

Her heart hammered against her chest. She resisted the urge to kiss him as he pulled away from her ear. It took everything in her not to. The only reason she didn't was because of his *complicated relationship*. He had said no more about it, and she didn't know where he stood. What she did know, was that if they kissed again, she wanted him to be the one to initiate it—even if she had thought about it every day for the past two and a half weeks since it happened.

Like right now.

But Paul didn't linger. He took a deep breath and then went back to work wrapping the fencing around the run.

~

Cheryl and Taylor came by later with a basket full of dinner. Taylor came running down the backyard to find them.

"Me and Mimi brought dinner," she said proudly. "Rigatoni."

Paul feigned surprise. "My favorite," he said and then gave her a wink.

"Yeah, but you can't have any," she said to him, followed by a giggle that let them both know she didn't mean it.

"Is that right?" Paul said.

Taylor nodded seriously, but her giggles gave her away. Paul launched forward, snatching her up, and spun her around, tickling her as he set her down.

As Luella watched Taylor giggling and Paul smiling, it made her heart swell, and her throat go dry. He'd make the best dad. Taylor obviously adored him, and she wasn't even his.

A pang of guilt hit her in the chest as the three of them walked back toward the house. She needed to tell him about the pregnancy. It was only fair. But was she ready for everything that came with that?

It didn't matter. She'd tell him before he left.

They sat around the table, exchanging stories with one another and making small talk over dinner. Helen was pleasant, even though she and Luella still weren't speaking to each other. She barely looked at Luella.

Paul must have noticed, because at some point, he reached a hand under the table and squeezed her leg. When she looked over at him, he gave her a small smile in solidarity.

But Helen freezing her out was the last thing on her mind. Her heart pounded as they cleaned up after dinner. A nervous flutter surfaced in her stomach as Paul said his goodbyes and he and Luella walked outside toward his truck.

"Thank you for today," she said, not knowing where to begin.

"I'm glad to help. I should have been doing more than just dropping off groceries. Should have done it for Helen before now."

"Well, you're here now and that's all that counts," said Luella.

His eyes softened as the corners of his mouth turned up in a slight smile. "So are you."

Tears welled up in her eyes, though she wasn't sure why. She didn't allow herself to think too much about everything. Being back at the farm. Paul. Helen's lymphoma. Her current predicament.

If she thought about it too much, she was afraid she'd fall apart. But there were moments that caught her off guard, like right then.

Paul wrapped his arms around her, and she sank into his embrace. He smelled like cedarwood and sweat. She closed her eyes against the overwhelming relief she felt in his arms.

How could a person feel so much like home?

Standing there with him felt like nothing else mattered in the world except the two of them.

Did he feel it, too? Or was it just nostalgia?

He pulled back and brought his hand up to her face. He traced the scar on her cheek and then swept his thumb gently across her face.

She waited for him to lower his lips to hers. Wishing that he would. But he took a deep breath instead and let it out. Then, he pressed his lips against her forehead and kissed her softly.

She needed to tell him now. Needed to blurt it out before she could convince herself otherwise.

But she didn't.

She simply watched as he walked around to the driver's side of his truck and hopped inside. Then, he was down the driveway and gone before she knew it.

*Nice going*, she chastised herself. *Really great job telling him.*

What was she going to do now?

# twenty-four

By the middle of March, Luella had been going on with life like she wasn't twelve weeks pregnant. As if ignoring it could make it go away.

But this was one thing she couldn't avoid. Especially with all the doctor appointments. Thankfully, she didn't need an ultrasound this time. Just checked her vitals and listened to the heartbeat with one of those little dopplers. She'd have monthly appointments now.

She told Helen she was spending the day with Meggie—which wasn't technically a lie because they did plan to get lunch together. She made sure Cheryl knew that Helen was alone at the farm in case she needed anything. It surprised Luella that she felt a bit of guilt over the lie.

She knew she was eventually going to have to tell Helen. She'd start showing soon. Thankfully, it was still chilly enough to get by with oversized sweaters. Even if she did sweat a little every now and then while wearing one.

As she drove away from the health clinic, through downtown Addison, she spotted an adoption agency sign outside of a small brick house.

She turned the Wagoneer into the parking lot so fast that she almost flipped it into the ditch.

The woman at the reception desk asked if she had an appointment. Luella told her no, that she just wanted a little information so that she could consider all her options. That she just wanted to see what the process looked like for someone who was expecting.

That's how she said it.

Like she was expecting a surprise, or any assortment of things. She couldn't follow it with the word baby because that felt too real. Made the panicky feeling in her stomach rise until her neck and chest became covered in hives, because that was how her body dealt with things, it inflamed. She had been trying hard to keep herself calm. She hadn't had a panic attack in years, but this was sure to bring one on.

The girl's eyebrows went up, like she could sense Luella's anxiety, too. Her smile was sympathetic as she asked Luella to wait while she checked to see if one of the adoption counselors could speak to her.

They made time for her, even though she didn't have an appointment. Luella wondered what the receptionist had said. Probably that there was a pregnant woman in the office freaking out and covered in hives. If that's what it took, so be it. Luella was thankful.

The adoption counselor that was available was a tall woman with short, curly, black hair. She had a buttery soft voice that offered comfort. Which meant that she was fantastic at what she did, or she just had a lot of experience with freaked out pregnant women. She brought Luella into her office and closed the door. She asked her to sit and offered her a cold bottle of water from the mini fridge in the corner. As Luella twisted the cap, she noticed the adoption agency's emblem and a silhouette of a pregnant woman on the label.

The woman listened as Luella explained how she came to be in the situation she was in. She didn't give the woman specifics; just told her it was a one-night stand situation that resulted in a pregnancy. A lapse in judgment. The woman asked about the father.

"He doesn't know. I doubt he would even care," said Luella.

The woman gave her a sympathetic look. "Georgia law is very

strict about birth father rights. You'll have to err on the side of caution. If you choose adoption, you're going to need his consent. There's just no way around it."

If she gained his consent, there was much more to consider. Like whether she wanted an open adoption or closed adoption. One meant being a part of the child's life, while the other meant no contact entirely. She could also hand pick a family. They had albums and videos. It sounded so transactional to her. Like she was picking out paint colors and got to take home swatches to see which one fit best. Once she decided on a family, she could get to know them before handing her child over to them forever.

She liked the idea of being able to choose, being able to hand pick the kind of family she always wanted for herself. One with a father and a mother that were happy together. Pizza dinners on Friday nights. A wrap around porch, and her own bedroom all to herself.

A family like Meggie's. Like the ones from the storybooks. The kind that lives happily ever after. That's what she wanted for her child. A fairytale life.

She felt too much guilt about bringing a baby into her life as it was now. She didn't have a job, didn't particularly like the baby's father at all, didn't want her child to feel the weight of that every day of its life, and she couldn't promise herself that she would be a better mother than Mya had been.

What did she know of mothering when her own had left her? She hadn't been around babies.

She had been around a lot of kids growing up, but never babies. Women talked about how the mothering instinct just kicked in when their babies were born. What if hers didn't? What if she didn't have it in her? That wasn't fair to a child. She wouldn't do it. She couldn't do it.

The woman handed her several pamphlets and told her to call her with questions or concerns. She encouraged Luella to tell Benjamin about the pregnancy and gain his consent so she could move forward. She ended her spiel by telling Luella about the benefits of adoption for the baby. Among which were a loving family who will always love and cherish him or her, as well as the ability to grow up and become the person he or she is meant to be. But the woman didn't press. She said that Luella was the only one who could decide what was best for her baby and if adoption was the right answer. She encouraged Luella to think about what kind of life she wished for her child to have.

She didn't have to think about it.

She wished for the kind of life she always wanted. The kind of family she only dreamt of. A mom and a dad in a home where she thrived. Where she was the center of their world. Where the mother stayed and cooked dinner and dressed her little girl in the cutesy clothes and matching bows. With picture frames filled with pictures where everyone was smiling or laughing, and it was obvious that they all belonged to each other.

In a home where, at night, she could lay her head, breathe deep, and feel completely safe and loved.

That's what she wanted for her child . . . to never know how it felt to be unwanted.

She shoved the pamphlets into her bag and thanked the woman for her time. Then, she got up from the chair and walked as fast as she could out of the office. She didn't look at a soul as she left.

Inside the safety of the Wagoneer, she took a deep breath—like she was at the bottom of the ocean and had finally come up for air. She pulled her phone out of her bag and opened Facebook. She searched for Benjamin and clicked on his profile. His smug face smiled back at her, but she felt nothing but indifference.

What would it look like if Luella contacted him now? Would he even care? It didn't really matter because she needed his consent if she decided on adoption at all. Forget everyone else's feelings. This wasn't about any of them. It was about the life that she carried inside of her.

She hit the home button, and Benjamin's face disappeared. She noticed the time. Meggie said to meet her at noon at the best little barbecue spot in town. Luella was twenty minutes late. No surprise there. She was always late. But Meggie knew that. Luella was sure that she would still be waiting for her when she got there. Luella hadn't told her about the pregnancy yet.

Meggie's life was extremely busy, so they mostly communicated through texts and phone calls. She had only seen her twice for lunch since she got to town. They were adults now after all.

That was the beauty of their friendship, though—being able to pick up exactly where they left off. No guilt, no shame.

Luella backed out of the parking lot and headed toward the restaurant.

~

Walton's BBQ was a Chipley Creek staple. A family owned and operated barbecue restaurant that was passed down for generations, known for its vinegar-based barbecue sauce and Mrs. Mae's famous banana pudding. There was no beating it. It was the creamiest banana pudding Luella had ever tasted. People begged her for the recipe, but she never budged.

People filled every spot they could for the lunchtime rush. Luella looked around the cramped restaurant for Meggie's face. She found her in a corner booth, smiling and waving, just waiting for Luella's eyes to land on her. Luella rushed over to her, keeping her eyes down as she did. If you accidentally made eye contact in a town like Chipley Creek, then you'd be stuck having a forty-five-minute conversation that lulled into another fifteen minutes of goodbyes.

Meggie smiled as Luella made her way over. She was almost at the booth when an older woman gasped and called out to her. "Luella McCrae, is that you, hon?"

Luella turned around to see that it was her high school English teacher. She hadn't changed a bit. She still had those enormous glasses that sat a little crooked on her nose, with eyes that seemed like they were scanning a person's soul—or at least that's how Luella felt about them. Luella smiled at her. "Hi, Ms. Whelan, how are you doing?"

The woman got up from her booth and wrapped her arms around Luella. "How long has it been?"

"Eleven years," said Luella.

Ms. Whelan leaned in close, as though they were best friends about to swap secrets, and said in a low, hushed voice, "I used to read all your columns in *Scandalanta.* I knew you'd go places. I always told you that you'd be a writer someday."

Luella smiled at her. She wouldn't exactly call herself a writer, but having your name attached to anything with a readership over a hundred would count in these parts.

"You need to come speak to my class about your experience working in the big city," Ms. Whelan said with a proud smile, like Luella was her greatest accomplishment.

Luella just nodded and smiled. If only she knew. But that was another thing about Chipley Creek—no matter a person's circumstance, they saved face and brushed it under the rug so that their life appeared shiny and perfect from the outside. She looked over at Meggie, who smirked at her behind Ms. Whelan's back. Just like she did in high school. Luella smiled as the woman pulled her into another hug. "It was good to see you, darlin'."

"You too."

When Ms. Whelan let go, her hand accidentally knocked Luella's purse strap off her shoulder, sending her purse crashing to the ground and scattering the contents onto the concrete floor.

"Oh, hon, I'm so sorry. If my back wouldn't lock up on me, I'd bend down and help you pick all that up." Ms. Whelan stood there just looking at the spilled contents.

Meggie got up from the booth and came over to help Luella pick up the stuff that had fallen out. Luella frantically grabbed her things, but Meggie's hands landed on the pamphlets first. Luella looked up at her as she looked them over before handing them back to Luella without a word. Ms. Whalen kept apologizing, and Luella told her it was fine, that it was nice to see her again.

Luella and Meggie scooted into opposite sides of the booth. Luella busied herself looking at the menu, trying not to give herself away. Meggie swirled her straw around a cup of water while staring at Luella. Her eyes bored into her. Luella finally looked up. "What?"

"Come on. You already knew I was going to ask," she said. "What are those pamphlets for?"

Luella sighed and looked away from her as she sank back further into the booth. She wanted to tell Meggie everything, but she felt ashamed she hadn't told her already, ashamed she was considering adoption, and still scared to say it out loud because that would make it feel all too real. "I was just curious about some things."

"Oh no," said Meggie. "You're not getting off that easy. I thought you didn't really care about having kids." When Luella looked up at her again, her eyes said everything she couldn't say. Meggie's mouth fell open. "You're not?"

Luella nodded. Meggie put her hand over her mouth, like it could cover up the shock written all over her face.

"Yeah . . . that's how I feel about it, too," said Luella. Then, she slumped forward and put her elbows on the table.

"How far along?"

"Twelve weeks," said Luella.

"But who?" asked Meggie, still unable to make complete sentences.

"This guy from the city. It was a big mistake, and it only happened once."

"Does he know?" Meggie asked.

"No," said Luella. "But if I decide to put this baby up for adoption, then I'll have to tell him and get his consent."

Meggie reached across the table and took Luella's hand in hers.

"I haven't told anyone yet. I'm afraid what it might cost me," she said, thinking of Paul.

The server came over and took their order. After she left, Meggie took both of Luella's hands in hers and looked her square in the eyes. "I'm here for you no matter what," she said.

"Whatever you need, you just ask. I'll support you no matter what you decide to do. Adoption is a beautiful thing, and you shouldn't feel guilty if that's the route you want to take. There is no shame in not wanting kids. Better to put the baby up for adoption so that a family who desperately wants a child can love it, rather than taking on that responsibility when it's not something you're sure you want. Babies are hard work."

"I'm not sure what I'm going to do yet. I'm going to have to tell Helen soon. I can't keep hiding it while living under the same roof."

"How is Helen?" Meggie asked, changing the subject.

Luella was thankful for shift. She shrugged. "She had a bad episode a few weeks ago. But she seems to be alright for now."

Meggie nodded. Luella looked up and saw the server walking toward them with a tray full of food. Meggie gasped again, so loud that Luella nearly knocked her drink over. "Speak of the freaking devil," she said, looking toward the door.

Luella followed her gaze and saw Paul standing with two other guys in their uniforms at the door, waiting to be seated. Heat filled her cheeks, but she couldn't pry her eyes away from him.

As if he could sense her gaze, he looked over, and their eyes locked. Luella's heartbeat picked up its pace, thumping wildly against her chest.

"I haven't seen this much drama unfold since the last time I saw an episode of *This Is Us,"* said Meggie. Luella shot her a look of annoyance. "Oh, he's coming over here."

Luella pushed the food around her plate with a fork. Suddenly, she wasn't very hungry. She looked up when Paul stopped in front of their booth. He smiled, and it reached his eyes, making both his dimples appear. Those dimples always got her.

"Hey, Lue," he said to her. Then, he looked over at Meggie and said hey to her, too.

"Fancy seeing you here," Meggie said with a smirk.

Paul gave a little laugh and said, "I know. It was a hard decision with all the many restaurant options that Chipley Creek has to offer."

Luella smiled. There were exactly two restaurants in town. Walton's BBQ and Waffle House. They didn't even have a Starbucks. One of his coworkers called out for him. The server was taking their orders.

He nodded and said, "Well, I should probably get back to them. It was good to see you Megs . . . I'll see you later, Lue."

And then he walked away from their table.

Luella kept her eyes on him the entire time, admiring the way he looked in his uniform. Luella could feel Meggie's eyes on her again. When she looked over at her, she smiled big at Luella and said, "Oh girl, you are in so much trouble."

Luella rolled her eyes. "I know it."

# twenty-five

April first brought with it a beautiful spring Saturday. The sun shined brightly overhead as the trees swayed from the subtle breeze.

Luella sat on the steps, soaking up the sun, when Gus came trotting down the gravel driveway. He stopped in front of Luella and sat down.

"And just where have you been?" Luella asked the dog. She laughed at the fact that her social life had been reduced to speaking to a dog as if it were a person. Gus stared at her with his tongue hanging out, panting away.

She looked around the quiet yard and the beautiful day and decided she needed to get out. To go do something other than sit around the farm. She was itching to write *something*. Her body buzzed from the need to let creative energy out.

Inspiration could be found anywhere, but she would not find it sulking around the farm. Helen was having a good day, so it was the perfect time to take advantage. She shot up from the steps and went inside, Gus following on her heels.

Helen sat in the kitchen reading a book and drinking a cup of tea. They were on neutral ground with each other now. Neither mentioned their attic fight. They were both too stubborn to apologize, so they moved right past it.

"Let's get out of here today," said Luella, coming up to the table.

Helen looked up from her book. "What for?" Helen was the kind of person who only went somewhere if it was a *required* trip. A doctor's appointment. Groceries. That kind of thing.

"Let's get out of the house," she said. "What is something that you're just itching to do?"

Helen put her book down on the table and thought about it. Then, she livened up and almost seemed excited. "Well, it is time to plant some things . . . I've been wanting to spruce up the flowerbeds and get some new bulbs in the ground."

It wasn't exactly what Luella was hoping for. She wanted to go to a bookstore or the next town over and do some shopping. But maybe it was a good thing Helen didn't want to, considering Luella's dwindling bank account. She didn't need much money while she was staying at the farm, but she didn't like the way it felt every time she saw a little more deducted from her account.

Luella could see the excitement on Helen's face, though. It was a good thing. They would do exactly as she wanted. Helen hardly left the house these days.

"Alright," said Luella. "Where do we go for that?"

~

Forty-five minutes later, they were driving down the road headed to Pike Farms. The Pike family had been in the farming and produce business for decades. They had only been in the business of blooms for about eight years, which is when they switched up their brand and started offering more for the community. People came from all over Georgia just to visit Pike Farms—especially in the fall. They had a pumpkin patch with a corn maze, and it was a beloved destination that brought people to their tiny town.

Pike Farms was down the county highway on the prettiest stretch of land in Chipley Creek. As they turned onto the long gravel road, Luella could see its appeal and understand why Helen's face lit up when she mentioned it.

A long beautiful white barn sat in the middle, housing the plants. Two huge grain silos sat just behind the barn. A medium-sized silo had been converted into a concession stand. A greenhouse made of windows stood beside it. Twinkle lights hung above a community area filled with corn hole boards, picnic tables and chairs. There was a small stage with church pews lined under a white tent, where a man in cowboy boots played an acoustic guitar. There were a few other tents with vendors selling things like candles, wooden signs, and t-shirts.

The farm was already filled with people at just barely ten o'clock in the morning. Helen held her head high with a smile as wide as the sea as they walked toward the entrance. Luella watched the way Helen's spirit lifted as she greeted the Pike family at the entrance. There was an area filled with wagons for customers to load up with whatever they found. Helen told Luella to grab one for her.

Then, Luella followed her down the aisles of spring bulbs, ferns, and rows of fruit trees. Helen looked like a kid on Christmas morning as she picked up several black-eyed Susan plants, Shasta daisies, zinnias, and a few hanging ferns for the porch. She'd twist them here and there, inspecting them to find the best ones.

At the concession silo, they each got a cup of homemade peach ice cream. Helen smiled after taking a bite. There was nothing like homemade ice cream. They sat beneath the willow trees and the hanging lights as they ate, watching a young mother a few feet away trying to wrangle her four kids and eat her own ice cream at the same time.

Helen let out a small laugh. "It's tough, tending a bunch of kids."

Luella looked over at the woman and thought back to Helen and all the kids she had cared for.

"Why'd you do it?" she asked.

Helen looked over at Luella through furrowed brows.

"Foster," Luella clarified. "Why did you start?"

Helen sat back in her chair and let out a breath as she considered her answer. After a moment, she spoke. "It was Fred's idea, really. Fred and I couldn't have any more kids. My body just wouldn't do it again. He saw how badly I wanted to give him more children and how distraught I was when I couldn't. He thought it'd be a good idea. So, we did it."

"When?"

"I think your mother was about thirteen when we took in our first child. She didn't love the idea of it. I hoped she and I could have had a better relationship than I did with my mother, but we didn't. So, it goes. She got pregnant with you a few years later and left a few months after that." Helen paused and took a breath while Luella looked down at the ground. "I thought maybe that would give y'all the relationship that we never had . . . I'm sorry it didn't."

A lump formed in the back of Luella's throat. She tried to swallow against it as tears brimmed the edges of her eyes. She didn't want to cry in front of Helen. Luella sniffed against the emotion and gave Helen a half smile instead. Helen put her hands on the sides of her chair and pushed herself up. Luella followed, pulling the wagon behind her.

~

Back at the farm, Luella unloaded the plants and carried them to the back side of the house where Helen wanted them to go. The sun was still shining, and the birds chirped away in the trees. She looked around the farm and marveled over how serene it was.

Maybe it was because she was older and could finally understand everything that she couldn't back then. Back when she couldn't wait for the time to pass so that she could go live her life the way she intended—under the hustle of a city sky. Where there wasn't any room for silence and pitiful thoughts. Now she understood the peace of the suburbs. The way sitting outside on a sunny day could stretch out time until you felt like it wasn't ticking by at all. The beauty in making a wish and blowing a dandelion, watching through marveled eyes as the tiny pieces floated through the air, wishes sent out into the universe. How many had she sent growing up? Most of them, wishing to be anywhere other than the farm.

She told Helen to sit on the swing, which made Helen fuss, but she listened and sat down. Luella knew that Helen liked things done in a particular way, but Luella convinced her to let her plant the flowers for her—with Helen's guidance, of course.

Helen scoffed but agreed.

Luella grabbed Helen's wheelbarrow full of supplies and rolled it over to the area Helen wanted them planted. She set the tools on the ground one at a time and then picked up the gardening gloves and put them on her hands. Helen let out a laugh as the swing creaked back and forth.

"What?" Luella asked, looking over at her.

"Don't you want to go change first?"

Luella looked down at the clothes she was wearing. She had on her nicest jeans and a cream waffle knit top. "No," she said. "It can't be that bad. A little dirt won't hurt. It'll wash out."

Helen laughed, louder this time. "Go on then," she said, still giggling.

Luella got to her knees on the ground and looked at the tools, wondering what she should do first. She had never planted anything before. That was always Helen's job. She prided herself on it. Grandpa Fred used to give her a hard time about it because she wouldn't let anyone near her flower garden. He always joked that she should grow flowers competitively.

Luella looked over the tools and decided on the small hand rake.

"That's your second step," said Helen.

"Okay . . . what's the first?"

"That hand cultivator. The one with the three prongs. That'll get rid of large objects and rocks."

"Alright," said Luella, grabbing the hand cultivator. Then she raked it back and forth.

"What's going on between you and Paul?" Helen asked out of nowhere.

Luella froze with the rake midair. "What do you mean?" she asked, dragging the rake over the ground again. She knew what Helen meant. Helen wasn't oblivious.

"I mean that you two seem like you're reconnecting is all," Helen said.

Luella sat back and looked at the rectangle that she cleared in front of her. Then, she looked over at Helen and smiled. She couldn't help it.

Helen nodded in approval. "Looks good."

Luella picked up the hand rake and ran it across the area. "We're reconnecting," she said, and then paused the raking and sat back on her legs. "It's weird, though. Because sometimes it feels like time hasn't passed at all. Like we're exactly who we were eleven years ago. But then it still feels new and exciting getting to know who each other is now." She set the hand rake down. "Now what?"

"Use the trowel to dig the holes," Helen said. "Dig 'em a little bigger than the flowerpot."

Luella picked up what she thought was the trowel.

"You mean this shovel?"

"It's called a trowel," Helen said.

"Same thing," said Luella. Then, she picked up the black-eyed Susans and set them down on the freshly raked dirt. She dragged the shovel around, outlining the circle, moved the pot, and started digging. Luella picked up the conversation from where she left off. "Sometimes I wonder what might have happened if I hadn't left. How different things might be. Would we be married with kids? Would we even still be together at all?"

Helen swayed back and forth in the swing, the old chains creaking as she did. "Don't do that," she said.

"You can't go back and change yesterday, but you can learn from it."

Luella considered her words. She and Helen had never had a conversation like this before. It was the kind she imagined having with Mya. Sometimes she'd even pretend she was having a conversation with her in the mirror. But that was just make-believe. Helen was here, and they really were having that conversation. A deep ache welled up inside of her—regret for having never tried to have one before now and joy that she finally was.

"I'm sorry for how I left," she said. "You deserved more than me sneaking out and leaving a letter on my pillow."

Helen stopped the swing. She opened her mouth like she wanted to say something, but she pressed her lips tight and, after a moment, started swinging again. "Thank you for that," she said in a low voice, but there was sadness in her eyes. She opened her mouth like she wanted to say something else but closed it.

"What is it?" Luella pushed.

Helen took a deep breath and let it out. "I'm sorry you never felt loved here . . . by me, I mean."

Luella pulled her bottom lip in through her teeth and then spoke hesitantly. "I thought you hated me because I reminded you of Mya. Always wondered why anything I did was never good enough . . ."

Helen shook her head subtly. "It's selfish, really. Not long after we started fostering, I learned to close myself off from getting too close. Then, Mya left, and it's like I shut that part of my heart off completely. Focused on providing a stable home and kept my distance emotionally."

Though it didn't take the sting of those adolescent feelings away, she could understand Helen's reasons. Could understand the numbing feeling of cutting off emotions. After she was in the city for a few weeks and it was clear that Paul wasn't coming after her, she shut a part of herself off, too. That's why she never let anyone close to her. Why she didn't have any friends, except for Mac, but she even kept him at a distance.

After a moment, Luella picked up the plant and delicately pulled it out of the pot. She set it down inside of the hole.

"You have to break up the root ball first," Helen said.

Luella sat back. "What do you mean?"

"Hold the plant between both of your hands and use your fingers to bust up the bottom, where the roots are."

"Why?"

Helen sighed and leaned forward, resting her arms on her legs. She looked out over the field, like she was weighing her words. "Because it helps to encourage growth. Not doing it can cause the plant to continue to be root bound . . . meaning it won't spread its roots. They'll grow upward, inward, or around themselves, which stunts growth."

"Oh," was the only word Luella could manage to say. For a moment, just a moment, she wasn't sure if Helen was talking about the actual plant or Luella leaving home. For a fleeting second, Luella felt like Helen was implying that she understood why Luella left. In her own Helen kind of way.

Helen must have felt it, too, because she smiled at Luella, and it felt like a weight had been lifted off Luella's shoulders. *Poof, gone. Just like that.*

She'd never forget the way the sun beamed down over Helen as she sat swinging back and forth, the old chain creaking like a melody in the wind. Luella blinked back against the wetness welling up in her eyes.

She dug her fingers into the root ball and set it inside the hole. Helen told her to add some soil to the ground. She opened the large bag of soil and reached in and scooped out a shovel full. Helen told her to water it first before packing it back in. She dragged the water hose over and sprayed it around the plant. Then, she pushed the soil and dirt around the plant, covering it up in its new home. She planted the rest of the flowers and sat back, inspecting her work.

"Nice job," Helen said, looking at the flowers in the ground.

Luella sat back and took off her gloves. It was the first time Helen had said that to her. She had no idea what those two words meant. Luella looked over at Helen. "Your birthday is in a few weeks," she said, wiping sweat from her forehead.

Helen made a disapproving sound. Luella knew she'd slide past that one without another thought. She hated celebrating her birthday. For as long as Luella could remember, Helen had cut June sixth out of every calendar that had ever hung on the kitchen wall. It always confused Luella when she was a child. Who didn't love birthdays? But the older she got, the more she came to understand the urge to plow right past it.

Helen got up from the swing. Her hand flew to her side, and she grimaced.

"Does it hurt?" Luella asked.

Helen waited a moment before responding, like she was waiting for the pain to pass or catching her breath. Then, she nodded her head just slightly. "I think I might need a little help getting inside."

Luella shot to her feet. It was the first time Helen was asking for her help. Luella put her arm around Helen's waist, and Helen put her arm around her shoulder, leaning some of her weight onto

Luella, who was more than happy to bear some of it for her.

"I think I overdid it today at Pike Farms."

"Probably," Luella said, feeling that sinking pit that came in waves now back in her stomach.

She and Helen danced around the truth as if saying what was really happening would shatter the work they'd done piecing their relationship back together.

Neither of them was ready to face what was surely coming their way.

# twenty-six

The late afternoon sky was hazy as Luella sat on the back porch swing swaying back and forth with a blank legal pad in her lap. She sighed as she looked down at it.

Her hair was twisted up and held in place by a pencil. She had been trying to write for hours.

Something. *Anything.*

She was growing restless the longer she went without a job and the income that came along with it. While she knew she didn't really need the money, it was simply the principle of it. And being at the farm meant that she had time on her hands. Time that should be spent trying to write the story that Cathy wanted from her. But something was fogging her brain up. Probably pregnancy hormones, but she wasn't sure if it was only that.

She hoped putting pen to paper the old-school way would help break her writer's block.

But the words just wouldn't come. Not like they had that day after the attic fight with Helen. Those words were heavy and calculated, fueled by anger. Good for processing feelings, but not good for getting published in a revered magazine.

And even Luella could admit that wasn't the kind of story she wanted her name on. Not anymore.

Her mind had been a jumbled mess since she arrived. Words swirled around like a tornado in her mind. She couldn't quiet the storm long enough to make sense of anything.

Probably didn't help that Paul was coming today. He hadn't said what time he'd be there, and she couldn't take her mind off it all day, making it hard for her to concentrate on anything else. She had other things to preoccupy the space in her mind. Things like Helen, the farm, the pregnancy . . . but she always came back to Paul.

He'd been extremely busy the past six weeks since their work day on the farm. Whenever he did stop by, it seemed they never had a moment alone together. Either Helen was there with them, or Taylor was tagging along.

Luella wondered if his complicated relationship had smoothed itself out and he just didn't have the heart to tell her.

Finally, the rumble of his truck echoed down the gravel driveway. She waited for him to find her on the back porch.

When he did, he stood in front of the screen door, just staring at her through the screen.

Her cheeks grew hot and that flutter in the pit of her stomach returned. She could hardly handle the way he was looking at her. "What?" she asked, finally.

"Nothing," he said with a smile that sent chills down her spine.

She pushed her glasses up on top of her head as he stepped through the screen door.

"Just seeing you here like this . . . it's nice." His eyes scanned over her, making her heart beat faster. She fumbled with her notepad. He must have sensed her nerves because he chuckled. She looked up at him with an icy glare, which only made him smile wider.

Helen stepped out onto the porch. "I didn't know you were coming by today, Paul." She looked over at Luella like she had purposefully left her out of the loop.

Paul stepped forward and wrapped his arms around Helen in a hug. Helen gave him one hard pat on the back and pulled away. "Come inside," she said, more like a command than a request. "It's chilly out here."

Paul and Luella exchanged glances. It was the end of April. It was warm more often than not, but Helen was hardly more than bones.

"Well, I was actually gonna see if Lue wanted to get out of here for a little while."

Helen's eyebrows went up, and she looked between the two of them curiously. "Alright then," she said, turning back toward the door.

"You sure you'll be alright?" Luella asked. "We won't be gone long."

Helen rolled her eyes. "I can take care of myself. I am not some sad sop that needs to be watched all hours of the day. If you think so, then I will gladly go check myself into the assisted living facility down the road." With that, she stepped inside the house and let the door slam shut behind her.

"Well then," Luella said, looking up at Paul. "I think we're good to go." She got up off the swing, and they walked around to the front.

Paul stepped ahead of her and pulled the passenger door open. She smiled at his chivalry and hopped in. Luella looked out the open window as Paul walked around to the driver's side.

The smell of rain was in the air. It was one of Luella's favorite scents.

As they drove down the road, Luella stole a few glances at Paul. They had never ridden in a vehicle together. She had been on buses filled with people, had been the passenger with other people before . . . but sitting in the truck next to Paul in such a confined space felt oddly intimate.

She wondered if he sensed it, too.

They drove about two miles down the road to the park they used to go to as kids. When Paul turned the truck into the entrance, Luella laughed. Paul looked over with the widest grin on his face.

Hudson Mill was more like a nature preserve, with hiking trails and three small waterfalls.

There was a playground and picnic area. But Luella's favorite part had always been the bridge that led to the biggest waterfall that spilled over into a large swimming hole. Helen and Grandpa Fred would load them all up when they were little and take them down the road to Hudson Mill. They'd park, and all the kids would go racing down across the bridge to the swimming hole.

"Man, I loved this place," Luella said, as Paul cut the engine off.

"Me too. Wanna go for a walk?"

"Rain's coming," she said.

"Chicken." He smiled at her. She pushed his shoulder with her hand and then hopped out of the truck. They walked side by side toward the bridge. Neither of them said a word, but they didn't need to. Silence wasn't uncomfortable for them.

When they reached the bridge, Luella stopped and leaned against the rail as she stared down at the waterfall. Something was different. It didn't look nearly as big as it had when they were kids. As she stood there staring at it, she marveled at how incredibly ordinary it was. It had been magical when they were kids—their own private ocean down the road.

Her brows furrowed at the thought. What a weird experience it was to see things differently as an adult. Like the magic had faded. Or rather, she just outgrew it.

She looked over at Paul, but his eyes were already on her. Heat rose in her cheeks.

"I'm sorry I haven't been by much lately . . . I've just been a little in my head and confused about things."

"I know what you mean." Luella picked at the chipping paint on the rail.

Paul slid closer to her, and their elbows touched. Luella's heart started beating faster. How could such a tiny thing have such a big effect on her?

"You being here has thrown me off. I never expected you to come back . . . you're messing with my mind, Luella McCrae."

She bit at her bottom lip. "Is that a bad thing?" she asked without looking up at him.

He turned to face her, and she looked up at him then. His eyes scanned her face, stopping only when they landed on her lips.

She had never wanted to kiss him more than she did right then.

He must have felt it, too, because he stroked a strand of hair hanging by her face and pushed it back behind her ear. Then, he placed his hands delicately on her cheeks, like he did the first time he ever kissed her.

He stepped closer, pressing against her. He softly brushed her cheek with his thumb. She closed her eyes against the sensation coursing through her. She never wanted it to end.

As he leaned closer, the sound of footsteps came loud and fast behind them as a group of teenagers came running down the bridge. He dropped his hand and stepped back as they passed, but his eyes stayed locked on hers.

She looked away first. They both leaned against the rail and watched as the kids went running up the trail beside the waterfall.

Thunder rumbled overhead. It had gotten darker especially down in the woods. She looked up at the moody, dark gray sky.

"Wanna head back to the truck?" Paul asked.

"Probably not a bad idea. It looks like it's about to pour."

They made it halfway back before rain started gushing from the sky. Luella gasped as it soaked them both. Paul laughed and grabbed her hand. They ran back the rest of the way and hopped inside the truck, both breathing heavily from the run.

Rain beat against the roof—the sound rhythmic and comforting. The windows fogged up, making the inside a private little oasis.

Luella watched a raindrop trickle down Paul's nose and fall into his lap. From the side, he looked like a boy again. Or maybe it was just her mind playing tricks on her. Or her heart.

"I can't stop wondering what would have happened if I'd never left . . . If I had just stayed, then maybe—"

"Don't," said Paul. "You can't change it."

She noticed the sharp edge in his voice. "But I wish I could."

"Well, you can't," he said, his voice a bit harsher this time.

He stared out of the truck windshield in front of him. His jaw tensed. "I've played that game in my mind for the past eleven years. What would life have been like? Would we have gotten married? Stayed in Chipley? You can play out one scenario after the next, but it changes nothing. And if I'm being honest, I go back and forth in my mind between being glad that you're here and bitter because of it. Seeing you has been harder than I thought it would be."

"Paul . . ." she pleaded.

He looked over at her—his eyes full of conflict. "I want to give you a pass. I want to give in to the part of me that is so happy that you're back, but then there's this other part of me that never recovered from you leaving. How could you just leave like that? Leave *me* like that?"

There it was. The thing he must have wanted to ask since the moment he saw her again. She thought they had barreled right past it as though it didn't occur—but everything rises to the surface eventually.

"I don't know," she said, shaking her head. She knew it was a deflective answer, but she wasn't sure what to say. Because the truth was, she had felt guilty about it every day since.

Why had she left? It was a loaded question. One she hadn't had to explain in complete sentences before.

She started planning it after Helen sent Paul away. She hated Helen for it. In her eyes, Helen kept her from Paul and from Mya, giving none of herself in exchange for what she took.

Luella got a job at the grocery store when she was sixteen. She started saving her paychecks and putting them in the tin beneath the floorboard by her bunk. She told Helen she was saving it for college. Helen said that was a smart, disciplined decision. If she had only known what Luella was planning.

Meggie helped Luella keep in touch with Paul, even took her to see him a few times. He had Meggie's cell phone number and would call whenever he could. She only saw him a handful of times after he left the farm. Each time at a burger stand on the edge of town.

The last time Luella saw him, she told him about her plan. Begged him to come with her. He laughed like she wasn't serious, but Luella was more serious than she had ever been in her entire life.

On the morning of her eighteenth birthday, she left a letter for Helen on the pillow of her bunk. It was more a note than a letter, really. It simply said that she was leaving and Helen shouldn't bother to look for her. Then, she grabbed her bag and crept out of the house long before sunrise. Meggie picked her up at the end of the driveway and drove her to the bus station where they said a tearful goodbye and made promises to stay close and keep in touch. If Meggie was against her leaving, she never showed it. She supported Luella no matter what.

Before Luella got out of the car, she handed Meggie a letter for Paul, telling him where she'd be and how he could contact her in the city. She had a feeling he wouldn't show up at the bus stop. She wished with all her heart that he had. Whether to go with her, or even to stop her from leaving.

Paul's voice cut through the memory. "You know I spent every day for a year convinced that you'd come back. I told myself you just needed a little time. And when you didn't . . ."

Her mouth went dry, and she swallowed against the lump forming in the back of her throat. She never meant to hurt him.

"I loved you more than I've ever loved anyone."

Luella closed her eyes as a tear fell down her cheek. "I loved you too. I never *stopped* loving you," she said with a quiver in her voice. "I tried. I really, really tried. But I never could."

Paul reached out, covering her cheek with his hand. "I should have stopped you. Or at least came after you. I guess a part of me was mad at you for leaving, even though I knew why you needed to do it. But it still hurt. Like you were leaving *me*."

Luella leaned into the warm, calloused feel of his hand pressed against her cheek. Their eyes searched each other's desperately as if silently asking one another for forgiveness.

For all they wished they had done, what they wished they had said, and for all they had lost.

In one swift move, Paul leaned over and brought her face to his. He crushed his lips against hers like it was the last moment they had on earth together.

The electric sensation Luella felt intensified with the hungry way Paul kissed her. She'd never get her fill of him. Paul's tongue pressed into her mouth, sending tiny sparks exploding all over her body. She let it consume her. Chemistry was never their weakness.

This moment was the one she had been dreaming about, wishing for, and hoping would happen again one day.

At first, she didn't even notice it. She was too lost in the moment with Paul.

Then, it happened again, harder this time, just below her belly button. A forceful flutter against the wall of her stomach. More than just butterflies.

A tiny little kick.

The first one she had ever felt. Her doctor told her she might begin to feel them soon, but no one could have prepared her for how it would really feel.

She gasped and pulled away from Paul. Her hand instinctively flew to the spot on her stomach where the baby had kicked. Then, she pulled it away just as fast.

"What's wrong?"

"Nothing." She forced a smile and adjusted the baggy sweatshirt she was wearing and prayed that Paul hadn't noticed the way her stomach was rounding out.

She would have to tell him soon before she couldn't hide it anymore. But she wasn't sure how he would react. It would complicate things. And she wasn't ready to give him up again, not yet.

She had been living her days like this baby didn't exist. Until now, she could even convince herself of that because she didn't feel any different physically.

But that changed at eighteen weeks along.

All it took was one little kick in her belly to remind her what was there, refusing to be ignored.

# twenty-seven

Helen's birthday landed on a Saturday. Perfect for a surprise party.

Luella enlisted the help of Cheryl and Taylor, who made it their mission to make it the best surprise birthday party there had ever been. Helen would hate it. She hated attention, but Luella let Cheryl and Taylor go wild with the planning anyway.

It was just supposed to be a small gathering. Luella, Cheryl, Taylor, Paul, and Helen. But Taylor insisted on a big party with more than just the usual dinner attendees. So, Luella invited Helen's Sunday school class and hoped Percy would come. That would also make Helen furious, but at least she'd have to wait until after the party was over to complain. If the party was a success, hopefully Helen would have a good time and forget to be mad by the end of it.

Taylor said they needed a theme, that all the best parties had themes. They tossed around several ideas, which included a luau, a fiesta, and a tea party. But none of those screamed Helen.

Luella was the one to decide on Halloween as their theme. It was Helen's favorite holiday. It was the only one that she went all out for decorations. Spider webs across every shrub and shutter. Her infamous skeletons, Henny and Lenny, were always dressed up and left somewhere outside of the house. How she posed them was always a charade—kept the neighbors laughing.

Once, she put Lenny out by the mailbox in fishing gear, complete with a fishing pole and a skeleton fish attached at the end.

Another time, she placed Henny in a cowboy hat and boots in a rocker on the front porch. It scared a delivery man so badly that he fell down the steps. He was fine, but Helen was reduced to a fit of laughter.

She had more Halloween decor than Christmas decor. Not only did she love draping Halloween everywhere, but she loved to pull pranks on Luella and the other children the entire month of October.

She'd hide outside a door and pop out, scaring them. Or she'd wear a Halloween mask and stand still somewhere, waiting to be found. She and Grandpa Fred used to throw the biggest Halloween party for the entire street.

After all the kids finished trick or treating up and down the road, they'd come to the farm and have a bonfire. The kids would play while the parents gathered. Helen would always dress up, regardless of if the other adults did.

It was the one day of the year that Helen let loose, and Luella always wished she'd stay that way forever.

She only did homemade costumes, though. The same went for Luella and the other kids. Helen couldn't stand all the store-bought costumes, said it sucked the fun straight out of it.

There were three huge storage boxes full of accessories up in the attic. She'd pull them down and let the kids go through them and come up with costumes. She promised a morning of no chores for whoever won the costume contest at the Halloween party.

So, it was an obvious choice to make it their theme.

Taylor counted down the days to June sixth. The plan was for

Cheryl to take Helen out for lunch and then bring her back to the party. Meanwhile, Luella and Taylor would get everything ready and welcome the guests—who were instructed to park over at Cheryl's house. That way Helen wouldn't have a clue. Cheryl's house was two houses down from Helen's, so Helen wouldn't be able to see the cars and get suspicious. Luella and Taylor would shuttle people from Cheryl's house on a golf cart so that they wouldn't have to walk.

Luella and Taylor worked hard that morning, blowing up balloons and making a beautiful balloon arch of black, orange, white, and purple. They set up tables borrowed from the church and threw tablecloths and centerpieces made up of pumpkins, cauldrons, and skeletons. They also rented a fog machine. Luella smiled, thinking about what Helen's friends from church would think of that.

They set out finger foods along with a cauldron full of green punch. Then, they got dressed in their costumes. Taylor spent hours gluing multicolored pom-poms onto a shirt so that she could be a gumball machine. Luella had simply picked out a gold sequined masquerade mask with feathers at the top to wear, along with jeans and a baggy sweater. Taylor insisted Luella also wear a golden cape that she found in one of Helen's bins, which Luella only agreed to because it would help hide her bump.

After they got dressed, they headed over to Cheryl's to wait for guests to arrive. Luella was pleased to see so many show up in costumes, all smiles and excited about the party. They had already made several trips back and forth in the golf cart when the rumble of a truck grew louder and louder.

Luella saw Paul's black truck coming down the road, and smiled. He said he'd try his best to make it. She wondered what kind of costume he'd be in. Her eyes stayed glued to his truck as he pulled into Cheryl's driveway.

It wasn't until they pulled closer that she could see someone beside him in the passenger seat.

A woman.

Luella's heart thumped wildly inside of her chest. What was happening? She suddenly wished Meggie could have made it to the party. She needed her best friend.

The woman looked familiar, though Luella couldn't quite figure out why. Heat flushed through her body at the sight of someone else sitting in the place she had sat kissing Paul not even five days ago. Her stomach twisted.

Taylor ran over to Paul as soon as he stepped out of the truck. She wrapped her little arms around him in an embrace. When he let her go, she proudly stepped back, hands on her hips, and asked, "Do you like my costume? I'm a gumball machine."

Paul laughed. "I love it."

The woman slid slowly out of the truck like a snake and shut the door. As she walked around the truck to Taylor and Paul, Luella tried to figure out how she knew her. It was like a word on the tip of her tongue that she couldn't quite get out.

She watched the way the woman beamed as she stood next to Paul, her strawberry blonde hair glinting in the sunlight. Luella suddenly felt sweaty. The cape around her neck aggravated her. She resisted the urge to rip it off.

Paul looked up at Luella, his face begging for forgiveness.

Her stomach tensed and got queasy, like she might throw up right there on the pavement as the three of them walked toward her.

The closer they got, the clearer Luella could see the woman's face. Why did she look familiar?

Neither of them wore costumes, which made Luella feel like a clown standing there in front of the two of them.

"This is Claire," said Paul. "Claire, this is Luella."

Luella's body froze in place. She knew that name. Why did she know that name?

Claire. Claire. *Claire.*

The nurse from her doctor's appointment.

Luella suppressed a gasp. She was suddenly thankful for the mask she was wearing, no matter how silly she felt standing next to Claire. Luella prayed she didn't recognize her. If this was Paul's complicated relationship, she might not take too kindly to Luella, which meant she might use whatever she could against her. But Claire simply held her hand out for Luella to shake. Claire smiled. Whether or not it was genuine, Luella couldn't be sure.

Another car pulled into Cheryl's driveway, and Luella couldn't have been more thankful for the divine intervention. "Y'all want a ride?" Luella offered, praying they'd say no.

Paul shook his head. "No, we can walk."

"Alright," said Luella, diverting her eyes from his. "See you over there."

They turned to walk down the driveway. Luella felt dizzy as she watched Claire's hand reach out and grab Paul's. Nausea overtook her body as she saw the way Paul's fingers laced together with hers.

After everyone had arrived, Luella texted Cheryl to let her know it was safe to come back to the farm. Cheryl sent her a warning text when they were on the street and Luella quieted the small crowd in anticipation of them walking around to the back of the house. As soon as Helen's eyes landed on them, everyone yelled, "Surprise!" and whooped and hollered until a smile finally appeared on Helen's shocked face, her eyes giddy as she looked out over all of their costumes.

Several of her friends rushed toward her with Halloween accessories to glam her up. Luella looked down at the food table and noticed that both chip bowls were nearly empty. She grabbed them off the table and walked up the back porch steps as someone turned the music up.

She looked back at the party, at Helen laughing and dancing with her friends, and couldn't help but smile. They had pulled it off. And

Helen wasn't even mad. At least, she didn't *look* mad.

In the kitchen, Luella set the bowls on the counter and slid the mask up on top of her head. She grabbed a bag of chips to refill the bowl. The back porch door slammed shut, and she heard footsteps coming toward the kitchen. When she looked over her shoulder, she saw Paul slinking slowly toward her. She turned away from him and started dumping chips into the empty bowls.

He stopped behind her. "Lue," he said, willing her to turn around. She wouldn't, though. And Lue? He used her full name earlier. Why not use it now, too? She grabbed the now full bowls and turned, intending to walk right by him, but he was right there in front of her. She wouldn't look up at him. "I didn't invite her," he said.

Luella scoffed and rolled her eyes. "I take it that's the complicated relationship then?"

Paul nodded, his eyes full of conflict. "She showed up at my apartment, and I told her I had plans, but she insisted on coming so we could talk about things."

"So, you've been seeing her?"

"No." His eyebrows furrowed together. "She's been texting and calling me like crazy. She wants to fix things. Obviously, I don't." He reached out, trying to grab her waist. She pulled away so he couldn't.

"Why did you bring her?"

"I told you. She came over to talk. And she kept talking. I told her we'd talk about it later, that I had somewhere to be. But she hopped in the truck and refused to get out. I didn't want to be late."

Luella searched his face. She wasn't sure she believed him. She huffed. "When she grabbed your hand, you took it."

"What?" he asked, confused.

"When you were walking over to the house. She reached out to grab your hand, and you took it."

He let out a frustrated sigh. "It wasn't intentional," he said. "I was trying to get her away from you. I haven't told her about us yet."

"Not really a good plan, Paul," she said with an air of sarcasm. "How did you intend to keep her away from me when you were bringing her to my grandma's party?"

"I don't know. I'm sorry . . . I screwed up. Let's just get through this party, and I'll take care of it."

Luella looked up at him, trying to hide the hurt that she felt. His face softened. He stepped as close as he could get to her. It was suffocating, and he knew it. "I'm so sorry." He stared down at her and smiled.

*Those darn dimples.* Luella caved, couldn't help smiling back at him. He stared down at her lips. "I know two things for sure. Claire and I are over . . . and you and I owe it to each other to see where this thing is going."

He leaned his head down and kissed her lips softly, which made every inch of her body soften like butter. She'd never get over that effect. She wanted to put the bowls down and kiss him harder, but someone cleared their throat behind them. They both looked behind him.

Claire. Her arms crossed, and her face was furious. "They're about to sing 'Happy Birthday,'" she said. Luella tried to slide the mask down over her face in time, but Claire had already seen her. Her eyes grew wide in recognition, but she didn't say a word. She stomped off back outside.

Paul took a deep breath and let it out like he was preparing himself for battle. Luella stepped past him with the chip bowls in her hand. "Lue," he said.

"We should get back."

Outside, Luella placed the bowls on the table in their missing spots. Everyone was still talking amongst themselves. Paul came down the back porch steps and sulked back over to where Claire stood, staring Luella dead in the face. Claire's cheeks were red, and her eyes fuming. Luella was trying to watch their conversation unfold when Estelle walked over and put her hand on Luella's arm.

"I think it's real nice what you did today for Helen. Real nice," she said.

Luella smiled at the woman and was about to thank her and step away nicely when Cheryl stood up on a chair, put two of her fingers between her lips, and whistled loudly for everyone's attention.

"Thank you all for coming," she said. "It's time to sing 'Happy Birthday' to the beautiful Helen McCrae, fiercest woman I know and the most loyal friend to all of us here today."

Everyone clapped. Cheryl led a countdown and then everyone started singing. Luella looked back over at Claire and Paul, who were still busy fussing, barely audible over the singing. As their argument escalated, several guests at the party noticed and stepped away from them uncomfortably. Paul noticed the people watching them, and his face grew bright red. He tried to lead Claire away from the crowd, but she yanked her arm away.

What happened next was a blur. In the same second that everyone stopped singing, Claire's voice yelled at Paul. "Luella's pregnant!"

It was obviously an accident. Anyone with eyes could see that from the shock and embarrassment written all over Claire's face when she realized.

Estelle gasped and covered her mouth with her hand.

*Wonderful.*

There was a collective intake of breath and silence amongst the crowd. Luella looked at the ground and dared not look at a single soul, least of all Paul. She felt naked to these people, even behind a mask.

She didn't blame Claire. It probably ate her up from the second she realized who Luella was. But she probably thought she had the upper hand, being here with Paul. Until she caught them kissing.

Luella felt sick to her stomach. When she finally looked up, it was Helen's face that she saw. Her eyes lingered a few moments, trying to figure out what it was on Helen's face. Empathy? Sadness that Luella hadn't told her herself? Compassion that Paul was finding out this way when things were finally going good?

Percy stood up from his chair and climbed onto it like Cheryl had—though it took him a bit longer. When everyone was looking over at him, he said, "Who wants cake?" and slapped both his knees and clapped. *Bah-duh-bah*. The perfect punch line.

Luella couldn't have loved him more at that moment. Some laughed, some snickered amongst themselves, but the party went on and voices filled the awkward silence. Luella looked over at Paul. His eyes met hers. Eyes filled with hurt and confusion, like he was waiting for her to come over to him and say that it wasn't true. That she wasn't carrying another man's baby. But she didn't. He looked away from her quickly and walked up to Helen, gave her a hug and said something in her ear before walking toward the driveway. Claire followed behind him, looking rather mortified herself.

Helen and Cheryl walked over to Luella. Cheryl placed her hand on Luella's back and rubbed back and forth as a mother would to console her child.

"How pregnant are you?" asked Helen.

"Almost five months."

A look of surprise appeared on Cheryl's face but was quickly wiped away with a pasted-on smile. Cheryl squeezed Luella's shoulders. "You're gonna have a baby," she said with a smile.

Luella shook her head. "I'm not keeping it."

Cheryl's brows furrowed. "What do you mean you're not keeping it? What does that mean?"

"I mean adoption," she said. When Helen and Cheryl just stared at her without saying a word, she felt the need to defend herself. "I think this baby deserves a normal family. A family that wants a baby and can take care of it. One that won't mess it up like I will."

"Oh, honey, that's not true," said Cheryl, now rubbing circles on Luella's back.

Helen looked over at Cheryl and spoke. "I'm tired. I'm gonna go rest. Let everyone know I appreciate them coming."

"Sure thing, doll." Cheryl watched through worried eyes as Helen walked up the steps of the back porch and let the screen door slam shut in the face of her party. Cheryl gave Luella a sad smile and squeezed her shoulder before walking off to let the guests know.

Luella sighed. She had ruined it. All of it. Helen's party. Things with Paul. She should have confronted the situation before it got out of hand and ruined everything. She should have told Paul. Should have told Helen.

So many *should-haves,* and now it was too late.

# twenty-eight

The party died down quickly after Helen went inside. One person after another left until it was just Cheryl, Luella, and Taylor.

The sky was darkening, and there was a chill in the air. Luella and Cheryl cleaned up the necessities and left the rest to be cleaned the following day.

Luella told Cheryl and Taylor goodnight, took a deep breath, and walked into the house.

A *Golden Girls* episode played on the television as Luella walked past the living room into the kitchen. She dumped the dishes in the sink and turned around, leaning against the counter.

She knew she needed to get it over with and go speak to Helen, but she didn't even know where to start.

She had a birthday gift for her. Maybe it would be a good buffer. She grabbed it off the table and went into the living room.

Helen sat on the couch watching television with her feet propped up on the coffee table in front of her. She looked up when Luella walked into the room, but her eyes didn't linger. She went right back to watching *Golden Girls*.

Luella sat down on the loveseat next to the couch.

"I always loved this show," Helen said right after Sophia made a snarky comment to Blanche. The corners of her mouth went up just a little.

Luella wanted her to say something about the party. About how Luella ruined it, or maybe even ask why she didn't tell her about the pregnancy. She wanted Helen to be furious. That's what she expected. So, when she didn't act that way, Luella felt out of sorts sitting there on the loveseat.

She cleared her throat and picked up the gift, which she had wrapped in brown kraft paper with a lace bow. She held it out for Helen. "I didn't get to give you this earlier."

Helen eyed the package and leaned out to grab it. "I thought I said no gifts."

"It's really not much. And you know people don't really listen when someone says that, right?"

Helen unwrapped the lace bow and tore off the brown paper. Underneath was a large, framed picture that Luella had blown up and framed at Bradley's photo center. She found it the day they picked up the scattered pictures in the attic.

In the photo was a young Helen holding a baby Mya. Helen's face beamed with pride and happiness. It was the prettiest picture of Helen that Luella had ever seen. She loved how glorious she looked standing there, holding her new bundle of joy. The corners of Helen's mouth lifted a little, and her eyes softened as she looked at the picture like she was looking at a long-lost friend. A few seconds later, her smile faded. She looked lost in a trance, or rather—lost in a memory.

"I thought you looked so pretty in it. I know you and Mya don't get along, but I couldn't get over how proud you look in that picture with her."

Helen's eyes flitted up to meet hers. "That's not Mya in the picture . . . it's *you.* That's you and me, kid."

Luella's mouth fell open just a little, and she looked from Helen's face to the frame in her hands. Helen noticed and held the picture out for her. Luella took it and studied everything about the picture, flabbergasted by the revelation. How had she not known? But then, she had never seen a picture of herself as a baby before. "I just assumed it was Mya," Luella said.

"Your mama had you when she was fifteen years old. Do you remember what it was like to be fifteen? The world revolves around only you, and it spins at an unhurried pace. You can't see farther than you can throw. A choice she made in the heat of a moment changed her life."

Mya had never talked about it. Luella didn't even know who her father was, and she knew better than to ask.

Luella put the picture on the coffee table. "Why didn't she get an abortion or put me up for adoption if she didn't want me?"

Helen took a deep breath and let it out slowly. "It wasn't that she didn't want you, Luella. She was just a kid herself. Knew nothing about taking care of a baby. She did the best she could."

Luella thought about it. Could even understand Mya little better in that moment. "I'm not making the same mistake she did. I know I wouldn't be a good mother."

"What about the baby's father?"

"Not in the picture. Besides, it wasn't anything. It happened in the heat of a moment, just like Mya. A very, stupid moment. If I'd have known . . ."

A quietness crept in between them and stayed for a few moments. "Well, you're not fifteen. You have plenty of sense of mind to know what you want and don't want out of life, and if kids aren't it, then that's your decision."

Luella sighed. "I wish it were a simple decision. I think it's what I want and then sometimes I think about Meggie and her girls and how she never wanted kids. You can't miss the way her eyes light up when she talks about them. She changed her mind."

"You'll figure it out," said Helen. She sounded certain. Luella wished she had that kind of confidence. Helen opened her mouth again and then closed it like she was finished, but Luella had a feeling that she had more that she wanted to say. "Anything else?" she asked, letting her know it was okay if she wanted to say more.

Helen's mouth twitched like she was thinking about whether she wanted to say it or not. "I just also want to say that you have no idea what kind of mother you'd be. You're assuming. That assumption goes flying out the window the moment they put that baby on your chest. You'll never know what kind of mother you'd be until you become one. And let me tell you a secret . . . none of us get it right. There's no such thing. There's only doing the best that you can do."

Luella's eyes stung as tears filled them.

Helen got up from the couch and handed Luella the remote to the TV. "I'm turning in for the night," she said, starting toward her bedroom.

Luella called out to her, "Helen?"

She turned around, her eyebrows raised.

"Happy birthday."

Helen rolled her eyes, but she smiled a little too, which made Luella happy. When she was gone, Luella turned off the TV and went to her room.

She sat down on the floor beside the bunk bed and crossed her legs. She shimmied the loose piece of wood from the floor and reached in and pulled out the tin box. Then, she opened it and took out the five letters she had from Mya. She sat back against the bunk and looked them over, studying the intricate cursive handwriting, as she tried to imagine where her mother probably was and what she was doing when she had written them. There was no return address. Luella imagined she was in another state, busy working. Or perhaps she was at the beach visiting friends. She couldn't shake the feeling that wherever Mya was when she had written them, it probably wasn't over fifty miles from the farm. Close enough to visit instead of write.

Luella read the letters repeatedly, analyzing the content and trying to give Mya the benefit of the doubt for how she chose to parent.

Fifteen years old. That meant that she was only twenty-two when she left Luella at the farm. Luella thought about who she was at twenty-two. She could barely take care of herself, was scraping by with no sense of here or there. She did whatever she needed to do to make ends meet. At twenty-two and at twenty-nine. Not much had changed. She couldn't imagine having a baby at that age, let alone a seven-year-old.

Maybe Helen was right. Maybe Mya had done the best that she could with what she was given. It could have been far worse had she stayed with Mya. All those men that came in and out of the house on rotation. It could have been far, far worse.

When she looked at it that way, she was thankful that Mya had left her at the farm.

~

The next morning Luella hid in her bedroom hoping that Helen would head to church without her, even though she knew that wasn't likely. She couldn't bear to show her face. Helen's footsteps were loud as they approached her bedroom door. Luella pulled the covers up over her head as if they could hide her from Helen's sight.

When the door swung open, she heard Helen sigh. "Better get dressed quickly. We leave in twenty minutes."

"I can't go," Luella said, pushing the covers off. "Not after what happened at the party. And Estelle was there. I'm sure everybody in

Chipley knows by now."

Helen walked over to the bed and sat down. "Luella. The only way to get in front of things is by doing just that. You need to go. Show your face. You can't hide from the things that try to break you down and wear you out. You'll find more strength in facing things head on than you ever will by running away from them."

Luella felt a kick that made her gasp. A small flip in her belly for the second time.

She placed her hand on the lower part of her stomach.

"What?" asked Helen.

"It moved," said Luella with a hint of amazement in her voice.

Helen smiled. "At least someone's listening to me this morning. Smart girl."

Luella looked up at Helen, a bit taken aback. "We don't know that it's a girl."

"Grandma's intuition," Helen said with a wink. Luella smiled, and Helen did, too. Then, she quickly sighed and said, "Now come on. Get dressed. We have to leave soon."

~

Thirty minutes later, they were walking up the steps of the church. Luella's face grew hot as she looked around at the people filing in through the doors. She couldn't help but feel like everyone's eyes were on hers. Watching her. Judging her. "Maybe we should sit in the back this time," she said to Helen. Luella could see several members of the church watching them as they stood at the back of the building behind the pews.

Helen turned around; Her eyes were full of determination. "No, we will not. We will sit up front like always. Church is not a museum for saints. It's a hospital for the broken. And we're all broken here.

Even the ones who look perfect to you. So, chin up."

She turned around and strolled to the third pew at the front of the church where they always sat. Luella followed her and did her best not to look at the people around her as she did. When they sat down, she looked across the room. Estelle was in the front row, leaned over, whispering to the woman beside her. No doubt filling her in about Luella.

That service felt like the longest one she had ever sat through as she fidgeted with her shirt the entire time, trying to keep it flowing away from her belly. Coincidentally, it was spring dedication day, *because of course it would be*. Luella watched as the couples filled the front of the church with their babies cooing and drooling as their parents dedicated them to Christ and pledged to raise them accordingly. Pastor Wynn was on a roll in his sermon, and he just kept going and going. Luella hoped it would be one of those Sunday mornings where the message was short, but no.

When the service was finally over, Luella shot to her feet and made her way out of the church, with Helen lagging behind. Luella made it halfway to the Wagoneer when she realized Helen wasn't behind her anymore. She turned back toward the church and saw Percy had stopped Helen at the bottom of the stairs. He looked nervous as he fidgeted with his hands while Helen stood in front of him, her Bible in her arms, swaying from one foot to the other.

They looked like a pair of kids in the schoolyard with an audience standing around, watching as they spoke. Luella smiled at the sight. She could tell by Helen's body language that she was uncomfortable. Helen hated being the center of attention, and Luella could only imagine what Percy was saying to her as he stumbled over his words. Helen had that effect on him. She had that effect on many people.

Finally, Helen began walking toward her. She looked over Helen's tiny figure to the people still standing on the church steps waiting to pounce on Percy like gossip fleas. One man clapped Percy on the back the way a proud coach would after his player had made a home run.

Luella didn't miss the ear-to-ear grin that Percy Webster sported on his face.

Helen walked past her and got into the car. Luella stood there for a second, wondering if she had suddenly become invisible. She got into the driver's side and turned the keys in the ignition. "What was that about?"

"Percy asked if I'd go to dinner with him."

Luella smiled. She had pegged Percy correctly. She knew he was sweet on Helen. "Well, what did you say?"

"I told him no." Helen looked out the window. She wouldn't look over at Luella.

Finally, Luella backed out of the parking spot. "I can't believe he finally asked, and you told him no."

Helen scoffed. "I told him no, that I would not go to dinner with him. I said if he would like to have dinner, he could come to my house, and I would cook a proper meal, and we could have dinner the old-fashioned way."

Luella's mouth fell open. She stared at Helen in shock.

"Mind the road," Helen said, pointing in front of her. When Luella looked away, Helen said, "I don't mind having dinner with a friend, but I refuse to be the talk of the town, as the people in Chipley Creek would surely watch us the entire time we were eating if we went to a restaurant."

"You have a dinner date," Luella teased. She couldn't stop herself from smiling.

Helen rolled her eyes. "Luella McCrae, you stop that right now, or I will call Percy and cancel."

"Alright fine," she said, but she didn't stop smiling. She also noticed the way Helen fidgeted in her seat, like she might have been a tiny bit nervous about the dinner.

# twenty-nine

Several days later, Luella pushed the cart behind Helen as she made her way around the produce aisle, picking up vegetables and inspecting them before placing the ones she wanted delicately in the shopping cart.

Helen walked slower that day compared to usual. She'd take small breaks like she had to catch her breath but pretended to be looking at something so Luella wouldn't notice. But she did. Luella had tried to convince Helen to make a list and let her run to the store and grab everything that she needed. But no. Helen insisted on going and picking out what she needed herself.

It took over an hour to grab the ingredients she needed for just the one meal. Helen was picky, but she was also weak and tired and too stubborn to admit it. Luella wished she hadn't pushed Helen about Percy. Maybe it was a bad idea. Luella would never say that out loud, though. Besides, at least Helen had done it on her terms.

The rest of the day went by in no hurry. Helen seemed on edge and antsy with each passing hour. She rested and watched some television for a while after they got back from the grocery store.

But as each hour ticked on, Helen couldn't seem to sit still. She'd fidget, or she'd get up and have to walk around a bit.

She was ready to cook around three-thirty that afternoon. Percy wasn't due to arrive until five-thirty or six, but Luella didn't say a word. She just followed Helen into the kitchen.

Helen had decided on a pasta dish. She grabbed a cutting board and a knife, and made Luella chop up an onion while she grabbed a pan from the cabinet. She set the pan on the stovetop and turned to find Luella mutilating the onion.

"Stop." Luella did and looked up expectantly. "Have you never chopped an onion before?" Helen asked.

Luella shrugged. "I've never really cooked for anyone." Helen's eyes widened like what she said was unbelievable. "Believe it or not, some people don't like to cook."

Helen put a hand to her chest like she was offended, which made Luella laugh. "That should be a crime," said Helen. "What are you ever going to do if you find yourself in a position where you need to host a dinner?"

Luella thought about it. "Probably order in."

"No," said Helen, shaking her head fervently. "If you only learn how to cook one meal, then that's enough. So, here we go. This is the proper way to chop an onion." She grabbed the knife and onion from Luella and showed her. "Think you can manage to finish?"

Luella rolled her eyes. Helen handed the knife back over to her. She finished the chopping while Helen cut the sausage into small chunks. The pan hissed as Helen dumped the cut-up bits of onion and sausage into it, then she looked back and nodded toward the stove, summoning Luella from her seat at the table.

She stood beside Helen as she worked and explained what she was doing and why and for how long. Luella's throat grew dry and her eyes welled up when Helen placed a hand on her back for just a second, encouraging her to take over. She couldn't remember the last time she had even hugged Helen—if she ever had.

The last time she stood in that kitchen cooking, was when Grandpa Fred had taught her to make pancakes. That was two weeks after she arrived at the farm. It felt circular somehow, being there with Helen and seeing how far they had come.

Helen tapped the spoon on the pot and covered it to simmer on the stove. Her eyes darted around the kitchen like she was making little mental notes. Luella was sure her head was probably spinning from everything running through it. She told her to go get ready, that she would take care of setting the table. Helen reluctantly agreed.

Once she was out of sight, Luella walked over to the China cabinet in the corner of the dining room and opened the double doors. She took out two of the floral lined plates, along with two long stemmed clear wine glasses. She opened the drawer and took out two placemats and linen napkins and set them on the table.

*Now it's a date.*

When she was done putting it all together, she grabbed a scented jar candle from the kitchen and placed it in the center of the table on a wooden tray. She'd tell Helen it was just so the room would smell good. She stepped back to admire how it all came together, and smiled.

In the kitchen, she cut up a loaf of French bread and placed the pieces in the oven. Helen walked into the kitchen, and Luella tried to keep her mouth from falling open in surprise. Luella had never seen Helen so dressed up before. Not even for church. She had on a pair of flowy black pants, with a floral wrap around blouse. She had fixed her hair and even put on a touch of makeup. Not too much, just enough to liven her cheeks and bring out her big brown eyes.

"You look beautiful," Luella told her.

Helen waved a hand at Luella, but her eyes softened, and her lips pouted just a little. "It's been a long time since I've had a first date."

Luella nodded. It was a big step. She was proud of Helen.

There was a hum in the air as the sound of Percy's car on the gravel driveway traveled through the open window in the kitchen. They both turned toward it.

Luella stood up. "I'm gonna take the Wagoneer to town and get some food . . . maybe go by Meggie's. If that's okay with you."

Helen looked panicked. Luella could tell she didn't want her to leave, but it was an evening meant for space and privacy. She felt awkward staying, and she didn't want to be the excuse that Helen found to end her date early.

"Okay," Helen said, a little unsure. "But you really don't have to leave."

"Don't worry. It'll be great. You're just having dinner with a friend. Don't overthink it."

Helen took a deep breath as the doorbell rang. "I'll let him in. I'll be back in a few hours."

Helen nodded, and Luella left her standing by the oven in the kitchen, fidgeting with her blouse. She looked back and smiled at her, though Helen wasn't looking. Then, she grabbed her purse off the entryway table, along with the Wagoneer keys, and pulled open the heavy, oak door.

"Good evening," Percy said with a hum in his voice and an ear-to-ear grin on his wrinkly face. Luella noticed his bottom row of crooked teeth, but it didn't diminish his smile—just added character.

"Hello," she said back to him with a smile. "She's all yours. I hope you two have a wonderful dinner. It smells delicious."

Percy's face grew bright red. They moved past each other. Luella through the door and down the steps, and Percy into the house, shutting the door gently behind him.

Luella opened the door of the Wagoneer and hopped inside. She could see them through the kitchen window. They stood like awkward preteens in front of each other, anxious and excited and unsure of themselves all at once. There was something to be said about the anticipation of new relationships and what they could bring.

Luella took out her phone. 5:55 p.m. She hadn't heard from Paul since the fiasco at Helen's party five days earlier.

He went radio silent. No doubt sorting through the past few days and wondering how she could keep something like that a secret from him. He may even have been waiting for her to contact him. She wanted to give him space, but she also had so much that she needed to say. So much that she wanted to explain. She sent him a text asking if they could meet and talk.

It felt like hours as she sat there and watched the text bubble appear and disappear as he tried to decide whether he wanted to see her or not.

Finally, a text popped up that read: 6:30 at Jerry's.

~

After Helen sent Paul away, his new foster home was just outside of town. Luella would call or text him from Meggie's phone whenever she was with her. The waiting in between felt like agony. He had been living under the same roof as her for ten years. They lived on different sides of the house and were hardly ever alone, but there was a comfort in knowing he was there if she needed him. Just seeing him made her feel better. When she could no longer walk to the other side of the house to see him anymore, it felt like the worst kind of pain a fifteen-year-old girl could imagine. She hated Helen for it, refused to speak to her for weeks.

Paul aged out of the system a few months later and moved into a subsidized building owned and operated by a transitional housing program that was offered by the state. He had a long list of requirements and rules to follow so that he wouldn't get kicked out of the program. Rules that kept Luella away from his apartment and gave him a strict nine o'clock curfew.

Whenever they could meet, they met at Jerry's. Meggie would give Luella and Paul space whenever they did. She'd order a burger and sit outside while Luella and Paul sat in her car and talked. Sometimes they would spend the entire time they had trying to get their fill of each other and sneak in conversation between kisses. Who knew how long it would be before they could see each other again. They went on that way until Luella's senior year.

Until she decided she was leaving Chipley Creek.

She tried to convince him to go with her. To get out of Chipley and go start their life together somewhere else. Somewhere new. She told him she didn't care where, as long as they were together. He had kissed her after saying that, which made her believe he was fond of the idea.

But Paul was methodical in his thinking. Luella could only see what was right in front of her. She got frustrated with him every time he brought her back to reality with his logic. He'd be leaving behind a life that was reliable. One that was helping him advance in life. Not that he didn't love her or want to be with her, but he thought they needed a more solid plan.

She'd sulk whenever he'd try to convince her they just needed to wait. Sometimes she'd cry, and Paul hated it when she did that. He'd get quiet and apologize, pull her close and kiss the top of her head, telling her they would figure it out. That they would find a way to be together. It was only a matter of time.

They argued the last time she saw him.

Luella was three days from her eighteenth birthday, and Paul wanted to celebrate, but Luella picked a fight instead. She'd told him she had a plan, and she was sticking to it. That she had already written the letter she planned to leave on her pillow for Helen. She had her hidden floorboard money in a safe spot and already packed a bag. Paul nodded his head indifferently, but his eyes betrayed him. He told Luella to do what she needed to do.

Luella begged him to be there at the bus stop three days later at sunrise. She'd bought him a ticket, too. For Atlanta. She wasn't sure what she'd find there, but she said there were more possibilities in the city than she could ever find in a place like Chipley Creek. She wanted more than being a waitress at Walton's or a teller at the bank. When they parted ways that night, there was an uneasiness in her stomach that she couldn't quite settle. Looking back on it, she would say that it was her heart's way of preparing her.

Three days later, she sat at the bus stop waiting for him to show up. She waited as long as possible before boarding the bus. The driver had already waited ten minutes later than he should have when he finally told her he couldn't wait any longer. She had to make a decision. To step foot on that bus, or to stay and be with Paul.

Before she knew it, she was walking up the bus steps, giving the driver her ticket and promising herself she would make Paul understand. That they would be okay no matter what. She'd convince him to meet her in Atlanta. She'd go on ahead and get everything ready. If she was being honest with herself, she'd have known that she was making excuses for leaving him behind.

~

She pulled into the tiny gravel parking lot at Jerry's. It wasn't exactly a stand. It was more like a small shack. The sun was still shining, though it was dipping just below the trees. There was a pond behind Jerry's that Luella and Paul used to joke about skinny dipping in one day. They never got the chance, though.

Several people sat eating at the tables beside the small building. Luella was glad to see that Jerry's was still beloved. She always thought it deserved more recognition. It was a hidden gem in

Chipley. There weren't many of those, either.

Luella looked around, waiting for Paul. He finally pulled in about ten minutes later and parked two spots down from her. She waited until he got out of his truck and then she got out too and waited at the back of the Wagoneer for him. He walked toward her with his hands in his pockets. He still had his uniform on. They stood there awkwardly in front of each other for a moment. Paul spoke first.

"Hungry?" he asked. Even though she hadn't eaten all day, she wasn't. She couldn't eat. Her stomach was in knots, and she wasn't sure how she would keep anything down. She shook her head. "Right. Well, I just got off shift, and I'm starving, so I'm gonna get something if that's okay."

"Of course," she said, but he was already stepping past her.

She walked over to the picnic table furthest away, down by the pond. She sat down and waited for Paul, trying to decide what to say first.

His eyes found her, and he made his way down the small hill and sat across from her. He picked up his burger and took a bite, never looking up at her.

"Paul, I'm sorry. I never wanted you to find out that way."

He wiped his mouth with a napkin. "Seems to me like you never wanted me to find out at all."

"That's not true. I've been trying to figure out what I'm gonna do about it, and also worrying about how to tell you when things seemed like they were going so well."

His eyes searched her face. "This isn't some minor hiccup, Lue. This is a big deal. It's a baby. It's a life. How could you keep that from me?"

"I wanted to tell you . . ."

"What about the baby's father?"

It caught her off guard. She put her face in her hands and rubbed her forehead. "He's not in the picture. And he's not going to be. It was a mistake. A one-time thing that never should have happened."

"Does he even know?" Paul asked.

Luella shook her head. She didn't want to talk to him about Benjamin. Didn't want him to know about that part of her life. The part that she wasn't proud of. "I doubt he'd care. I'm gonna have to tell him, though. If I want to move forward with putting it up for adoption."

Paul sat back fully in his seat. "Adoption?"

"This baby deserves a proper family. A mom and a dad that love each other and will dote on him or her, and a house with a white picket fence. Something that I can never give it."

Paul scoffed. "That's an excuse, and you know it. You still don't get it. You never have. Families come in all shapes and sizes. And thank God for that. Otherwise, I wouldn't have one if not for Helen and Fred."

"I didn't mean—"

"Yes, you did. You've always been so blinded and bitter about what you never had that you couldn't see the value in what you did have."

"Paul," she pleaded. He had never been this hard on her before. Maybe he had thought these things, but he had never said them out loud to her. Her stomach twisted, making her feel nauseous.

"No. The only thing that matters is how you choose to see it. You don't have a husband? So what? You don't have a house and a white picket fence? Who cares. Can you love and care for this baby? Yes. Can you make sure that baby feels everything you never got from Mya? Yes."

Her eyes studied the wooden table in front of her, as tears brimmed the edges. She didn't want to look up at him. He was right, and it stung a million times harder coming from him.

But there was another part of her that wondered if she was like Mya—willing to give it up because she wanted Paul more. She wanted her own happiness more. At that moment, she forgave Mya a little. Understanding how she must have felt. Stuck. Wanting something else. Wanting *someone* else.

Paul was right. She could have this baby, make it work if she tried hard enough. Her heart was full of so much confusion. A tear fell down her cheek. She lifted her hand and wiped it away quickly.

Paul sighed, and his face softened. "Look at me," he said, which only made her tears fall faster. He leaned over the table and wiped the wetness from her cheeks. She looked up at him. "It's gonna be okay. Whatever you decide. I just want you to know that you *are* enough for this baby. It's your choice, of course. But I know you. That baby would be lucky to have you as its mama."

She gave him a small smile and wiped her eyes as he pulled back. She gazed at a group of ducks crossing the pond while Paul finished his dinner.

She wasn't sure where that left them, but maybe it wasn't the time to figure it out. As much as she wanted to ask or bring it up, she decided not to. She'd let the dust settle and see how things panned out. It was an odd sort of feeling, finding herself in the same situation she was in eleven years earlier, in the exact same place, wondering what the future held for her and Paul.

When he was done, he threw a few pieces of bread to the ducks as they made their way over to where Luella and Paul were. Probably smelled the food. Paul smiled when one of them squawked. Luella wanted to reach out and touch the dimples that she loved so much, but she stopped herself.

She decided right then and there that she would fight as hard as she had to, to not lose him again. This time she wouldn't run away. She'd stay and fight for what she wanted. Something that she hadn't done in a long, long time.

Luella followed Paul up the hill as he threw away his trash. Then, they strolled side by side over to Paul's truck. "Thanks for meeting me. I just needed to tell you face to face that I'm sorry. I should have told you sooner."

Paul stiffened. "I get why you didn't. It just caught me off guard. Came out of nowhere."

"Yeah, kind of like you bringing Claire," said Luella.

Paul looked up at her a bit surprised. She felt a little guilty for sliding that bit in there, but she just couldn't help herself.

"Claire and I are done. For good. I told her about us. About how things were going really good before that night . . ."

"They can still be good," Luella said, reaching for his hand. His jaw tensed, but he wrapped his fingers around hers. She stepped closer to him and looked up into his honey-colored eyes. "I still love you."

He took a deep breath and closed his eyes. When he opened them again, Luella saw the conflict they held. This wouldn't be an easy fix. It was going to take time.

"I just need some space," he said. Luella felt like the wind had been knocked out of her. She couldn't even muster up a response.

Paul leaned down and placed a kiss gently on her forehead. Then he stepped around her and got into his truck to leave.

~

That night when she walked in the door, Helen was waiting for her in the kitchen. She sat at the little round table, drinking a cup of hot tea. Gus was laying on the floor beside her feet. It was barely nine o'clock, but Percy was already gone, and Helen had changed into her pajamas.

Luella had driven around for almost an hour after she left Paul because she was sure Helen and Percy would still be enjoying their evening.

"How was dinner?" Luella asked.

"Fine," Helen said.

Luella slumped down onto the chair in front of Helen. "Just fine? That's it? I kind of expected him to still be here."

"We're not teenagers," said Helen. "We had dinner, a lovely conversation, dessert, and then he left."

"Did he kiss you goodnight?" Luella asked, smirking. Helen's eyes shot up, and Luella smirked. "I'll take that as a no then."

"I wouldn't kiss and tell anyway," Helen said, taking another sip of coffee. "How did your night go?"

Luella shrugged her shoulders. "I met Paul at Jerry's. He says he needs space."

Helen nodded. "That's understandable."

Luella knew it was, but it wasn't what she wanted to hear. She wanted Helen to tell her it would be okay in the end. That it would work out. Because that was easier to hear. "I know . . . maybe we're just forcing this. Maybe it's not really meant to be, and this is the hint I'm not taking."

Helen blew out a breath. "Giving up is the easy part. You know what's harder? Working it out. Nothing worth having ever just falls into place. It takes work and commitment. It takes an honest effort every single day on both your parts. Because real love is worth the work. Once that honeymoon phase you feel at the beginning of a relationship passes, that's when you know. That's where you'll find out the nitty-gritty part of it."

"You think me and Paul are meant to be?"

Helen nodded her head just once. "I always have. You two will work it out. It'll all be okay."

Luella's throat went dry, and her eyes burned. Helen would never know how much that single statement coming from her had meant to Luella.

Just a few months ago, she would be itching to get up from the table and go to her room to be by herself—uncomfortable in Helen's presence. But now she found she wasn't ready to turn in for the night. She wanted to linger a little longer around the small kitchen table with Helen, soaking in her presence as long as she could.

# thirty

Luella sometimes wondered about the children who passed through the farm. Who were they now? Did they ever think about this place? If they did, how did they remember it? Was it anything like she remembered it?

She always found it incredibly interesting how subjective experiences were. How one person could find something beautiful, while another thought it horrible.

At the end of June, she got an answer when one of Helen's foster children showed up on Helen's doorstep. She was a petite thing with mousey brown ringlet curls and a gap in her teeth. She couldn't have been more than twenty. Luella had never seen her before, so she must have come through after Luella had already left. When she asked to see Helen, Luella led her into the living room where Helen sat watching television. "Helen, someone's here to see you."

Helen looked up groggily.

"Hey, Mom."

Helen looked her over as if she was trying to remember her. When the girl smiled, Helen shot to life. "Susie! What are you doing here?"

The girl leaned down to give Helen a hug, and Luella noticed the way the girl lingered. When she pulled back, tears were streaming down her face.

"Oh, stop that," said Helen, wiping at Susie's cheeks.

"I'm sorry. Didn't think I'd cry. I promised myself I wouldn't."

"It's alright as long as they're happy tears," Helen said with a smile.

Luella was glad the girl had come. Helen needed this visit. She had been pushing everyone away. Luella read that might happen eventually and would be an indicator of declining health—pushing away loved ones and cutting themselves off so it would be easier when the time came.

Helen didn't want to see anyone, so it was a good thing Susie showed up unannounced. Luella turned to leave the room, but Helen stopped her.

"You don't have to leave, Luella. You can stay and chat."

When Luella turned back toward them, Susie smiled timidly, but Luella could see the hesitation in her eyes. She didn't know Luella, and she probably came looking to have an intimate visit alone with Helen. Especially if she knew Helen was sick. "I'm just gonna go make you some tea. Would you like some tea, too, Susie?"

"That would be nice. Thank you."

Luella nodded and walked toward the kitchen. She stopped behind the wall and listened to Helen ask Susie about her life.

Susie was doing great. She moved to Mobile, Alabama, with her older sister and gotten a job at the local department store and was on her way to becoming the store manager. After that, her sights were set on becoming district manager. She was proud, and she wanted Helen to be proud, too. Helen congratulated her and told her she knew she could do it. Susie said when she heard Helen was sick, she cried for days. She wasn't sure she'd be able to come back and see her, but she told her sister and her boss she just had to. The farm was her home. The only one she ever had.

Luella wasn't sure how much time Helen had left, but she couldn't imagine driving to a visit knowing it was probably the last time you were going to see someone you loved. How does the heart process that? Perhaps in shock so the mind keeps the body moving in order to make it happen. Luella was sure Susie's heart would process it all the way back to Alabama.

She stopped listening and walked over to the stove to make the tea. When she finished, she carried the mugs back into the living room.

Susie's eyes were red and her face blotchy like she had been crying. She held a tissue in her hand, wringing it back and forth. Processing. Luella sat with them, and Helen made the conversation flow with stories about Susie's time at the farm.

When the conversation lessened and Helen's eyes looked tired, Susie noticed and said she should get going. She had a long drive back to Mobile. Helen nodded, grateful for Susie's discernment.

Luella walked Susie out to the driveway. When they reached her car, Susie turned around and looked at the farmhouse like she was memorizing everything about it.

If a house could talk, what would it say? If a house had feelings, how would it feel?

Susie closed her eyes and smiled fondly, like the house itself had whispered a tender goodbye in her ear. Luella looked back at the house just to be sure it hadn't.

After she left, Luella walked back into the living room. Helen looked over at her. Her face looked more sunken in than usual. She needed to rest. But Luella knew better than to say so.

"Susie's always been a sensitive soul," said Helen.

Luella nodded. She didn't know Susie, so she couldn't agree. She had to take Helen's word for it. "Do you remember them all?"

Helen waited a moment before answering. "Yes, I do," she finally said, proud. "Every single one."

"How?" asked Luella. She couldn't imagine how many children had passed through the house, let alone how Helen would remember them all. Helen leaned over to the small table beside the sofa, pulled the drawer open, and reached in, pulling out a worn-out leather Bible.

She flipped through the pages until she came to a folded-up piece of paper. She held it out for Luella, who took it and unfolded it.

There on the notebook paper, line by line, was the name of every child she'd ever fostered, along with their age and the dates they were hers. There had to be at least a hundred in all. She looked up at Helen. "Why do you have this?"

"To remember," said Helen. "I still pray for every single one of them by name." Luella sat frozen, staring at Helen. "I pray for where they are, for what they're doing, but mostly, for who they've become."

"Even the bad ones?" asked Luella.

Helen rolled her eyes like Luella had said something silly. "There are no bad ones. We're all bad. We're all good. We're shaped by what happens to us and how we choose to see those things."

Luella studied the paper that was smudged and tattered from years of being folded and unfolded. She went down the list, recognizing a few names as she went. But the one that stopped her eyes from scanning further was *Rebecca Blevins.*

"What ever happened to Rebecca?"

Helen furrowed her brows as she thought. "She met someone and moved up to North Georgia around Blairsville, I believe. She calls me now and then. Seems to be happy, which is a good thing because she wasn't a happy child."

"She hated me," said Luella. "I never understood why."

Helen sighed. "Before your mother brought you here, your grandpa and I had spoken a few times about adopting Rebecca. One of those times, I caught her eavesdropping on us. But after you came, life got a little crazy, and we never followed through. I've always regretted that."

It all made sense after that. Rebecca blamed Luella. If she had never come to the farm, Rebecca would probably be a McCrae. But Luella came in, already a namesake, and stole that opportunity from her. *How ironic*. They weren't that different after all. They both just wanted a family to belong to. Rebecca almost had that chance, while Luella took hers for granted.

After dinner that night, Luella picked up both their plates as she got up from the table. She set them down beside the sink full of dishes. When she turned the water on, Helen interrupted.

"I've got something to show you," she said, getting up from her chair.

Luella looked back at the sink overflowing with dishes.

"Don't worry about those right now. Just follow me," Helen said before turning and walking toward the living room.

Once there, Helen pointed to something in the corner of the room. A rather large object with a cream-colored sheet thrown over it. How long had it been sitting there? Luella hadn't noticed it before.

"What is it?" Luella asked.

"It's for you. You know . . . if you need it," Helen said, slowly lowering herself onto the couch.

Luella walked over to the object and gently tugged at the sheet. It fell to the ground, revealing an antique wooden baby crib. The sight of it made Luella's heart ache. She wasn't sure what she was expecting, but it wasn't this. She looked back at Helen and noticed the subtle way the corners of her mouth turned up. Luella looked back at the crib and ran her fingers along the walnut-colored rail. She marveled over the carved, ornate detail on the posts in the corners.

"This is beautiful," Luella said. "But I'm not sure—"

"I said *if* you need it."

Luella considered it for a moment and then finally said, "Thank you."

Helen nodded just once in response, but her misty brown eyes made Luella feel a rush of emotion she wasn't expecting. She swallowed against the lump in her throat and sat down on the loveseat beside the couch. After a moment she asked, "Where did it come from?"

"It was up in the attic. I had Paul bring it down last time he came by."

He had only come by two times since she saw him at Jerry's. He was distant, and unsure.

Luella wondered how they'd done it without her knowing. Couldn't stop herself from wondering what Paul had been thinking when he saw it, carried it, down the stairs for Helen, knowing she intended it as a gift for Luella.

She looked over at the crib again, wondering too about its history. It was in great condition, despite appearing well loved.

"Whose was it?" she asked.

"It was your mother's first, then you used it for a little while. After that, the few babies we had come through the house used it, too."

Luella wondered how long it had been sitting up in the attic, waiting for another baby to come along and need it once more.

She tried to envision herself standing beside it, looking down at a baby cooing back at her. But the vision was blurry and distorted, making her heartbeat quicken with panic and fear. She took a deep breath and let it out slowly, telling herself there was still time to decide. She brought her hands up to the front of her belly and let them rest there as Helen turned the volume up on the television, ending the night with their usual *Golden Girl* reruns.

Luella gazed over at Helen, noting how tiny her frail body looked against the backdrop of the old couch.

*There's still time,* she thought. There had to be.

# thirty-one

I don't know what they put in this tea," Meggie said, taking another sip of the pink drink she clutched in her hand. "But I know that after I drink one, I'm ready to conquer the world. I swear the last time I cleaned my entire house—baseboards, windows, blinds. Everything. How's yours?"

Luella took a sip of her milkshake. "Not bad."

Meggie had convinced Luella to meet her in town so they could visit with each other while she ran some errands. Luella agreed, even though the late June weather was sweltering hot and so humid it left a person gasping for air. But she didn't have any plans and took the opportunity to spend some time with her best friend because Meggie's life was so busy between all the hats she wore and the to-do lists she juggled.

Meggie had been raving about a new place that opened in town that sold meal replacement protein shakes and loaded teas—which were all the rage.

After they got their drinks, they walked two stores down to the local boutique. "You've really popped," Meggie said, motioning to Luella's belly.

"Yeah, it's getting harder to hide these days. We're a little over halfway now. Twenty-one weeks to be exact." Luella grabbed at her kimono, trying unsuccessfully to pull it tighter around her as they stepped into the small boutique.

A peppy young girl stood behind a counter made from the front end of a VW bus. She looked up and welcomed them into the store. Meggie perused the racks, grabbing one thing after another, piling it all in her arms. She pulled out a flowy peach peplum top. "You would look so cute in this."

Luella took another sip of her milkshake. "I'd look like a giant peach. I'd feel like one, too."

"If you say so," Meggie said, hanging it back on the rack. "Hey, how is your writing going?" She pushed aside hanger after hanger, looking through the rack as though it were a competition to see how much she could grab in a short amount of time.

"Not great. I feel stuck creatively. I haven't been able to write in months. Anything I start just doesn't feel right. It feels forced. I don't know if it's just being back here under the same roof as Helen or everything else . . . probably all of it. But I just can't seem to find my words anymore. I open my laptop and try, but nothing comes out." Luella rolled her eyes when she realized Meggie hadn't even looked up from her shopping. "Are you even listening?"

"Yeah, I heard you. Creatively blocked. Can't find words. They'll come to you; I know they will."

"You're a robot," Luella said with a laugh, flipping through a rack even though she wasn't really looking.

"No, I'm a mom. We're good at multitasking. You just wait until—" As soon as she said it, she looked up apologetically. "Sorry. I didn't mean . . ."

"It's okay," Luella said, quickly grabbing another top from a rack. She held it out for Meggie.

"I like it," Meggie said. She reached out and took it, stacking it on top of the already enormous pile in her arm. They made their way through the racks, back to the fitting area. Luella sat down on a vintage pink suede couch beside the five stations meant to be dressing rooms. The only thing in between the spaces were sheets of plywood and floral shower curtains.

"Give me a fashion show," Luella teased.

Meggie hung the mountain of clothing on the hooks, then lifted her eyebrows up and down as she yanked the floral curtain shut behind her.

A Goo Goo Dolls song started playing through the speakers, and Luella smiled. They were her favorite band, and it was her favorite song. It always made her think about the farm and about Paul. Something about grown up orphans and never knowing their names. She'd smile every time she heard that beginning acoustic riff come through the speaker.

Meggie yanked the curtain to the side. She had on a black and white stripped midi dress. "How about this?"

Luella scrunched her nose up and shook her head.

Meggie huffed. "You're right," she said before sliding the curtain back.

"So, what do you need this dress for anyway?" Luella asked, taking another sip of her milkshake. She could see Meggie's feet under the door as she dropped one dress and tried on another.

"Will's firm hosts a charity gala every year in Atlanta. It's a big shindig, and it means I get a night off to enjoy myself . . . and my husband." Meggie's voice billowed through the boutique as she tried to talk loud enough for Luella to hear. After a few seconds she asked, "How are things with you and Paul?"

"The same, I guess. I haven't seen him in almost two weeks. He said he needed some space."

Meggie yanked the curtain aside once more. This time, she had on a fancy sequin top with faux leather pants. Luella's eyebrows shot up. "Too much," she said. Meggie nodded in agreement and closed the curtain behind her.

The boutique door opened, and a bell chimed. The same peppy girl happily greeted the woman entering. When the woman turned her head to say hello back, Luella realized that the woman was Claire. She felt frozen in the seat. What were the odds? But that seemed to be happening to her a lot lately.

Luella turned away from her, hoping to hide herself from Claire's eyes. Meggie was talking away behind the curtain, and Luella kept the conversation flowing by saying *uh-huh* and agreeing with everything Meggie said, even though she wasn't paying any attention to what any of it was. She was too busy trying to keep eyes on Claire, so she could keep Claire's eyes off her. She watched Claire thumb through several racks, picking a few things up. Then, she walked up to the counter where the girl was sitting, and Luella heard her ask where the fitting rooms were. Her heart started racing. She had to get away from the fitting rooms fast. "Meggie, I'm gonna go to the bathroom. Be right back."

"Okay," Meggie said through the curtain, but Luella was already walking as fast as she could to the back of the store and out of sight. She went into the restroom, shut the door, and locked it behind her. Then, she took a deep breath and let it out. This was just another reason she had left town at eighteen. In the city, you could easily escape from people you didn't want to see. The chances of running into them at a random boutique store downtown were way slimmer than in a tiny town like Chipley Creek.

When she finally came back out, Meggie was hanging the clothes she didn't want on a rack beside the stalls. Luella looked around, but didn't see Claire. She assumed that meant she was in the only other closed stall, or she had left already. Meggie had two tops in her hand as she walked toward the register.

"There you are. You alright?" Meggie asked.

She nodded as she peered over Meggie's shoulder to the only closed fitting room stall. The curtain slid quickly to the side, and Luella saw Claire's eyes land on her. She imagined smoke blowing out of her ears like they did on all those Saturday morning cartoons she watched as a kid. Claire hung her clothes on the rack and stomped toward Luella. Meggie was too busy with her purchase and conversation with the girl behind the counter to notice.

"Hi, Claire," Luella said, as Claire came to a stop in front of her.

But Claire didn't say a word. She just looked her up and down, like she was assessing a mannequin. Her eyes stalled on Luella's protruding, rounded belly. She scoffed, like she was disgusted, which made Luella's cheeks grow hot. "You really should be ashamed of yourself, trapping a good man like Paul."

"I'm not trapping anybody."

"If that's what you want to tell yourself," Claire said, stepping past her and toward the counter.

Meggie came up and looked between the two of them as Claire turned to give Luella another look of disgust. The girl behind the counter busied herself scanning Claire's items.

"What's going on?" Meggie asked, but Luella didn't answer. She was still looking at Claire. Meggie put her hand on Luella's arm to break her from her trance.

Claire finished her purchase and turned to leave. She stopped in front of Luella and sucked in a breath of air and said, "If you really loved him, you'd let him go."

Meggie's face changed from a look of confusion to one of shock as she processed what was going on. When Luella said nothing in her own defense, Meggie stepped in front of her.

"Look here, how about you retract the claws and go on about your day like the grown up you're supposed to be. Mmkay?"

Claire smirked and walked past them toward the door. The bell dinged as it slammed shut behind her. The girl at the register looked around a bit awkwardly before disappearing to the back room.

"I assume that was Claire?" said Meggie, walking toward the door. When Luella nodded, Meggie went on. "Well, at least it sounds like Paul ended it for good. Because that girl was bitter." Meggie laughed as Luella's phone started ringing.

Luella stopped walking and fished through her purse, trying to find it. As she pulled it out, her eyes landed on Cheryl's name on the screen. She answered quickly.

Cheryl was frantic.

Luella could hardly understand a word she was saying. She asked her to slow down so she could hear her better. When Cheryl finally took a few breaths and started again, Luella had to catch her own breath.

"It's Helen," Cheryl said. "You need to come to the hospital."

# thirty-two

The drive to the hospital this time around had the same heaviness as before, only now it was vastly different in weight.

Six months ago, she felt like she had little to lose. But she couldn't say the same anymore. The ache in her chest let her know just how much Helen had come to mean to her. How she looked forward to their systematic morning routine and conversations over cups of hot coffee. Or their quiet evenings spent watching *Jeopardy*, followed by *Golden Girls* and reading books as they watched.

It wasn't enough time.

Had she enjoyed those moments enough? Cherished them enough? Funny how it takes feeling like you're about to lose someone to understand exactly how much they mean to you.

Luella looked out the passenger window, staring into space as the streets and trees and houses flew by. Meggie insisted on driving her there. Said she wouldn't chance Luella being too upset or frantic on top of being pregnant. Luella didn't have the energy to argue against it, so she gave in.

When they arrived at the hospital, Meggie barely got the van parked before Luella was pulling the handle and hustling her way into the building. Her heart raced as the Emergency Room doors slid open. As she walked through, her eyes landed on Cheryl, who flew up from her seat in the waiting room and rushed over. Taylor sat slumped down in the seat beside

Cheryl's, her sad eyes watching them as they spoke. Meggie walked past Cheryl and Luella and plopped down beside Taylor, striking up a conversation. Luella was thankful for Meggie's mothering instincts.

Cheryl grabbed Luella into a hug and then pulled back, wringing her hands as she spoke.

"They won't let me back there. They brought her here by ambulance. I was following them when Taylor reminded me I needed to call you. My head was in a million different places. I'm sorry I didn't call sooner."

"What happened?"

Cheryl shook her head. "We went over to take her a pie and found her slumped down on the sofa. I could hardly get her to come to. She wasn't making any sense, and I just knew something was wrong. I called 911 immediately. They came fast and assessed her. That's when they said she'd need to come to the hospital by ambulance."

"Where is she?"

"Back there somewhere." Cheryl looked over her shoulder toward the doors leading to the exam rooms. "They won't let me back there because I'm not family." She scoffed. "But I told them you were on your way. I don't know anything other than that."

"Okay," Luella said. "Thank you, Cheryl." She nodded as Luella moved past her and over to the reception desk. The man sitting behind the desk looked up. "My name is Luella McCrae. My grandmother was brought here by ambulance—Helen McCrae."

The man looked the information up on the computer. "She's in the fourth room on the right," he said, pushing a button to unlock the doors.

Luella looked back at Cheryl, Taylor, and Meggie sitting in the waiting room. Then, she took a deep breath and pushed the door open.

Nurses walked up and down the cold hallway. Luella could hear chatter in the other patient rooms. When she reached the fourth door, she knocked lightly and then pushed it open. Helen was laying in the bed asleep. There was an oxygen mask over her face and an IV hooked up to her arm. Luella walked slowly over to the bed. She put her hand over Helen's.

"I'm here. You're not alone," she said. Then, she pulled a chair over to the side of the bed and sank down into its worn-out cushion and watched the slow rise and fall of Helen's chest. A tear fell down Luella's cheek. "Please don't leave me yet," she whispered. "I'm not ready."

A doctor came in after what felt like hours. It was the same doctor Luella had seen the first time at the hospital. He looked over at Helen sleeping, and back at Luella. His lips pressed together in a thin line, and his eyes were unreadable.

"Is she gonna be okay?"

"She's very sick," he said.

Helen woke, pulling at the oxygen mask on her face. She pulled it down. "Don't talk about me like I'm not here."

The doctor smiled. *Typical Helen.* Even he was used to her antics. He stepped forward. "We're going to admit you, Helen. Run some tests. Get some answers. See what's going on."

"We both know what's going on," she said, looking him in the eyes.

He sighed; his eyes locked on hers. Then, he looked over at Luella and spoke directly to her.

"We're gonna run some tests and figure out what we need to do."

"I'm tired," Helen said, pulling the oxygen back over her face. The way she said it made Luella's heart ache, made her wonder if she meant she wanted rest or if she was tired of this battle altogether. She wondered how much longer Helen could go on like this.

The doctor nodded. "We'll get you moved up to a room as soon as we can."

But Helen's eyes were already closed.

"Thank you," Luella said to him. He gave her a sad smile and left the small room. Luella got up. "I'll be right back," she said.

Helen nodded, but didn't open her eyes.

She walked back out to the waiting room, knowing Cheryl, Taylor, and Meggie sat waiting for news. When the doors opened, she saw Paul sitting beside them now. Taylor leaned against him. They looked up as she approached. Cheryl shot up from the seat. "How is she?"

"I'm not sure. She's resting. They're gonna admit her and run some tests. See what's going on. I'll let y'all know something as soon as I do." She looked over at Meggie. "You should get home to Will and the girls."

"I need to know you'll be alright before I go," she said, looking at Luella through concerned eyes.

"I'll be okay," Luella said.

Meggie got up, grabbed her keys, and then hugged Luella. "Please don't be mad," she whispered in Luella's ear. "I had to call him."

She pulled back and made an apologetic face. Luella couldn't be mad at her. Helen was the only mother Paul had ever known. Luella should have called him as soon as she got off the phone with Cheryl.

"You call me if you need anything at all," Meggie said.

Luella nodded. "Thanks." Cheryl hugged her next. She held on a lot longer than Meggie did, and Luella knew it must have been eating her up, not being able to see Helen after how she found her. Helen was her best friend. If it were Meggie, Luella would feel the same way. "I'll call you as soon as I know anything, I promise."

Cheryl nodded; her eyes watery around the edges. "Come on, Taylor."

Meggie, Taylor, and Cheryl all walked out together, leaving Paul and Luella behind. Paul stood up, his eyes on Luella's as he stepped toward her. They stood there for a few seconds, just staring at each other. Her heart beat faster. They had been here before. It was a familiar ache, only this time, it was one they could see coming. It wasn't a curve ball like with Grandpa Fred. They were forced to live each day knowing what was coming with Helen. Luella wasn't sure which was worse. Knowing it was coming, or being blindsided by it, unable to say goodbye.

They were each their own kind of hell.

Finally, Paul wrapped his arms around her. She breathed in deep and let it out, and let go of what was happening between them, because it wasn't about them right now. It was about Helen.

She put her arms around his waist and held on to him as hard as she could, relishing the safety of being wrapped up in his arms.

When they finally let go of each other, she said, "I'm sorry I didn't call."

"It's okay . . . how is she, really?"

Luella knew he wanted the raw version, not the fluffed up one that she gave Cheryl and Meggie. And he deserved the truth. "I think she's hanging on by a thread . . ." Her voice caught in her throat. She sucked in a breath, pushed her shoulders back, and began again. "She's tired. The doctor said they'd run some tests, but it looked like he already knew. Like he was doing it because he had to. Helen even said they both knew what was going on. I was the only one sitting there in denial."

Paul's eyebrows furrowed, and the sides of his mouth turned downward.

She knew he didn't want to say it, either. Not out loud. As if holding it back could prolong the inevitable.

"I should get back," Luella said. "I don't want to leave her alone for too long. We'll be in a room soon, I hope."

He nodded at her words, but she could see the anguish in his eyes. "Okay," he said. "But I'm gonna stay. I'll be right here if you need me."

She threw her arms around him again and held on to him as if he were a lifeline, charging up her strength.

"Tell her I love her," he said.

~

Two hours later, they were finally moved to a room on the Med-Surg floor of the hospital. Paul came up and saw Helen for a few minutes. Just long enough to lay eyes on her and see that she was, at least for now, okay.

The room was bigger, and Luella felt less stressed without the hustle and bustle of the Emergency Room. The sun was setting and Luella looked out the window at the cotton candy colored sky. Blue sky covered in clouds that looked more pink than white. It had always been her favorite. She pulled the blinds up so Helen could see it, too.

She was awake, watching television. Luella turned around and leaned against the windowsill.

Helen looked over at her. "You really don't have to stay with me. It's not necessary. They'll probably let me out of here tomorrow. The animals are probably starving."

"Cheryl and Taylor are taking care of it."

"Still," said Helen. "It doesn't make much sense for both of us to be here. It's not the most comfortable place to sleep." She looked at Luella's belly and back up at her face.

"I'm not leaving," Luella said, her head held high in defiance. She was, after all, Helen's granddaughter. If she inherited no other traits from the woman, they were neck to neck in stubbornness.

She sat down in the chair beside Helen's bed and watched old sitcom reruns with her until the sky was black and the night was thick.

Nurses came in and out every hour, taking blood samples and checking vital signs. It seemed every time she had just fallen asleep, there would be another one coming through the doors. Helen was right. It was the worst kind of sleep.

At three in the morning, Luella woke to find Helen awake, staring into space.

Luella leaned forward and put her hand on Helen's leg. Helen looked over at her. "Are you okay?" Luella asked, scooting the chair closer to her side.

"Mmm," Helen mumbled in response.

"Where were you just now?" Luella asked. Helen had looked lost in a trance. Luella knew that sometimes, before a person died, they would see things that weren't really there. Or maybe they were there, and it was others who couldn't see.

"Walking beside the ocean," Helen said. Then, she closed her eyes and smiled as if she was there again.

A peace came over her face that made Luella's heart ache. Luella watched her until her smile faded and her face relaxed from slipping back into a deep sleep.

~

The next morning, the doctor opened Helen's door. His face looked pinched, and his brows furrowed together as he said good morning and walked fully into the room. "We got some of your labs back," he said. "May I speak openly?" he asked, looking toward Luella and back to Helen. She nodded. "It's not good," he said. "Your body isn't responding to the medicine anymore. We could try a stronger treatment, but—"

"No." Helen said it adamantly.

Luella looked over at her. "But if a stronger medicine will help, then why not?"

"No." She said it louder this time, like they weren't taking her seriously. Then, she took a deep breath, as if it had taken every ounce of strength out of her. "Stronger medicine means stronger side effects. And there's no guarantee how long it will even work, if it does at all."

The doctor shifted from one foot to the other. "Sometimes it does, yes. But it may also give you more time." He looked over at Luella for just a second after he said it.

Helen noticed. She held her hand out for Luella, who took it with misty eyes. Helen leaned her head forward a little and said, "There will never be enough time. There's only now, and making sure it counts."

She understood what Helen was saying and nodded in agreement. They'd make the most of whatever time they had left. She had to respect Helen's wishes. After all, they'd already had years. It wasn't fair to pressure Helen into a decision she didn't want because Luella hadn't made the most of the years she had already been given. But that's the thing. You never really know what you've lost until you've lost it. Just like Mac had told her.

The doctor said he'd discharge her if she was sure. Helen said she was. She'd made up her mind. It was all about palliative care now. If she needed anything, he'd be there to provide it.

If she changed her mind, she knew how to contact him. He didn't urge her one way or the other. He was only concerned about what she wanted. Luella walked to the door with him and followed as he stepped into the hallway. His eyebrows went up in surprise and curiosity.

"Um . . . I'm just wondering what to expect. Toward the end. How am I going to know what to do for her?"

He took a deep breath. "Death from lymphoma is usually comfortable and painless. There are pain meds that can be given to lessen the severity should she need it." He reached into his pocket and took out a card, handing it to her. "Here's my card. You call me if you need anything."

Luella took it from him and nodded. Her voice felt stuck against the dryness at the back of her throat. He put a hand on her shoulder and then walked away. Luella tucked the card into her back pocket and pulled her phone out to send Paul a text: I need your help...

They would be discharged soon to go home. But Luella had no intention of staying at the farm for long.

# thirty-three

A plan was made. It was thrown together quickly, but it was a collective effort to make sure it happened.

Meggie found a house to rent, right on the beach in Fort Morgan. Her mother had insisted on paying for their three-day stay, which only made Luella love Wren that much more. Paul agreed to come along. Cheryl packed a bag for Helen, along with some things she thought she might enjoy, like snacks and magazines. Luella packed herself a bag and changed while they waited on Paul.

Helen was too weak to walk so he borrowed a wheelchair from work and rented an accessible van for them to drive.

When they told Helen, her eyes lit up.

Cheryl and Taylor came to see them off. Luella handed Cheryl a piece of paper with the address of where they were staying, along with the numbers she could reach them at, in case she needed them. Cheryl told them not to worry—they would take care of the farm and the animals.

When Paul's truck turned down the gravel driveway, Cheryl walked over to Helen to say goodbye. Tears streamed down her cheeks as she hugged Helen tight. No one knew what was going to happen next, or when. Luella could see plain as day that Cheryl was scared she was saying goodbye to her friend forever.

It was a four-hour drive if the traffic wasn't bad. Luella and Paul wanted to wait until morning to leave, but after Helen found out, she wanted to go as soon as possible. She said she couldn't wait until the morning. So, they loaded up and were on their way.

Helen sat in the front beside Paul, with her seat leaned back so that she could rest. She had Luella's headphones on, listening to an audiobook.

Luella sat in the captain's seat behind Paul. She wanted to have eyes on Helen the whole time. As Paul drove, Luella jotted down her thoughts on a notepad. Every now and then, she'd look up and find Paul's eyes on her in the rear-view mirror.

And every time, it made her heart skip a beat.

They made good time. They took a right off 59 and headed toward the tip of Fort Morgan. Luella had always loved the quaintness of the small beach town. The way the sun danced through the trees in welcome as they made their way forward, driving past the old church and all the historic houses.

There were only a few hours of daylight left and Paul wanted to find the house and get Helen settled. He said he'd run up to the marketplace for whatever groceries they needed. They found the beach house nestled to the right of several others, but still off to itself.

It was perfect.

Paul helped Helen up the front steps. She was weaker on her feet now than she had been before. It took all of her energy just to make it up the steps.

"Next time, I'm carrying you," said Paul, stepping over the threshold.

Helen snickered. "I'd like to see you try."

Inside, Luella helped Helen to the back of the house where the sliding glass door was. The curtains were shut, casting the house in shadows. Luella grabbed the cord and tugged it, sending the curtains sailing to the side. The room lit up, and the ocean came into full view. Beautiful clear blue water. Luella looked over at Helen. Her eyes were focused on the water, and she was smiling.

"Want to go out there?" Luella asked.

When Helen nodded in response, Luella slid open the glass door, helping her step through it and get settled into a blue cushioned Adirondack chair on the patio. She sat down in the chair next to Helen. The salt air whipped around them as they sat there in silence, soaking up the late afternoon sky.

Luella looked over at Helen. "Are you happy?"

"Very much," said Helen. Then, she took a deep breath and closed her eyes against the sun and smiled.

*There it was.* The same peace that fell over Grandpa Fred every time Luella had seen him close his eyes against the sun. She watched in a quiet awe until Helen opened her eyes again.

"I wish I was strong enough to run along the shoreline while the waves crashed over my feet. Those are the things you take for granted when you're young."

Luella wished she could give Helen her legs, her strength, and her health. She'd do it in a heartbeat. But since she couldn't, she sat in silence beside her instead, listening to the sound of the waves, until Paul found them an hour later.

He picked up groceries and ordered dinner from one of the restaurants in the small town. They sat around the dining room table and ate together like a proper family. Helen took small bites and mostly used her fork to push food around her plate.

Helen went to bed not long after they finished. It had been an exhausting two days, and she needed rest. She had gotten little of it in the hospital with the nurses coming in and out at all hours of the night.

After Helen turned in, it was just Luella and Paul in the quiet of the house.

Without Helen there, the tension between them was thick. Luella busied herself putting groceries away while Paul lugged their bags inside and set them down in the hallway. They insisted Helen take the master bedroom at the back of the house. The other two bedrooms were at the front, across the hall from each other. Paul took his bags into one, and set Luella's in the other. Then, he went into the bathroom.

She went into her bedroom to change clothes while Paul took a shower. Her body was full of anxious energy. She didn't know what to do with herself, so she grabbed her laptop from her bag and opened the bedroom door, telling herself it was so she could tell Paul goodnight, but that was only partially true.

He opened the bathroom door and stepped out in a pair of plaid pajama bottoms and a tight white shirt. Luella noticed the way it squeezed against his arms. He looked over at her open door, and his eyes landed on her sitting on the bed. She wondered if she should have left the door shut instead.

"Goodnight, Lue," he said, then walked into his bedroom, shutting the door behind him.

Luella sank back into the pillows. She wasn't sure what she wanted him to say, but goodnight was certainly not it. She got up and shut the door with a bit more force than intended and then switched off the light and got back in the bed.

~

The next morning, they sat on the back porch soaking up the early July sun before it got too high in the sky and scorching hot. Helen looked serene as she looked out over the ocean. A salty breeze blew by, and she pulled tighter on the blanket draped around her shoulders.

Paul sat on one side of her and Luella on the other, but it was like she didn't even notice they were there as she stared out across the water. "Fred always loved it here," she said.

Luella and Paul exchanged glances as a single tear fell down Helen's cheek. She wiped it away quickly, like she didn't want anyone to see it. Paul leaned over and held his hand out.

Helen placed her hand in his, and they sat like that for a long time.

Several families came out with their kids, claiming their spots on the beach with umbrellas and chairs. Children laughed and played and ran in and out of the water. A man helped his son get a red octopus kite flying high in the air.

Luella could tell that Helen was enjoying the view. She hadn't stopped smiling since they stepped outside. But a part of her heart still ached because she wanted Helen to feel the sand beneath her feet. She wanted her to be down there, not watching from afar.

Luella got up from her chair. "I'll be back," she said. "You need anything?" Helen shook her head and Luella looked over at Paul, who shook his, too.

Inside, Luella pulled out her laptop and opened it up. She was determined to get Helen down to that beach. She searched businesses in Fort Morgan, looking for anywhere that rented motorized carts or ATVs. When she finally found one, she jotted down the address.

After lunch, Helen was tired and decided to lie down for a while. Luella found Paul outside and handed him the piece of paper. "What is this?"

"I need you to go pick up one of these carts for me. I already called and arranged everything." He eyed her suspiciously. "It's for Helen."

That was all she needed to say. He nodded. "I'll go in just a bit."

"Thank you," she said. "Try to be back before sunset."

~

Helen woke up a few hours later. Paul wasn't back yet but would be soon. Luella didn't tell her anything about it. She wanted it to be a surprise. They waited on the back porch. When Paul finally came rolling up, Luella looked over at Helen. "I have a surprise for you," she said. Helen looked at her through cautious eyes as Paul bounced up the steps. "But you're gonna have to let Paul carry you down the steps for this one."

She scoffed, but let Paul help her to her feet. He swooped her up like she was weightless and then he carried her down the steps.

"What is this?" she asked, as Paul sat her down in the passenger seat of the cart.

Luella got into the driver's side. "Just you wait," she said, smiling.

"Lue, I hate to bust your bubble, but the owner said that these things aren't allowed on the beach."

She turned the key, and the cart hummed to life. Then, she looked up at Paul. "Don't you ever break the rules?"

"Lue . . ."

"Chicken."

Paul's face changed from annoyance to amusement as he stepped out of the way, opening the sandy pathway to the beach.

Luella looked over at Helen. She couldn't see her eyes from behind her sunglasses, but she could see her smile. It was ear to ear, and it reached all the way up to the sky.

"You ready?"

Helen nodded, and Luella pressed on the gas. They rolled forward onto the beach, toward the water. There were a few families still out, enjoying the late afternoon sun. She drove the cart right past them and down to the water, stopping just a few feet away from where the waves met the shore.

As she got off the cart, she noticed a few people staring in their direction. One woman stood with a hand on her hip and the other held against her forehead, shielding the sun.

Luella walked around to Helen's side. She had on linen pants, and Luella didn't want them to get wet. She bent down and folded the bottoms of the pant legs up so that they looked like capris. As she stood, she looked back at the house and saw Paul watching them from the back porch. Her heart swelled at the sight of him and how he knew this moment was just for her and Helen.

Luella reached out and held onto Helen's arm as she pressed her feet into the damp, compressed sand. The sun was slowly setting, casting out a burst of orange and pink and yellow across the sky. Helen smiled again as she stepped forward quickly so a coming wave could rush over her feet. When it did, she chuckled. Then, she squished her feet into the sand as the water rushed back toward the sea.

She looked over at Luella and laughed. Luella couldn't stop the smile that spread across her face. They stood there for a few moments as the waves came and went, pulling all the heaviness Luella felt back out to the sea.

After a while, Luella looked over at Helen and said, "Come on. There's more."

Helen's eyes lit up as Luella helped her back into the cart. Luella powered it on and turned it around, so they were facing the sunset. She made sure that no one was on the brief stretch of beach in front of them. Luella pressed the gas and drove as close to the water as she could get and then she pushed the pedal down as far as it would go, sending them flying down the beach.

Helen laughed, a boisterous sound that rolled up from deep within her belly. Luella couldn't help but laugh, too. It was *that* kind of laughter. The contagious, good-for-the-soul kind that feels so rare. Helen's hair blew wildly in the wind as she grabbed hold of the bar in front of her and held her other arm out beside her as if she was flying.

A lump formed in the back of Luella's throat. Her eyes welled up at the sight of Helen in the sunset.

Weightless, soaring; filled with nothing but happiness.

She knew she would always remember this moment in the days, weeks, and months to come. That this one memory would carry her through it all.

After a while, Luella turned the cart around and headed back down the beach toward their rental. As they got closer, Luella noticed a woman at the bottom of the steps by Paul, fussing at him. It was the hand-on-her-hip woman from the beach. She looked like a feisty chihuahua barking at a much bigger dog.

Luella parked the cart beside the back porch steps as an officer walked up. An officer. *You've got to be kidding me.* She twisted the key back, shutting off the cart, and tuned in to listen as the woman complained.

". . . and we locals work real hard to keep the beaches quiet and respectful. We don't want to have to worry about some crazy person flying down the beach on a vehicle."

"It's hardly a vehicle. More like a golf cart," said Paul.

The officer cleared his throat. The woman and Paul looked over at him. "I got a phone call about a vehicle on the beach," the officer said, less than enthused.

"Yes." The woman stepped forward and flicked her hand in Luella's direction. "This woman was flying this motorized cart at a ridiculous speed down the beach. She could have hit kids, or animals. It was unsafe and not to mention, illegal."

Luella stepped off the cart and walked over. "There was no one on the section of beach that we were driving on."

The officer sighed and stiffened, visibly wishing he were somewhere else. "Ma'am, vehicles and ATVs are not permitted on the beach."

"That's what I was telling *him* when you came up," the yappy woman snapped. "Us locals are tired of the blatant disregard of rules around here. It's an absolute—"

"Oh, shove it, blondie."

The four of them looked over at Helen, still sitting in the cart. When she lifted her chin in defiance, they knew it had come from her. The woman's mouth fell open. Paul choked back a laugh as Luella's eyes widened.

The officer suppressed a grin. "I can handle this, Mrs. Mahoney," he said.

The woman stormed off in the direction of her house. Luella looked over at Helen.

"What?" She shrugged her shoulders. "I'm dying, what do I care."

The officer's face softened, and he pushed his sunglasses up on top of his head. "I'm gonna give you a warning on this one." He looked over at Helen, his eyes sad as he took in the sight of her.

It was amazing how quick a person could pity someone, given the facts.

The corners of his mouth turned down, and he pulled his lips tight. "You folks enjoy your visit."

"Thank you," Luella said.

The officer nodded and walked back to his patrol car.

~

The three of them couldn't stop laughing about it over dinner that night. It felt good to laugh. Laughing made everything else feel lighter somehow—as if they could pretend they were just on vacation, enjoying a wonderful dinner together. It was the calcium carbonate to the acid, enough to curb the burning pain of what it really was just long enough for them to relish in that moment together.

After dinner, Helen's face grew serious. She ran her fingers along the fringe at the edge of her place mat. "Thank you both for bringing me here," she said with a faint smile of appreciation. "It's brought me more joy than I've had in a long time."

"It was all Lue's idea. Thank her."

Luella shook her head against Paul's statement. "It wouldn't have happened if he didn't help."

Helen looked between the two of them with her raised eyebrows. "Okay, I'm going to say something now, and that's all I'll say about it."

The two of them looked at her nervously.

"You need to figure this thing out between the two of you. I've never seen two people more meant for each other. You've been glued together ever since you were kids. Something like that doesn't come around often. It takes hard work to make a relationship ebb and flow. But the two of you have the most important piece of that. *Friendship*." She grabbed both of their hands and placed Luella's on top of Paul's. "I think you might be fighting this a little too hard."

She sighed and patted the top of Luella's hand before looking up at them both. Then, she pushed the chair back and said, "I think I'm ready for bed now."

Luella pulled her hand away from Paul's quickly. "I'll help you," she said, getting to her feet.

Paul sat quietly at the table, his face lost in a trance, like he was processing what Helen had said. She had never outright said anything like that before, especially to the two of them.

For all they knew, Helen didn't want them together. She viewed Paul as a son. He had told Luella once that a part of him always felt like he had betrayed Helen and Fred in some way for loving her. He was like their son, and she was their only granddaughter. Fred had died before Paul could confess his feelings about Luella. Helen never pried. She just watched quietly from afar.

For her to approve of their relationship now—to say so out loud to them, meant a lot. She must have known that.

Luella guided Helen into her bedroom, and turned on the lamp beside the bed. Then, she helped Helen into her pajamas. As the gown fell past Helen's head. Luella noticed Helen's eyes were more blue than green. She had never paid attention before. Never been close enough to tell. There was something else there, too.

The dimming of a spark they had always possessed.

Luella helped her into the bed. Helen sat with her back against the upholstered headboard. "I'm gonna read a little while to tire my eyes out."

Luella nodded and turned to step away, but Helen reached out for her. At first, Luella was a little unsure of what she was doing. She couldn't remember the last time that she had been affectionate with Helen—if she even had before.

Helen's hands motioned for her to come closer. Luella sat down on the bed, facing her. Then, Helen leaned forward and wrapped her tiny arms around Luella and held tight for several seconds. Luella leaned into her embrace, letting her hands rest on Helen's bony back. And there it was—a feeling she had never experienced. What it felt like in the safety of a parent's arms. Her eyes welled up. She closed them tight to try and stop the tears from spilling out.

When Helen pulled back, she saw them brimming over the edges of Luella's eyes. She reached out and cupped Luella's cheek and held her gaze for a moment.

Neither said a word. They didn't have to. Luella could feel it—a lifting that she couldn't explain. One that said *you're safe with me*. A love you didn't have to deserve. Love that had been there all along, buried beneath the hard surface like a precious pearl.

Helen leaned back against the headboard. "Chin up," she said.

Luella nodded through tears as she got to her feet. She wiped the wetness from underneath her eyes and reached for the doorknob.

"We'll be right out here if you need anything."

Helen nodded as she picked a book up off the nightstand.

Luella shut the door behind her and looked around for Paul. She found him in the soft glow of the porch light, leaning against the rail. She stood there admiring him through the glass door. The beard on his face from not shaving the past few days suited him well. Her heart fluttered when he looked over and saw her. She pulled open the sliding glass door and stepped out, closing it behind her. The night was breezy but warm. The moonlight was bright overhead. The waves crashed against the shore, singing a rhythmic lullaby for the night sky.

"She's right, you know," said Paul, his eyes fixed on the ocean.

"About what?"

He turned his head to look at her. "You and me." Luella felt her heart drop as Paul turned and cast his eyes back to the ocean. "I always believed that you were made just for me. And I hate to admit it, but I'm most thankful for the day your mom left you. Because it brought you to me."

Luella walked over to the rail, her eyes still on him, willing him to look at her. Her protruding belly separated them. It was the only thing in between them anymore. Not distance, not Claire, and not Helen. She looked down at the bump, instinctively bringing her hand to it. "There's so much I would change if I could."

It took him a few seconds, but then he stepped closer. Her eyes were still on the ground as he lifted her chin up with his finger. "But then you wouldn't be who you are. You wouldn't be this version of you . . . and I think she's pretty great."

A tear fell down her cheek. Her hand flew to her face to wipe it off. "These hormones are getting the best of me," she said, rolling her eyes as more tears fell. She finally met his gaze and smiled. Paul's eyes drifted down to her stomach. Luella instinctively wanted to pull for the cover of a kimono, but this was the first time she hadn't tried to cover it up. The first time she put on a maternity top with rouching at the sides that accentuated her swollen stomach.

Paul slowly pressed a hand to her stretched-tight belly.

She was unsure how she felt about it. A part of her felt ashamed. But another part of her liked it more than she cared to admit. She had always dreamed that one day she would carry Paul's baby.

But this baby wasn't Paul's. And though it wasn't a part of Paul, it was a part of her. She still hadn't quite worked out what that meant.

# thirty-four

They had three glorious days together at the beach. When they got back, Helen was in unusually good spirits. She had a burst of energy that made it seem like she was on the upside of the lymphoma.

For a few days, their lives went back to normal. Their routine picked up right where it left off, as if the beach had provided a kind of healing for Helen.

That's what Luella told herself.

On the fifth day back, they ate lunch together at the small round table in the kitchen, like they always did. Afterwards, Helen went to lie down, like she always did.

Luella went into Helen's bedroom just before dinner because she hadn't woken up yet. When she pushed the door open, Helen was still sound asleep in her bed. Luella walked over to her. "Helen," she whispered, sitting down on the bed beside her. "It's time to wake up. Dinner's done."

When Helen didn't move, Luella's heart started racing. She placed her hand over Helen's and still felt warmth. She looked for the slow rise and fall of her chest but didn't see it.

"Helen," she said, getting more frantic by the second. She knew then, but she leaned over anyway and pressed her ear to Helen's chest, listening for a heartbeat to prove her wrong.

But there wasn't one.

Luella choked back a sob. "No, no, no . . ." she said, pulling back. She shook Helen's body with her hands. "Please wake up."

Her eyes scanned over Helen's face as she tried to will it away. Helen's hair was tousled, and Luella reached out through watery eyes and smoothed it back. Her face was peaceful, now in an eternal sleep.

Luella looked at the empty space next to Helen, then at the plaid pajama bottoms on the floor. She told herself Helen had chosen exactly where she wanted to leave the world—in the bed she had shared with her husband for thirty-two years.

And now, they were finally together again.

What Luella would have given to have had the chance to say goodbye. But wasn't that what she had been doing all these months? Slowly saying goodbye?

Helen said things were better done quickly and unexpected, like ripping off a bandage. If you couldn't see it coming, you wouldn't feel the pain until after it was already over.

Luella called Paul first. She couldn't say it out loud to him, but she didn't need to. He knew. He told her to call 911, and he'd be there as soon as he could.

Paramedics arrived first. Then the coroner. Luella didn't stay in the room while they did what they needed to pronounce her dead. She didn't even stay in the house—couldn't bear it. She sat on the front porch steps. She didn't want to remember how it looked to watch them come in and take her away.

Paul's truck came barreling down the driveway like he was in a race against time. But he was already too late. He jumped out of the truck and rushed over to the porch. Luella stood up and staggered toward him.

She didn't cry out, but her chest heaved up and down while her body shook.

"I'm here, baby." His strong arms wrapped around her and held her tight. It took her a few moments to notice the quiet tears streaming down his face.

Cheryl came racing up on her golf cart. She knew from the ambulance and fire truck and the look on Luella's face what had happened.

Luella expected her to fall apart for what she had lost—her best friend, but Cheryl just took Luella in her arms and hugged her tight, rubbing circles on her back. Either she was in shock, or she was well acquainted with death. It was like Cheryl was a different person. Felt as though Helen had sent her stoic strength down the road to Cheryl as her earthly body left the world behind. Or that's what Luella chose to believe. Either way, she found it comforting.

~

That night, Cheryl stayed at the farm as late as she could, making them all cups of tea and cleaning to keep busy. She cleaned the entire kitchen while she was there, scrubbing the sink twice—so very *Cheryl* of her. She processed her feelings through acts of service and the smell of 409.

When Cheryl went to pick up Helen's favorite mug still sitting on the end table beside her spot on the sofa, Luella yelled out for her to stop. Cheryl's hand froze midair. She and Paul both looked over at Luella.

"Not that one," she said. "Not yet."

She finally understood why Helen had never moved Grandpa Fred's pants. Grief makes you do funny things.

Paul stayed over that night. It was the first time he had slept under the roof of the farmhouse since he was seventeen years old. He curled up on the loveseat after Luella fell asleep on the couch. The next morning, she found him with one leg scrunched up and the other dangling off the end.

The sun shined bright that day, and bitterness welled up inside Luella's chest as she busied herself around the farm. She felt the weather should match exactly how she was feeling on the inside: stormy and dark with no end of rain in sight. Still, she moved. Working the ground, tending to the animals, tidying up the yard. If she stopped for too long, she knew it would all come crashing down around her. Moving was imperative.

She met with Pastor Wynn and the funeral home. She made all the arrangements with Paul by her side. Millie Beams called—but Luella wasn't ready to talk to her just yet. Percy called. It felt like the entire town had called. Eventually, Luella unplugged the phone.

Gus walked from room to room, like he was searching the house for any sign of Helen. When Luella couldn't stand it anymore, she snapped at the poor dog.

"She's gone, Gus. She's not coming back."

The dog's ears went down. He made a disgruntled sound before jumping up onto the empty spot at the end of the couch where Helen always sat, which broke Luella's heart into a million pieces.

Paul was never far, but he gave Luella space, probably working through his own muddled thoughts and broken heart. Loss was nothing new to him, but this one was sure to hit the hardest. Luella had lost a grandmother, one that she had just come to love. But Paul had lost the only mother he had ever really known.

~

The funeral was at Friendship three days later. Luella and Paul stood at the front of the chapel as a line of people trickled through to say a last goodbye to Helen. She was cremated, per her wishes. She said she didn't want anyone staring at her dead body and crying when they had plenty of time to see her face while she was still alive. True Helen fashion. Luella had smirked when she said it.

Luella set the picture she had given Helen for her birthday beside the urn for people to see as they came and paid their respects. It had quickly become Luella's favorite picture, the one she'd cherish the most.

They had shaken too many hands and seen too many faces by the time Mya made it through the line in her tortoiseshell sunglasses and black lace dress. She looked like a long-forgotten ghost as she took Luella's hand in her own. Then, she pushed her glasses up on top of her head.

It took Luella a few seconds to realize she was staring at her mother's face. When she did, she yanked her hand back. "How dare you," she said furiously.

Mya looked around and then cast her eyes downward as everyone stared at them.

Paul moved closer to the two of them. "Not the time, Lue," he whispered, and then looked over at Mya. "You two can talk after. It's best if you just move along."

Mya nodded and moved down the line.

Luella watched as she took a seat in the very last pew at the back of the church. She tried to shift her focus on the people stepping in front of her, but it was hard knowing that Mya was sitting back there, having appeared out of thin air as if it was an ordinary Tuesday. There it was again.

*Tuesday.*

Pastor Wynn gave a beautiful speech about Helen's life, which made Luella wonder how much he really knew about his congregation besides what they showed him on Sunday mornings. Not that what he said was wrong. Helen was the same person every day of the week. That was probably why the whole of Chipley Creek respected her so much. Exactly why the pews were overflowing and people standing where they could.

It just felt surreal to hear someone talk about Helen's life in such an intimate way when Helen was an incredibly private person.

"Helen was beloved within this community. She spent many years fostering children in her home. I know a few of you stayed in this town after passing through the McCrae farm." He hesitated and then went on. "I want to do something a little different today. It just feels pressed on my heart, like I'm supposed to ask. And I know better than to ignore that push. If you were one of those children that lived at Fred and Helen McCrae's for a time, can I be so bold as to ask you to please stand up?"

Luella heard it before she saw it. The collective creaking of wooden pews as people rose from their seats. Cheryl covered her mouth with her hand. Luella turned around slowly. The sight of it took her breath away as her eyes welled up with tears. Almost half of the room was on their feet.

She recognized several faces, a few of which had knocked heads with Helen during their time at the farm. A few who society might have labeled as *troubled*. Helen would never have said that, though. Those were the ones she poured into the most.

There was one face in the middle of those standing that made her tears pour over.

Rebecca's.

As their eyes locked, a chill ran over Luella. Helen had only carried and birthed one child, yet she chose to take care of dozens she hadn't. And she loved them all the same.

The pianist began playing a slow, familiar tune. "Wow," said Pastor Wynn in astonishment. He cleared his throat. "If that doesn't speak volumes of a life well lived, then I don't know what could."

There was a quiet, palpable awe that fell over the room after that moment. Pastor Wynn said a prayer and then it was time for the eulogy.

Luella decided she should be the one to give it. She wanted to do it for Helen. She mulled it over in the days leading up to the funeral. Whenever she tried to write it out, the words wouldn't come. She knew winging it was a bad idea, but she hoped that standing in front of everyone, she would find the right words, and they would be simple and profound and say everything that she wanted them to know about Helen.

She got up from the pew and made her way to the stage, where Pastor Wynn stepped aside, making room for her at the podium. Her hands clenched the sides of the tall wooden stand, hoping it would steady her. She took a deep breath that echoed through the microphone. Then, she cleared her throat.

"I . . . um . . . as most of you know, I'm Helen's granddaughter." Her hands started sweating as they clung to the podium for dear life. "I'm a person who loves words, but oddly enough, I couldn't find them when I sat down to write this eulogy."

She looked out at the faces staring back at her. Faces she knew, and some that she didn't. They stared at her expectantly—like a blank white page waiting to be eloquently shaped.

"Helen is . . . *was* . . ."

Her heart hammered against her chest. The words wouldn't come. She knew everything she wanted to say, but the journey from her mind and out of her mouth was closed off. Her face grew hotter by the second. She looked up and saw Mya staring straight at her. What was the look on her face? Luella couldn't tell, but she was dizzy and nauseous and needed to get off the stage.

"I'm sorry," she said, making her way woozily down the steps and back toward the very first pew.

Paul stepped out and helped her the rest of the way, then he turned back and walked up the steps to the stage. He stood in front of the microphone and picked up where Luella left off, able to say the things that she had wanted to but couldn't force out of her mouth. She sat in a stunned silence until it was all over.

Afterward, people said their condolences twice over, and the sanctuary emptied. She and Paul walked out of the church doors to find Mya waiting at the bottom of the steps. Paul looked over at Luella.

"It's okay," she said.

He nodded and gave Mya an uneasy look before walking past them toward his truck.

Mya's brows were furrowed, like she was trying to weigh her words. "I really am very sorry about your grandma."

Luella scoffed. "Like you care. Where were you the past few months? I told you she was sick."

Mya nodded, and her eyes welled up. She started to speak, but her voice quivered. Her hand came up to her mouth as if she was trying to steady herself. "That's my regret to carry now."

Luella took a deep breath. Here her mother was, finally, after all these years. Luella had wanted her to be a part of her life for as long as she could remember. She prayed, begged, and pleaded with God.

Now, here she was. Mya was right. She was the one who would have to live with the past. It easily could have been Luella standing where Mya stood on that day, if not for a single phone call. How would she have ever known? Would someone have called and told her? Would she have shown up after eleven years at her grandmother's funeral? She didn't have to think about it. Because Helen had given her a second chance. She had given her an offer, and that offer had brought her back to Chipley Creek—bitter as she was about it.

Helen, Paul, Cheryl, Meggie, Taylor, and even the entirety of Chipley, had nurtured her and welcomed her back without hesitation.

Now Mya stood before her, broken and bent, not asking, but hoping for a little grace. What would Helen have done?

Luella already knew the answer.

"Some people are coming back to the farm. There's mountains of food," she said. Mya looked up optimistically. "Why don't you come by and get something to eat."

The tiniest of smiles appeared on Mya's face. "I'd like that," she said. "But only if you're sure." Luella nodded in response, and Mya seemed pleased. "I'll meet you there."

Luella stepped past her and walked toward Paul's truck. Paul was standing beside the door, waiting for her. "What was that about?" he asked, as she got closer.

"I invited her back to the farm."

Paul didn't even try to hide his surprise. "You what?"

Luella shrugged her shoulders and pulled the passenger door open. She grabbed the handle above the door frame and hoisted herself up. It was getting a lot harder to do the farther along that she got.

Paul got in and pulled the door shut. He stared forward for a few seconds, feigning disbelief.

Then, he cocked his head to look at Luella like she was messing with him.

"Oh, stop. It's what Helen would do."

He turned the key and looked back at her. "You're right. It is. I'm proud of you. She'd be proud of you, too."

She gave him a sad smile and then buckled her seatbelt. He reached his hand out, resting it on her thigh. She put her hand in his and looked out the window as he drove, trying not to think about what was waiting for them at the farm.

# thirty-five

Parked cars lined the sides of the driveway and every free space of grass in the front. Some people asked if they could come, while others just showed up. Luella didn't have the heart to turn them away. It was as though being there was a form of therapy, or a final goodbye.

It's an odd sort of ritual—gathering at the house of a deceased loved one. But Luella guessed that must be why people amassed together afterward. So they don't have to sit alone with their grief. And being in the space that the person inhabited makes people feel close to them even after they're gone. Who was she to not let them have the closure they needed?

Plus, there really was an abundance of food.

Luella and Paul walked into the house, and it reverberated with idle conversations. Voices filled up every ounce of space in the house. Helen would have loved that the house was full of noise again. Luella smiled. It was the sound of her childhood, the house that she remembered. Like she had stepped inside a picture and got to talk with an old friend.

If a house could talk, what would it say? If a house had feelings, how would it feel?

She'd bet this one felt like a mother whose children had come home again after being gone for far too long.

Pastor Wynn and his wife were there. Sweet Percy Webster was there. Meggie and her family came. Luella hadn't even noticed them at the funeral, but it was all a blur. Foster children from different seasons of life were gathered there around the long wooden table, swapping stories of life at the farm. The table was full, and the conversations were deep and meaningful.

Luella looked back at Paul, who had a smile on his face. A man sitting in the living room shot to his feet when he saw Paul. He called out for him. When Paul saw the man, he rushed over, and they embraced. Luella left him to his conversation.

She headed toward the kitchen where Cheryl and Taylor sat at the small round table, just the two of them. Luella pulled out a chair and sat down with them. Her eyes met Cheryl's as they both tried not to stare at the only empty spot at the table. Her eyes said that she felt it, too. Taylor was too busy eating a piece of pound cake to notice.

The front door creaked as it opened, and Mya stepped slowly inside the house that was once her home. She shut the door behind her. Luella watched as she made her way awkwardly through the horde of people. Mya looked into the kitchen and spotted Luella. She walked toward the table.

When she reached them, Luella looked over at Cheryl. "Mya, this is Cheryl," she said. "Cheryl, this is Mya. My mother."

Cheryl set her mug of hot tea down and held out her hand. "It's nice to meet you," she said.

Mya smiled and shook her hand. "Why don't you sit down with us," Cheryl said, looking over at Luella like she hoped that was okay.

Mya pulled out the chair and sat down, looking around the kitchen. "Nothing has changed," she said.

"Helen wasn't a fan of change," said Cheryl. "Believe me, I tried. I wanted to update her entire kitchen one Christmas for her, but she wouldn't let me. She was stuck in her ways, that one." She laughed at the memory.

"Yes, she was," said Luella with a deep sigh. There was an awkward silence as they sat there, not knowing what to say.

"How far along are you?" Mya asked, a little hesitantly.

Luella put her hands on her belly. "Twenty-three weeks."

Mya smiled but said nothing else.

"Make yourself a plate of food," said Luella. "There's plenty here. I'm just feeling a little claustrophobic. I'm gonna get some air."

She got up and walked through the dining room to the small hall beside Helen's bedroom. It led to a covered porch on the backside of the house. She gently shut the screen door behind her as she stepped out, hoping no one would find her out there. She took a few deep breaths, trying to soothe the parts of her that were wound up tight. The sinking feeling that came and went ever since Helen's ER visit.

She looked around at the old, dilapidated porch. Helen loved to sit out on that back porch when it rained. Grandpa Fred had covered it with a tin roof so they could hear rain hitting the roof right outside of their bedroom window. Luella wondered why she hadn't sat out there more. It was the perfect spot to escape.

After a few minutes, she decided she needed to get back inside before anyone noticed she was missing. She pulled open the screen door and made her way back down the little hallway.

A movement in Helen's room caught her attention. She peeked in and saw Mya sitting on the bed, looking around. Her face was blank, but her eyes couldn't hide their sadness.

Luella leaned against the door frame. "I'm sorry you didn't get to see her before it happened."

"Don't be," said Mya. "I made my choices."

That was fair. It was also the truth. They had all made choices.

Luella was glad she had taken Helen up on her offer and didn't have to feel the way Mya must have been feeling.

"How long had it been since you'd last seen each other?" Luella asked.

Mya sighed and looked up at the ceiling as she thought about it. "I can't even remember," she said.

Mac's words resonated in her mind again. *You never know that you've been robbed until it's too late.* Was it too late for her and Mya? Could they somehow patch up the past between them and start anew? If the past few months with Helen had taught her anything, it was that people will surprise you. That sometimes the only thing standing between you and forgiveness is a first step.

Luella wondered what Mya thought about them starting over. "What do you—"

"Look," said Mya, interrupting her. They both smiled awkwardly at their collision.

"You go ahead," said Luella.

Mya pressed her lips into a thin line. "I was just gonna say that I'm sorry for the way I just dumped you. I was young and selfish—a magnet for bad decisions."

*There it was.* An olive branch. Luella took it as a sign they could move forward from this. Maybe Helen somehow knew they could, too, and that was the point of all of this. Of her bringing Luella back to Chipley. Luella shrugged. "I have the letters at least. As soon as I got one, I couldn't wait for another."

Mya's brows furrowed. "Letters?"

"The ones you sent. I kept them all."

Mya's eyebrows went up as a smile crept across her face. "Oh," she said, rocking back as she did. "Good. I'm glad."

They could move forward. Luella was sure of it. "I'm gonna get back," she said, pointing toward the other end of the hallway. Mya nodded, and Luella left her sitting there, no doubt needing just a little while longer in the place that was so intimately Helen's.

The living room was full of people. Both sofas and all the chairs were occupied, while others stood. Paul and Taylor sat in the corner playing checkers. The sight of them made Luella's heart swell. Cheryl strolled over to her. "How are you doing, doll?" she asked, running her hands up and down Luella's arms like she was trying to warm her up.

"As good as can be I guess." The baby kicked the lower part of her belly, sending a sharp pain into her side. Luella put her hand on the side of her stomach and took a deep breath.

Paul jumped from his spot in the corner and rushed over. "You alright?" he asked.

Luella dismissed his serious tone away with a wave of her hand. Then, she placed her hands on the sides of her bulging belly. "She's restless, is all."

Both Cheryl and Paul's eyes widened. Cheryl smiled.

"She?" Paul asked.

Luella let out a quiet laugh to herself. "Helen thinks it's a girl," she said, thinking about that morning before church, grateful that she had that memory. Her eyes cast downward onto the wooden floor beneath her feet. "Thought," she corrected. "I wonder if it will ever feel normal to talk about her in the past tense."

The three of them stood in silence together for a few moments.

Cheryl sighed and looked over at Luella. "I don't think it will ever feel normal, and that's okay. Because she'll always be present in our lives, in this space, or when we do things that remind us of her. She'll never stop being present with us. We move forward with her in mind." She smiled a sad smile as her eyes welled up. Then, she took a deep breath and looked away from them. "I'm gonna make a cup of tea."

And she was off toward the kitchen. Luella knew eventually the reality of it all would hit Cheryl. If she ever stopped moving long enough, it would come crashing down on her like a mountain of bricks. Luella only hoped Taylor wasn't there to see it. Or maybe it would be better if she was. She wondered how different things might have been if she had seen the things that Helen was going through while she was growing up. The things she didn't come to understand until she was an adult. Things some adults try to hide away for their own reasons, but mostly because they think children can't handle it. But children can deal with a lot more than adults give them credit for. They extend grace so much easier than grownups do.

Which was why it was a very unfortunate thing Paul was standing next to her when Millie Beams came walking up. Had Luella known who she was, she could have sent him to get her a drink or check on Cheryl or Gus. But she didn't know then that the tall woman with short, dark brown hair walking toward them was Helen's lawyer.

"Miss McCrae?" asked the woman. When Luella nodded, the woman extended her hand. "I'm Millie Beams, your grandmother's lawyer."

Luella shook her hand. "It's nice to meet you."

Paul smiled and held out his hand and introduced himself. She shook his hand and then looked back at Luella. "I'm sorry about Helen."

"Thank you," said Luella. She looked around for an out—anything she could use to pry her away from Millie Beams and Paul. But everyone was talking amongst themselves, and she couldn't come up with a valid reason. Her heart started beating faster.

"I've got some things for you to sign, and some things to go over if you want to come by my office in the next few days," said Mrs. Beams.

"I'll come by tomorrow," Luella said, hoping that would be enough. She stepped back a little to let Mrs. Beams know that she was finished with the conversation.

Mya stood a few feet from them, sipping on a drink while

watching. Mrs. Beams looked over at Mya and must have recognized her. Luella backed away, but the woman was relentless. She reached out for Luella's arm to stop her. "One more thing," she said. "It'd be best if you came alone. Per terms of the arrangement."

Luella froze. How she wished she would have just kept walking, no matter how rude it may have been. She nodded again.

"Perfect," said Mrs. Beams. "I'll see you then."

And the woman was out the door within seconds. Luella stood frozen to the floor. She didn't want to look over at Paul, but she could feel his eyes on her. She looked up at him hesitantly.

"Arrangement? You only came back because of an arrangement?" But he didn't give her time to respond. His eyes filled with anger as he tried to piece it together.

"Paul, I can explain . . ."

"Save it," he said, looking around the room. Luella noticed all eyes were on them as they stood near the entryway. This time, he didn't care if anyone was listening. "Every time I think I have you figured out, you surprise me again." He shook his head in disbelief and then stormed out of the front door.

Meggie got up off the couch and walked over to her. "You alright? What was that about?"

Luella hesitated, but then nodded her head. Her body felt heavy, yet weightless at the same time. The past few days had taken all of her energy, and yet somehow it always seemed to get worse. Why couldn't things just be easy and stay that way? Why did she always do this?

"I just keep messing things up," she said without looking up to see the pity she knew she'd find on Meggie's face.

~

After everyone left, it was just Luella and Mya, alone in the house. It surprised Luella to find her still there after the crowd had disappeared. Luella stood in the kitchen, putting food in containers and trying not to check her phone every five seconds. She had no messages from Paul. He didn't come back after storming off. She assumed that meant he needed more space. She thought they had finally closed the gap between them. That nothing else could come out of left field and blindside her. Luella was lost in thought when Mya walked up, jarring her back to reality. She jumped.

Mya laughed. "I didn't mean to scare you. Can I help?" she asked, pointing to the mounds of food and plastic containers strewn out on the small, round table in the kitchen.

"Sure," Luella said. Mya went to work opening containers and loading them full of food.

"How long are you in town?"

Mya shrugged. "I'm not sure yet."

Luella felt like it was more of a question than an answer. She couldn't help but feel like a large part of it hinged on what Luella wanted. But she wasn't even sure she knew what that was. She wasn't sure of anything anymore. Being with Helen here at the farm had grounded her and helped her feel okay with just being still for a while. She didn't have that feeling now that Helen was gone. Loneliness seeped through the cracks like fog, obliterating all logical thought. "You should stay here tonight," Luella said.

Mya stopped what she was doing and looked over at Luella for a few seconds, her face full of appreciation. "That would be nice," she said. "I'm not quite ready to leave."

"Good," said Luella.

Then, they went back to work packing food up. She didn't know why, but it eased the loneliness just a little.

Luella made small talk, asking about Mya's life now.

She was currently unemployed, but Luella was too, so who was she to judge a person for that. She was eight months sober after waking up in someone else's apartment with no memory of the night before and all the contents of her wallet stolen. Having nowhere else to go, she walked herself down to the nearest rehabilitation center and checked herself in. She'd been going to AA meetings ever since. Luella couldn't help but wonder if Helen knew. No doubt that if she did, she'd be proud.

They talked about Luella's life in the city, although Luella was sparse in her details. She didn't need Mya knowing every sordid aspect of her past. She just gave her enough to fill in the gaps.

After they were up to speed on each other's lives, a comfortable quiet set in between the two of them as they finished cleaning up the kitchen.

Perhaps they could start again in this place that had been a fresh start for so many others. After all, it had given Luella a new beginning with Helen. Why couldn't it do the same for her and Mya?

Looking back, Luella would say she knew better than to be that naïve.

# thirty-six

Luella found Mya in the kitchen the next morning, where she had made breakfast and set it out nicely on the small table in the kitchen.

Luella hesitated, but pulled out the wooden chair anyway and sat down. "This looks nice. You didn't have to do this."

"I wanted to," said Mya, picking up a hot biscuit and slathering it with butter and jelly.

They ate like any other family at any other table. Luella found it odd how easily they slipped into the roles of the average mother and daughter sharing conversation over a breakfast table.

Until reality smacked her in the face.

"What kind of arrangement did you and Helen have?" Mya asked nonchalantly, taking a sip of coffee.

Luella swallowed the bite of biscuit she was chewing. "What do you mean?" she asked, taking a bite of eggs.

"I overheard you and that lawyer yesterday . . . I was just curious." Luella noticed how she didn't look up even once as she spoke.

"It's nothing," said Luella. Then, she took a sip of orange juice.

Mya nodded. "Does she have a will?"

Luella set the cup on the table with a thud and put her hands in her lap. She ran them over the tops of her thighs. So that was it. That's why she'd come. "Yes, she does. Is that why you're here?

"Of course not," Mya said. "I was—"

"Just curious," Luella finished the sentence for her. Mya nodded. Luella scooted her chair back. "I've got to go get ready."

"Okay," Mya said, getting up from the chair. "I'll clean this up."

On her way out of the kitchen, she turned around and looked back at Mya scraping the plates off and cleaning up the mess she made by cooking breakfast. Luella felt a pang of guilt for jumping on her like that. Maybe she really was just curious.

In her bedroom, Luella picked her phone up off the dresser and looked at the messages. Still nothing from Paul. She had sent him several texts and tried to call him, but he never responded.

If he had just given her a chance to explain instead of jumping to conclusions.

She opened the closet door and stared at the clothes hanging in front of her. It had taken her months, but she finally hung them up instead of leaving them scattered on the dresser and in the suitcase she had brought them in. She did it one night after Helen told her it was good to have her *home* again. Looking at the clothes hanging in the closet now made the hurt come crawling up from the pit of her stomach to rest heavy on her chest. She yanked a shirt off a wire hanger and grabbed a pair of jeans.

After she got ready, she walked out of her room and heard rustling coming from Helen's bedroom. When she opened the door, Mya was rifling through Helen's things. Her jewelry box was open in disarray atop the dresser. She looked almost frantic.

"What are you doing?" Luella asked, furious.

"She has to have a copy here somewhere," said Mya, without even looking up from her investigation.

"A copy of what?"

Mya looked up. "Her will," she snapped.

Luella scoffed. She knew it. She freaking knew it. Mya didn't care that she knew it, either. She just kept rifling through drawers and looking through books, trying to find what wasn't there.

"Get out," Luella said. But Mya kept going. Luella rushed over and pulled at Mya's prying hands. "Get. Out."

Mya snatched her hands back. Her face was no longer that of a caring, empathetic mother. Selfish Mya had returned. The woman that always wanted more, took more, and manipulated in order to get the things she thought she so rightfully deserved. She stepped toward Luella, her face red and angered. "You're no better than me, and you won't be any better for that baby," she said, casting her eyes down to Luella's belly.

"I won't tell you again," said Luella. "Get out of this house."

Mya smirked as she walked toward the door of Helen's room. Then, she turned back and said, "You can just send me the money for whatever she left me. I don't want anything else."

Then, she left just as quickly as she had appeared. Only this time, Luella was relieved. She heard the front door slam shut as she put Helen's things back into the drawers. She fixed the jewelry box and stepped back to make sure everything looked just as it was before. Then, she took a deep breath, grabbed her purse, and left for Millie Beams' office.

~

The office was in one of the old historical homes in downtown Chipley. The receptionist asked her to take a seat. She didn't wait long before Mrs. Beams stepped out of her office and told her to come in.

"How are you today?" she asked in a tone a bit too chipper for Luella, given the circumstance.

"I'm fine," she said, running her hands up and down her thighs again.

"Good, good," Mrs. Beams said. Then she began the process, pulling paper after paper out for Luella to sign. She explained the arrangements of Helen's will and wishes. Luella only half heard what she was saying because it was so much information to process.

Luella would be given the deed to the house, the land, and the other assets as well, which she could choose to liquify or keep. There was a trust set up for Mya that would release funds monthly into an account that had already been set up for her.

It made Luella furious that Helen had done that for Mya. If she could have seen the way Mya had gone through her drawers like she was executing an FBI search, then Helen may have thought twice about what she left for her. But Luella knew that wasn't true, either. That wasn't Helen. Mya would always be her daughter. And Helen had told Luella that there were some things she simply wouldn't understand until she became a parent herself. That it took experiencing that kind of love to understand it.

When the paperwork was finished, Mrs. Beams picked up a manilla envelope and held it out for Luella, who grabbed it reluctantly. "What is this?"

Mrs. Beams shrugged. "I'm not sure of the contents, but Helen left it for you. She asked me to give it to you after everything had been finalized."

Luella grabbed it and examined the envelope in her hand. There was no writing on it, and the envelope itself felt weightless, like it contained nothing at all. "Thanks. Do I need to do anything else?"

"No, I think that's everything."

Luella left the office as quickly as she could. She set the envelope beside her in the Wagoneer as she made her way back to the farm. The ache in her chest came back as she pulled down the long gravel driveway and parked the Wagoneer beside the porch. Gus barked angrily outside the car door. "Yeah, yeah. I hear you." Luella grabbed the envelope and got out of the car. Gus followed close behind as she made her way to the porch, rushing through the door as soon as Luella opened it.

The silence was so loud that she feared it would swallow her up. The last time she was alone in the farmhouse was the morning she picked Helen up from the hospital. That felt like a lifetime ago. She felt like a completely different person now, standing alone in the house again. She threw the keys in the bowl on the entryway table, walked into the living room, and sank into the loveseat's cushion. Gus jumped up in Helen's spot on the couch and turned a full circle before lying down and staring blankly at Luella.

She stared at the manila envelope in her hands, unsure if she was ready to open it. Though she had no idea what she'd find inside, she knew it would be the final goodbye. She took a deep breath and then gently tore open the glued down flap, reached her hand in, and pulled out a small key attached to a chain. She flipped it over in her hand. Helen had taped a piece of paper to it with the words *safety deposit box* written on it. She didn't even know Helen had one of those.

She set the key in her lap and reached in again, this time pulling out a single envelope. As her eyes caught sight of it, her mouth fell open.

Baby blue with a floral crest.

She'd know that stationery anywhere. It was the same one from her mother's letters. But how? She ripped the envelope open and pulled out the letter it contained. When she unfolded it, a flood of emotions came over her at the sight of the familiar handwriting.

*Helen's.*

It had been Helen all along. She had written those letters, not Mya. It's why Mya looked confused when Luella mentioned them. A sob rolled up from the back of her throat, and this time, she couldn't stop it. She let it out. All that pent up grief she had been trying to push down. All the misguided resentment she felt toward the past. She cried so hard that she was sure Cheryl would hear and come running through the door at any second.

She couldn't read Helen's words through the tears. She held the paper to her chest as she sobbed. Over what she had lost. What had always been in front of her, but she'd never seen. But mostly, she sobbed over what she had gained. She had never been more thankful.

Helen was the grandest mother she could have ever had.

No one was perfect. But she was perfect for Luella. She was everything she had needed all along. Luella read Helen's words through tears.

*Dear Luella,*

*If you're reading this, then it means that I'm gone. Don't be sad. Be grateful for the time that we had together. I know I am. More grateful for that than anything else in my life. I'm sorry I lured you back through an arrangement, but I wasn't sure you'd come if I had been the one asking. I'm sorry that it took me finding out that I didn't have much time left to realize how precious life is.*

*I should have looked for you sooner. I'm so happy you agreed to come back to the farm. I hoped we'd have the chance to reconcile our differences before it was too late. So that I could make up for the past.*

*Your life was my life's greatest part. I am so proud of the woman you have become. And you're wrong. You will be an amazing mother one day. If that's what you want. But don't give it up just because you think you have nothing to offer that baby. Because you do. You. You are enough.*

*All my love,*
*Helen*

*P.S.—Please take care of Gus for me.*

Gus jumped down off the sofa as if summoned and walked over to the loveseat. He jumped into Luella's lap and laid down. Tears poured out of Luella's eyes and down her face, spilling onto the letter.

Helen was the one who wanted her to come back. And it wasn't because she needed help. She used that as an excuse to bring Luella back. All along, she just wanted time with Luella. Time to make amends.

When she had no more tears left to cry, she set Gus down beside her, got up, and grabbed her notepad and pen. Then, she walked into the kitchen and sat at the little round table that she and Helen had sat at so often, and she began writing.

Everything she wanted to say at the funeral but couldn't. All the ways that Helen had made her a better person. How she made others better. What Helen meant to her. What she had become.

The sun danced through the trees and onto the table as she wrote. As she poured out everything she meant to say, she felt Helen's presence so deeply that if she only looked up, she might have seen her sitting right across the table from her.

It was cathartic. Words had never poured out of her the way they did at that table as she eulogized Helen the way she had wanted to but couldn't out loud. She had never been good at communication. Putting pen to paper had always worked better for her when she needed to sort out how she felt.

Helen had given her that, and this was her way of giving it back.

# thirty-seven

Almost a week went by with no word from Paul. Luella didn't contact him, either. It seemed they both needed space to work out their grief and come to their own conclusions about where they stood.

July dragged on like a garden snail, moving at a glacial pace. Luella wanted nothing more than to see it end. July had robbed her of so much.

On the last day of the month, Luella was down at the barn feeding Boots when she heard the deep rumble of Paul's truck coming down the driveway.

The sun was slowly setting over the pine trees as he parked his truck.

She pulled her phone out of her back pocket and sent him a text letting him know she was down at the barn.

He stepped out of the truck, and she watched as he looked at his phone and then down to the barn. She waved a hand, so he'd see her.

As he made his way closer, she noticed his hands were shoved into his pockets. Never a good sign with Paul. She turned back toward Boots and pressed her hand against his nose, trying to calm the rapid beating of her heart. Boots blew a breath out. She heard Paul's footsteps behind her.

"Hey," he said.

She took a deep breath and turned around to face him. "You've got your serious face on," she said.

His silence told her that she was right. He bit the side of his cheek and looked around the old barn. "We used to love it down here, didn't we?"

"It was always our spot," said Luella. She got the feeling Paul was trying his best to look anywhere else but her face. The push and pull of their relationship since she'd been back was draining. Maybe it wasn't supposed to be that hard. Maybe there was a reason so much seemed to get in the way of them being together. Whatever it was, she couldn't take it anymore. "I get the feeling that there's something you came here to say."

He nodded, looking down at his boots, and then lifted his face to look at her. "I got a job offer. It's one of those traveling positions. I put my resume in thinking that they'd never call. But they did, and they offered me a position in Birmingham."

Her heart dropped. "I see," she said, taking in the weight of his words. Alabama wasn't that far away. Just a couple of hours. It wasn't across the country. They could make it work. Did he want to make it work? She wasn't sure anymore. "Is this because of what Millie Beams said? Because of the arrangement?"

He blew out a breath and stepped toward her. His eyes were full of confliction. "Yes, no, and maybe."

Luella stepped back and leaned against the wooden beam of the barn. How many times had they stood beneath this barn talking about the things they were going through? Conversations she loved. She couldn't say the same about this one.

"I've spent my entire life in this town. It might do me some good to get out like—"

"Like I did." She finished the sentence for him. He nodded in response. "I understand," she said. "I really do."

And she did.

She understood his need to try on a different city with unfamiliar sights, fresh sounds, and new people. But she couldn't quiet the selfish part of her that didn't want him to leave and find that he liked his life better out there, away from her. She had wished for so long that one day life would bring them back together, and she thought he felt that way, too.

Sometimes she even wondered if that was what Helen had intended the entire time—to bring them back together since it was her that had separated them in the first place. But it wasn't her fault. True, she sent him to a different home, but it was Luella who boarded that bus. And if she was honest with herself, she knew he might not follow. She chose to step on that bus despite that fact. Now it was Paul's turn to be the one doing the leaving. That was only fair. She wondered if some small part of him got even the tiniest satisfaction from it. Leaving *her* behind this time.

"Lue," he said, pulling her out of her thoughts and back to the present. "About us . . ."

She put a hand up to stop him and shook her head. "It's okay. Maybe all of this was meant to happen just so we could get through losing Helen together. I don't know what I would have done if you weren't here."

He stepped as close to her as he could get and took her hands in his. He pressed his forehead against hers and closed his eyes. "I've loved you my entire life. I never stopped, and I never will. But I have to do this for myself. I know you understand how that feels."

Luella blew out a breath and rubbed her lips together to keep herself from crying. She hated goodbyes.

What an odd sort of feeling to be the one being left behind. First Helen. Now Paul. What a cruel twist of fate. She let go of his hands and pulled away before he could see that she was upset.

"What are you going to do?" Paul asked.

"About what?"

He shrugged. "Everything."

She took a deep breath while she considered it and looked out at Boots in the field, grazing the grass as his tail swung back and forth behind him. Looking up at the farmhouse, she thought about how old and run down it was now. But this was her home. She looked at her belly, now twenty-eight weeks along. There was still some time to decide. She didn't have to make a decision just yet. Finally, she said, "I'm not sure yet."

Paul walked beside her back toward the house. They were quiet as they walked, letting the breeze and the sound of the trees swaying be the only sound between them. That was what she had always pictured. She and Paul being together again, enjoying the slow, monotonous things in life.

If you had asked her at fifteen where she saw herself in ten years, her response would have been somewhere with Paul. The rest didn't matter. But he was leaving now. He was choosing to leave her when they finally had their chance to be together. But life was intrinsically complex, like Helen had said.

Maybe his heart was just conflicted, or maybe it was all just too much.

Luella stopped a few feet from his truck. She looked over at him. "For whatever it's worth, I came back because of the arrangement, but that's not why I stayed. I stayed because of you. And because of Helen and what I found here with her."

Paul let out a slow breath, like he was taking in her words. He shook his head. "I can't stay just because you flew away and then found out you liked it better where you were. I haven't taken any opportunities away from here because I always wanted to be here just in case you came back to Chipley."

"But I did," she said, stepping closer to him. "And I'm still here. And we can finally be together like we always wanted to. That someday we always talked about . . ." Luella stopped herself. That was all she would give him. She refused to be a woman who begged a man to stay. She'd watched Mya do it, even at the expense of what it had cost her—the only daughter she ever had. The only chance at being a mother she had. Luella wouldn't do it. That's where she drew the line. Even with Paul.

When he didn't say anything else, didn't step toward her, she lifted her chin and asked, "When do you leave?"

He looked at the ground. "Tonight."

"Wow," she said, taken aback.

It punched her in the gut. So, this was it. This was why he had come. Their goodbye was happening right now.

"Lue," he said, barely above a whisper. He knew it was going to hurt her.

She walked over to him and placed her hands on his chest to steady herself. "Goodbye, Paul."

She lifted herself up and kissed him gently on the cheek. When she stepped back, he grabbed her wrist, holding her there, and closed the gap between them.

His eyes looked into hers, saying everything the two of them refused to say out loud. Then, he looked down at her lips, and his shoulders sagged.

They met in the middle, leaning in at the same time, their lips crushing together. Paul's hands came up to her cheeks and cradled her face as he kissed her without hesitation.

Like he was getting his fill of her before he left. But it would never be enough for Luella. Tears stung the edges of her eyes, and she let them spill out.

Paul pulled back with sad eyes and pressed a hand softly to her belly. She wished. Oh, how she wished.

In a different world, the baby in her belly would be his. And that kiss wouldn't have been goodbye, but one that said hello every day for the rest of their lives. If only she could have figured out how much she wanted that reality just a little bit sooner.

But life doesn't work that way. The baby in her belly was not his, and the kiss they shared said goodbye, not hello.

There was nothing else to say. No sense in dragging it out.

She watched as he got into his truck and turned the engine on. It was probably just a reflection in the glass, but she could have sworn she saw tears in his eyes, too, as he turned the truck around and drove away.

This was not how she thought her day would end—saying goodbye to the only boy she ever loved.

That made two things July had taken away from her.

# thirty-eight

In the middle of August, Luella found herself back in the city. She contacted Cathy, asking for a meeting after she finished revising what she had written about Helen after the funeral. She could have emailed it, just like she could have the first time. But there was a reason she needed to do it in person. A reason she needed to go back to the city.

Well, two reasons.

Walking through the busy streets set her nerves on edge. Whether from pregnancy hormones or the fact that she hadn't been around that many people in almost eight months, she didn't know. And even though she had spent eleven years of her life here, the sounds were jarring to her now. They weren't the comforting white noise she had found them to be before. That's what she needed to see. What she needed to find out.

When a person feels they've outgrown something, there's a desire to put it on again to try it on for size, just to be sure that it no longer fits. Sometimes it takes doing that in order to let go of it for good.

Luella opened the door to The Coffee Shack and stepped inside. Cathy sat at the same table she had on Christmas Eve. As she walked over, she couldn't help but smile at the feeling of déjà vu.

Cathy's eyes went wide when she landed on Luella. "Okay, Meggie did not prepare me for this," she said, looking at Luella's belly. "She is good at keeping things to herself."

"Nothing prepared me for it, either," Luella said, sitting down. "A lot's changed in the past seven months."

"I'd say so." Cathy took a sip of her coffee, her eyebrows still raised in surprise.

Luella didn't want to waste too much of Cathy's time. She reached into her bag and pulled out a folder. She took the stapled paper out of it and slid it across the table to Cathy.

"What's this?"

"It's what you wanted. I didn't want to write it because of what it would ask of me. To revisit old wounds. But I realized that it was never about me, or the fostering, or the farm . . . it was always about her. About Helen."

Cathy looked up and gave her an empathetic smile. "I'm sorry about your grandma." Then, she put on her reading glasses and settled back into the chair like she had the first time.

Luella should have been nervous. But she wasn't. Not even a little. Something had shifted inside of her. She wanted Cathy to print this story. She hoped that she would. For Helen.

But her every hope didn't hinge on it like it had before. At their first meeting, it was about a steppingstone, a foot in the door to bigger opportunities. This time, it was because she wanted to share Helen with the world. She thought Helen deserved that after everything she'd done for Luella and every child that came through her home. Luella wanted to give that to her, even if she'd never know about it.

It was what Cheryl had said, about moving forward with the ones that we lose. Keeping them present in our lives so that they are never past tense. Helen would never be far from her now. Luella felt her presence with her even right there in the coffee shop.

She waited patiently as Cathy read every word. When she finished, she looked up at Luella, her glasses hanging on the tip of her nose. Luella held her breath. When Cathy finally smiled at her, she let it out.

"This is it," said Cathy, tapping the paper. "This is what you've been trying to find."

"What do you mean?"

"Your voice."

Luella's mouth suddenly felt dry. She couldn't swallow past the lump forming in the back of her throat.

Cathy said it would be perfect for the anniversary edition of *The Georgian*. That she would show it to the editors, and while she couldn't promise anything, she felt good about this one. "It's a beautiful tribute to your grandma."

Luella thanked her for the encouragement. Cathy took her glasses off and tilted her head up like she was analyzing Luella. "You seem different, and I don't mean just because you're pregnant. I don't know. I can't put my finger on it."

Luella smiled. "I feel different."

They didn't make small talk this time. Luella had somewhere else she needed to be.

Mac's Diner was just a few blocks away. Luella enjoyed the breeze as she made her way down Marietta Street. When she got to the street corner, she looked up at her former apartment complex.

Nothing could make her want to walk up those stairs and into that building ever again.

She rushed across the street, smiling up at the familiar sign that stood like a beacon in her life during the eleven years that she lived in the city.

The bell dinged as she pushed open the door. Mac stood behind the counter, cashing an older couple out at the register. His eyes lit up when they landed on her. "It's my lucky day!" he exclaimed. Half the restaurant turned to look at her, and she felt her face get red as she made her way over to the counter. She couldn't help but smile, though.

When he finished with the couple, he pulled up the piece of counter that separated them and walked through it. He wrapped his arms around her, and she leaned into his hug. It felt good to be hugged by him. She didn't miss a thing about the city. But she missed him fiercely.

"Where have you been?" he asked. He didn't look down at her belly, even though it stuck out like a sore thumb. "We've been missing you."

She smiled. "I went home and saw my family."

A wide grin spread across Mac's face. The kind of smile you give when someone says they loved your favorite book, or rather the one you give when someone actually takes your advice. "And?"

Luella looked past him for a second while she thought about it. Then, she placed her hands on her belly and said, "A lot has changed."

Mac looked down at her belly and then met her eyes. "I was just waiting for you to mention it. Didn't want to bring it up if you didn't want to talk about it."

"Well, it's kind of hard to miss," she said. "And it's the reason I'm here. I'm meeting someone."

"Ah," he said, nodding a little as he did.

"I needed a safe place to do it."

"Well, kid," he said, patting her on the back, "I'm right over here if you need me."

"Thanks Mac," she said.

Then, she found an empty booth and scooted inside to wait. She watched the servers walk up and down from here and there, refilling drinks and bringing food out on trays as the diners enjoyed their conversations over lunch. A group of teenagers crowded in a corner booth, no doubt enjoying the end of their summer. On the far side of the diner, a kid placed a quarter in the jukebox machine and a pop tune started playing through the speakers.

As soon as the bell on the door dinged, Luella felt a knot begin to wind up in her stomach.

She ran her hands over her thighs as Benjamin made his way toward her.

It wasn't until he got to the booth that he noticed her swollen stomach. His eyes grew wide, and his body language told her that he wanted to turn around and run. His mouth opened like he was about to say something, but Luella spoke before he could. "I don't want anything from you. I just want to talk."

Benjamin thought about it for a second and then sat down hesitantly. "Look, I don't know what you're expecting here, but me and Harper got back together, and we're trying to work it out, and this is the last thing that I need right now."

It surprised her how defensive she felt over the little life growing inside of her. And she couldn't believe he had gotten back together with Harper, but that was his business, and she didn't want any part of it. She didn't want him to be a part of this baby's life anyway, but she had to at least give him the chance to make that decision for himself.

"I just need you to sign this," she said, reaching into her bag and pulling out a folded-up piece of paper. She held it out for him.

"What's this?" he asked, taking it from her.

"If I decide to put this baby up for adoption, they'll need your consent."

He unfolded the paper as she pulled a pen out of her purse and handed it over to him.

"All I need from you is a signature."

He clicked the pen on and off as he read over the paper. He hesitated for a moment when he reached the bottom where the signature part was. He looked up at her and then down at her belly.

"Are you sure this is what you want?"

What were the other options? Co-parenting with Harper and Benjamin? What a nightmare that would be. Letting Benjamin have this baby to raise? A selfish part of her didn't want him involved at all—like that would make her decision easier somehow.

Luella nodded.

Benjamin hovered the pen over the signature line for several seconds like he was considering it. Then, he signed his name at the bottom and slid the paper back over to her. "Is that it?"

Luella let out a breath. "Yep," she said, grabbing the paper off the table and folding it back up. "That's it."

"Alright, well . . . I don't see the need to drag this out." Luella nodded.

"Bye, Luella," he said. Then, he was out of the door quicker than he came in.

Mac must have been watching, because not even a minute later, he was walking over to the booth with a strawberry milkshake. He set it down in front of her and then slid into the booth across from her. "Thanks, Mac," she said, pulling the cup closer and taking a sip out of the straw.

"You alright?" he asked, his eyes full of concern. She waved his worry away with a flick of her hand and a nod. "You're gonna be alright, kid," he said, placing his hand over hers. The caring way that he did it made her want to cry.

She knew she'd be okay, no matter what. But inside, she was conflicted. She was lonely, too. She felt different, more whole than she had before, but it was possible to be both whole and lonely.

"You sticking around?" Mac asked.

She could if she wanted to. There was nothing stopping her from staying in the city. But her heart was no longer here. It had never really been here to begin with. Now she knew where she belonged. She had *somewhere* she belonged. Luella lifted her eyes to meet his, and shook her head. "I'm going back home."

# thirty-nine

It woke her up around midnight. Just a dull ache at the top of her belly on the right side. But the baby's kicks had been harder and harder lately, so she wasn't too worried about it. She was more annoyed than worried because she had finally fallen into a deep sleep—something that had taken a while for her to get back into.

It must be some rite of passage that the closer a woman gets to her due date, the harder it is to sleep. Many mothers say it's the body's way of preparing you for life with a newborn.

Luella got out of bed and went into the kitchen to make some chamomile tea. Something Meggie suggested would help with the sleep.

She laid back down in bed, hoping the discomfort would ease and sleep would find her once again, but it never came. She threw the covers off and got to her feet and paced the wooden floors over the next few hours. The pain never lessened, no matter what she tried. Stretches didn't help. Putting her feet up and drinking water didn't help.

She was only thirty-four weeks. Something didn't feel right. Something in her bones told her she needed to phone her doctor.

At four o'clock in the morning, she finally did. The on-call obstetrician told her to come quickly. Luella knew she couldn't drive herself, as the pain was getting worse and worse. She wanted the comfort of her best friend but decided to call Cheryl instead since she was closer. It took several rings, but Cheryl finally picked up the phone. She must have sensed it, too. She didn't even say hello. Once she picked it up, she immediately asked what was wrong.

Her car was in the driveway within minutes. Thankfully, she didn't have Taylor that night, so she just threw on some clothes and rushed out the door. Gus barked as Luella threw things into a bag, just in case. She hadn't prepared. These were the things she wasn't ready for, things you couldn't expect.

"Shh," Luella said to soothe Gus, who must have sensed her panic. "It's alright. I'm gonna be alright," she told the old dog who was right on the heels of her feet.

They got to the hospital thirty minutes later. Luella slouched forward in pain. Cheryl called ahead, and the nurses were waiting at the door when they arrived. Cheryl reassured Luella that she'd be right in.

The nurses wheeled her through the doors and got her set up in a room. Cheryl was there a few minutes later, worry written all over her face.

They ran some tests and informed Luella that she was in the early stages of preeclampsia. Cheryl's face grew scared when the doctor said it, which made Luella even more anxious.

"It's gonna be fine," said the doctor. "But it is serious, and we need to monitor you closely."

The nurse came in with a needle full of steroid solution.

"What's that for?" Luella asked, panicked.

"It's to help the baby's lungs just in case."

"Just in case of what?"

The nurse pulled her lips in a tight, thin line. "In case of labor."

Luella looked over at Cheryl for reassurance. Cheryl was right there, holding her hand and telling her that it would be okay.

The Labor and Delivery floor was almost completely full, so they discharged her with the understanding that she was on full bed rest, and if she got nauseous or felt flu-like, she needed to come back immediately.

*The flu?* She'd never had the flu before.

It was a bit of a blur, but they released her around nine in the morning, and Cheryl drove her back home and insisted on staying. She said Luella couldn't be on bed rest alone at the farmhouse. Cheryl called the parents of the girl Taylor was staying with and asked them to keep Taylor for a little while longer. Luella didn't want to be a burden. She tried to convince Cheryl she could simply call her if she needed her, but Cheryl shot that down real fast. Luella would come to appreciate that she had.

She sent Meggie a text detailing what had happened over the course of the night and then she sank into the bed and slept hard. The kind of sleep where you wake up and forget where you are.

She woke up Tuesday afternoon. She got up to get a drink of water, and that's when it hit her again. A wave of nausea. She barely made it to the bathroom in time. Cheryl called the L&D nurse, who told her to bring Luella back in immediately.

Luella threw up in a trash bag the entire drive back to the hospital.

This time she was scared. Everything about her pregnancy had been easy until that point. There were no signs of anything going wrong. No way of expecting something like this. Luella had specifically kept herself from looking up birthing stories or anything of the sort. She wanted to walk through this pregnancy blindly.

Everything from that point on felt like a fever dream. The doctor's words sounded far away and distorted as he said something about inducing immediately. But the baby wasn't ready. She wasn't ready. She was supposed to have a few more weeks before having to worry about the delivery and everything that came after.

The nurses came in and out, taking blood and running tests. Nothing was improving. A steady stream of drugs entered her body. Pitocin for the induction. Magnesium Sulfate to prevent seizures and strokes. Fentanyl every hour.

Pain.

Relief.

Pain.

They followed an angry rhythm until one overlapped the other. It went on for eight hours. The next round of bloodwork showed signs of HELLP syndrome—the breaking down of red blood cells, elevated liver enzymes, and low platelet count. The baby had to come out, and fast.

They would have to do a C-section. Cheryl was frantic. Luella begged her to be in there with her and Cheryl promised she would. They gave Cheryl scrubs and put a scrub cap on Luella's head.

Tears of panic fell down Luella's face as the doctors worked behind a sheet covering her from the waist down. Cheryl sat beside her, rubbing her forehead to soothe her. "It's gonna be okay," she said over and over. Luella wasn't sure if she was saying it to convince Luella or herself.

"I'm scared," Luella choked out. She tried to calm herself down, but she felt exposed laying there on the table, being cut open. She wasn't just scared of the reality of what was happening, but the fact that she wasn't ready. She hadn't decided about the adoption. Didn't have any of the things she needed. The baby wasn't ready, either. It terrified her. It was all happening way too fast, at warp speed, and there was nothing she could do to stop it. She focused on Cheryl's thumb as it moved back and forth across her forehead.

A crying sound came next. It was high pitched and rhythmic. Luella looked down toward the sheet, and the doctor held up a mucous covered baby. Luella thought it looked like a tiny alien as it kicked and squirmed and screamed. She couldn't believe that baby had come from her. That it was a part of her. It was tiny. They bundled it up in a hospital blanket covered in multi-colored ducks and blocks. Then, they put a little cap on its tiny head and brought it over for her to see. The cap had a perfect little bow on the front. "This is your daughter."

"It's a girl?" Luella asked through tears. When nurse nodded, she choked back a sob and looked over at Cheryl, who smiled through tears of her own.

Luella looked back at her brand-new baby girl. Given to her on a Tuesday, no less. She placed a kiss on her tiny face. Then, they took her away.

They moved Luella into a regular room. She told Cheryl she would be fine, that she could go home now. Cheryl left only once Meggie arrived to switch out with her. Meggie came in crying, and threw her arms around Luella and held her tight. It was good to see her, but it didn't soothe the ache she felt in her chest, because someone was still missing.

It took four hours before Luella could see her baby again.

Two nurses came in and helped her into a wheelchair. The medicines were wearing off, and the pain was intense, but she wanted to see her baby more than she cared about the pain. The nurse rolled her down to the NICU unit where the baby laid sleeping behind a clear plastic box.

There were holes on the sides where Luella could stick her hands through to touch her. She reached in and grabbed the baby's tiny hand, marveling over her tiny fingers and fingernails. She counted them one by one. Ten perfect fingers. It was hard for her to believe this tiny human had come from inside of her. That she had grown her and nurtured her.

Luella knew nothing about babies. But it's true what they say about the mothering instinct. Her heart swelled at the mere sight of her. Luella knew that there was no way she was ever going to let her go. She would figure it out.

She leaned as close to the plastic box as she could and said, "It's just you and me now, kid."

Tears spilled out as she watched the slow rise and fall of her tiny chest.

~

The nurse wheeled Luella back to her room an hour later so she could rest. As soon as the door opened, she saw him standing there in the light of the hospital window. Her heart raced at the sight of him, and her chest heaved as she held back a sob.

Paul.

His back was toward her, but he turned when he heard the door open, and their eyes met. He pressed his lips tight, and Luella could see relief wash over his face. He was holding back tears, too.

The nurse went to help Luella up from the wheelchair, but Paul stepped forward. He helped her to her feet and over to the hospital bed. The nurse smiled as she grabbed the wheelchair and left, giving them some space.

Paul sat down on the bed beside her. She couldn't stop the tears from coming this time. She didn't even try. The past twenty-four hours had been a whirlwind, and all she had wanted was him.

"How did you—"

"Meggie called this morning after she got your text, and then again after Cheryl texted her."

She smiled. Her best friend knew her better than she knew herself. Did for her what she was unwilling to do for herself.

"I left as soon as I could. She didn't know all the details, but her voice told me enough. I've never driven so fast in my life. I was so scared." Paul grabbed her hand and lifted it to his lips. He kissed it once, twice, and then again.

"We're okay," she said to him, suddenly wanting to ease all of his worries away.

He nodded and lifted his eyes to hers. "How's the baby?"

"She's fine." Luella smiled.

"It's a girl?"

When Luella nodded, a smile spread across his face. "Helen was right." His face grew serious then. "I'm sorry it took me so long to figure it out."

"Figure out what?"

He leaned toward her, and she tilted her face forward to meet his. He placed a delicate kiss on her lips. It was gentle and soothed the ache she had been feeling since the second he left. "That I don't ever want to be away from you again."

Finally, she felt complete. She felt safe. But she needed him to know everything. Her eyebrows furrowed, and she looked down at her lap. She ran her hands across the tops of her thighs.

"There's something you need to know first," she said.

Paul looked at her with cautious eyes.

"I'm keeping the baby."

He looked down at his hands for a few seconds and then back at her. Her heart clenched. What would it mean for them? How would he feel? She could barely take the thoughts looming around her mind. Finally, she looked up to meet his eyes.

A smile spread slowly across his face as a tear fell down hers. He wiped it away with his thumb.

"I was hoping you'd say that."

# forty

## six months later

Luella woke to the sound of the rooster crowing. She opened her eyes and saw the early light of morning creeping in through the window. Paul was still asleep beside her, his arm thrown over his head. She leaned over and ran a finger over his five o'clock shadow and then kissed him gently on the lips.

She'd never get over waking up next to him, or watching him be a dad.

She sat up on the bed. Nora laid sleeping in the bassinet beside her. Luella watched as her chest rose and fell gently, wondering if she'd ever stop worrying if she was still breathing.

She was no longer a preemie. Her little body had plumped up over the last six months, and her pediatrician said that she was in perfect health. No need to worry. But a mother always worries. Luella pressed a hand to Nora's chest and let the gentle rise and fall soothe her nerves.

They moved into Fred and Helen's room. They both felt that Fred and Helen would've approved. They started making renovations on the farmhouse, updating small things that needed fixing. They weren't ready to make big changes, and the subtle ones made it feel enough like it was theirs.

Luella pulled on her jeans and threw on a flannel button-up. She put on her socks and slid her feet into a pair of boots. Gus followed behind as she made a cup of coffee and then dumped a scoop of food into his bowl. He ate while Luella enjoyed her hot coffee. After she was finished, she set her cup in the sink and started toward the door. Gus followed fast on her heels.

She stopped at the bookshelf beside the back door like she did every morning. On the top shelf was the picture of Helen and her as a baby. Beside it, a framed copy of her tribute to Helen that had been published in *The Georgian*. She smiled as she pulled the door open and stepped out on to the back porch.

The sun was coming up over the trees, shining in all its glory. Orange and yellow spilled out across the sky like a watercolor painting. She stepped outside of the screen door, and it hit her in the face. Warmth that felt like peace.

She finally understood.

Life is a complicated, beautiful mess. In the end, all that really matters is that you leave this life having lived it well. You do the things that scare you, because that's how you find yourself. You can't go back and change yesterday, but you can learn from it. You love the ones that you get, the life you get, and it's how you live that life that matters. Helen had taught her that.

Luella closed her eyes against the sun and smiled.

# Author's Note

Even though this book is a work of fiction, I drew from certain elements in my own life when it came to the foster care aspect of this story.

My grandparents fostered children for a little over thirty years. They had probably close to a hundred children pass through their home in that time. I grew up with extra cousins to play with in a house that reverberated with noise. Some of my favorite memories are from that time. Several of those children were adopted and became my aunts and uncles, though we were already family without the titles.

Foster care is often stigmatized and portrayed in fiction from different viewpoints and experiences. We so often hear from foster parents, foster siblings, or foster children themselves, but an entire family is impacted by that experience.

I wanted to offer one of my own.

# Acknowledgements

This book took me three years to write. It was a collective effort of both myself and the community surrounding me that finally brought it to life. It takes a village to write a book and I'm enormously grateful to mine.

First thanks will always go to the One who created me. Thank you to God for this passion that runs through my veins. I'm not sure who I'd be without it.

To my husband, Brian. Thank you for being my anchor and letting me dream big dreams without ever trying to do anything other than support them. You're the real deal and I'd choose you again and again. To my sweet Sadie Grace, you will always be my first dream come true. Always, always.

Thank you to my parents for always loving me and supporting me in everything that I do. I've never questioned your love and for that I am thankful. To my brother, Justin. Thank you for being my biggest fan, and for always asking me how my book was going and where I was in the process—it helped more than you know.

To my wonderful in-laws, thank you for loving me like your own and always being so very supportive of me.

To all of my grandparents and grandparents-in-law, thank you for passing along your wisdom and enthusiasm for my dreams.

To my critique partner, Neely, you are the real deal. This book is so much better because of you. I'm serious when I say that you're never getting rid of me.

To my alpha readers—Macy, Hannah, Jessica, Becca, Jess, and Jamie. Thank you all for being both constructive and excited for this story. It has come a long way and that is mostly due to all of you. I'm so grateful.

To my mastermind peers—Neely, Adrienne, and Allie. I couldn't walk this journey without the three of you and what we have built together.

To every creative I worked with on this project. First to Karli, for loving this story and making my first editor experience a great one. To my copyeditor, Whitney, I'm sorry about the abundance of commas and incorrect plurals that you had to correct. So grateful to you. To my proofreader, Ellen Polk of Ellen Edits. You made sure this story was as smooth as butter and I am eternally grateful for your keen eye and attention to detail. To Kaitlyn, thank you for all your graphic design advice and always being there for feedback on the many versions of this book cover that I made.

I would also be remiss not to acknowledge how much of an impact the writing community on Instagram has changed my life. All of you. You know who you are. Before you, I created inside a bubble, and it was a lonely place. I credit so much of my determination to get this book finished to all of you.

And lastly, to Leslie. Not a day goes by that that I don't think about you. You were always so encouraging of my writing journey. Losing you affected me in ways that changed my perspective on life forever. I know threads of that grief are woven throughout the themes in this story. I'm so thankful to have known you.